THE OTHER SIDE

Nira was trembling from head to foot now. She dug her long fingers into the side of the bed.

"Are you going to try and make me believe it wasn't prearranged, that you and Cricket only met in town by accident? All the old stuff about staying late at the office, too."

He shifted from one foot to the other, uneasily.

"What's the good of all these recriminations? You're my wife. You are supposed to love me and where there's love surely there's forgiveness," he said grandly.

Nira almost bit through her lip. She didn't know whether to laugh or to cry. When she had said that he had cracked up their marriage she had meant it. There was a great big fissure through the mountain of content and happiness—the joy she had known before last night. The memory of Cricket's pretty, vicious face and that kitten-quality that made her so treacherous and unattractive in Nira's sight, damped her spirits.

Des said, "You don't *want* to forgive me. Is that it? Perhaps you're not so fond of me after all? I always imagined you were full of high principles. You used to talk so much about fidelity and romantic love. Have *you* always been faithful to me? I'm beginning to wonder. What about that evening you spent with Rob —alone in this house except for the kids. Or are you going to go on telling me you're just good friends?"

Nira gasped. Her breath quickened. She looked at him with positive loathing.

"You dare say a thing like that; about Rob and *me*? You know perfectly well there's nothing like that between us and never has been. Nor have I had an affair with any other man. *You know it*. It's the most awful thing for you to suggest. You're absolutely contemptible."

The Other
Side of Love

Denise Robins

CORONET BOOKS
Hodder Paperbacks Ltd., London

For Monica

Copyright © 1973 by Denise Robins
First published 1973 by Hodder and
Stoughton Limited
Coronet edition 1975

Printed in Great Britain for Coronet Books, Hodder Paperbacks
Limited, St. Paul's House, Warwick Lane, London EC4P 4AH,
by Cox & Wyman Ltd., London, Reading and Fakenham

ISBN 0 340 19479 0

"I hated now with a hatred more vital than indifference because it was the other side of love."

STRINDBERG

Nira and Des

I

NIRA WAS ONE of those people who wake up early and she was at her best in the morning, and more inclined to feel sleepy at the end of the day. On this particular April morning she woke at seven. Instead of getting straight out of bed to switch on the electric kettle and make the early tea, she lay quietly in the big double bed beside her still-sleeping husband and contemplated him — and life. Their life and those of their two children. Jonathan and Renira (her mother's name in full) were not yet stirring. No sounds came from the two rooms at the end of the corridor.

Nira stretched her long slender limbs, luxuriating in the warmth of the bed and of the masculine body beside hers.

Desmond Curtis lay on his side facing her. At times, when she first opened her eyes she would find his head on her shoulder, and he would be snoring very gently, though not loudly enough to disturb her. Sometimes he opened an eye and blinked sleepily at her then with sudden longing would draw her close and begin to make love to her.

Nine times out of ten she responded. She was still in love with Des. Their relationship had been a very happy one. The close association of eleven years had not yet extinguished the fire of the early days. Neither had parenthood destroyed the romance, even though it sometimes made it a little more difficult for them to be romantic. Tricky was, perhaps, the word. Not so easy to exchange passionate embraces while a crying infant, or inquisitive child, disturbed them.

Little Jonathan had suffered from night terrors from the time he was two. He often ran into their room for comfort. So it wasn't easy to feel relaxed and enjoy completely the ardours of the year before the first baby came.

Nira looked at her husband's face with fond approval. She was lucky to be married to a man like Des and he seemed well satisfied with her. Of course they both had their faults and moments of disagreement *and* there had certainly been one or two blazing rows. On the whole they tolerated each other's discrepancies and the infrequent quarrels were soon over, and followed by what Des called 'fun and games' in the marriage bed.

In sleep he looked very handsome, she thought. She put out a hand to touch the thick brown hair which he wore longer than he used to do; not too long. She couldn't stand that. But he allowed a nice tail to grow down at the nape of the neck and he had recently cultivated a small moustache. She had hated that to begin with, now she liked it. He was a tall athletic man and at his best in country clothes. She liked to see him in pullover and slacks striding over the golf course or driving off a tee with his tremendous vigour. He was a good golfer. They spent most of their week-ends on the local course which had pleasant surroundings and an attractive club house. They were fifteen miles from Brighton. Sometimes they played up on the Dyke. Nira played mainly to please Des — and to be with him. She dreaded becoming what they called a golf-widow. But she didn't really care for the game, and she wasn't very good. Des both teased and encouraged her and had been glad when she stopped using the children as an excuse for not leaving them. Now Susan, a local girl, came daily to take care of Jonathan and Renira when they were not at school, or in the evenings when Nira wanted to go out.

Des has a lovely straight nose, thought Nira, and she adored his large, dark-brown eyes, long lashes and rather full sensual lips. Asleep, he looked young despite that moustache. He had marvellous points. He was kind and attentive and a wonderful lover. Of course he had his weaknesses — for wine and women. He almost always beat it up at a dinner party and he was a frightful flirt. But Nira was not a jealous person. She was sure of his deep affection and certain of his fidelity. But she did wish sometimes that he wouldn't be quite so noisy when he'd had a couple of drinks or that he wouldn't make such outrageous passes at the good-looking girls who were all too anxious to say snap. However, she was fairly sure that the fun didn't go too far. Des always derided both the girls and himself once he was alone with his wife again.

"Attractive females amuse me, but you are the one I love," he'd say.

She had nothing to complain of, she reflected happily as she lay dreaming, watching the sun filter through the slats in the Venetian blinds. It filled the room with little golden slivers of light. It was going to be a lovely morning. It was Saturday, too. That meant Susan would be here early to take Jonathan and Renira off her hands. Golf, and lunch at the Club, and tonight they were going out to a dinner party.

A very pleasant day.

She began to think about what she would wear tonight. If it stayed fine she'd try out that new violet dinner-dress with the silver collar. She'd had her hair done yesterday—the way Des liked it best. It just needed a comb-out. Her hair was dark and silky. The best of the local hairdressers, an Italian, shaped it well. She wore it brushed back from her forehead high on top.

Suddenly she sprang out of bed. She wanted to take off her shortie nightgown and stand naked in front of her mirror. She did so, and contemplated her reflection. With the blinds still down and in that dusty gold sunlight, she stood a moment, staring.

She had always been on the tall side—four inches shorter than Des, who was six foot. She had kept her small waist and her smallish, rounded breasts. People told her she had a lovely figure. She could have been a model.

She was the same age as Des but looked younger. She had limpid eyes, greyish-blue, narrowing to slits when she laughed, and a slightly tip-tilted nose. Her mouth was moist and sweet. She had a pale fine skin and high cheek-bones. When she was made up she could look quite stunning.

She slipped into a white candlewick dressing-gown, tied the belt, then switched on the kettle. She was going to make tea and wake Des.

Now she could hear the children's voices. They were not allowed to come in here till half-past seven. Possibly by this time young Jon was out of bed and sitting beside his little sister. They got on very well, which was fortunate. Nira disliked brothers and sisters who were hostile to each other. It was usually out of jealousy. But she and Des had made a point of not causing this by showing favouritism. They prided themselves on being ideal parents.

Yawning, Nira dug a spoon into the tea-tin and made sure she hadn't forgotten Des's sugar. She didn't take it. She had a strong will and stuck to a reasonable diet. Des was putting on weight and she was cross sometimes when he refused to deny himself an extra slice of bread or lump of sugar, or those foaming tankards of beer he liked so much, and which were so fattening.

As soon as the kettle hissed and boiled she made the tea and called her husband.

"Wake up, lover."

He groaned and buried his face in the pillow.

"Too early."

"It isn't."

"Darling, it is. It's only quarter-past seven," his muffled voice slurred back. "Not a working day. Why wake? Come back to bed."

She leaned over him, shook the broad shoulders gently then dropped a kiss on his hair. She liked the odour of his hair tonic and after-shave lotion, and the faint rich smell of cigar smoke that still clung to him. A business friend had come back for a drink last night and given Des a cigar. He had enjoyed it. He liked expensive things. He meant to forge ahead in his business and eventually lead a life of luxury, and give her and the children all they wanted. That was one of the things Nira liked about him. He was so generous—too much so at times—inclined to be extravagant.

He was a business executive in an advertising firm, and after six years he was doing well and looked like making steady progress. They were always hard up—most young couples with children in their income group found it hard to manage—what with the steady rise in prices and disheartening taxation. But they were luckier than their friends the Hallings, whom they saw more of than anyone else in the district. Boyce Halling was a research engineer and he didn't seem to get either the salary rises or opportunities that gave Desmond an aura of success, yet Boyce worked just as hard. But his wife and small son had to economise and sometimes Mrs. Halling—known as Cricket, because of her petite figure and twittering voice—envied Nira.

Desmond gave a prodigious yawn, cleared his throat and sat up, running his fingers through tousled hair. He licked his lips and scowled.

"I drank too much last night. Why in God's name must you be so bright so early, woman?"

"Darling, you know we're having early golf, and that first of all we've got to drive Susan and the kids into Brighton and settle them with Gandy." (The children's nickname for old Mrs. Curtis was Gandy.)

"What a bore!" said Des.

"Well, your mother's taking Susan and the kids off our hands for the whole day, and you ought to be grateful."

Desmond swung his legs over the bed and rubbed his palms over his naked torso. He had a habit of wearing pyjama trousers but never the coat. The hairs on his chest were curly — chestnut brown like the thick hair on his head.

Nira looked at him with pride and pleasure. Her handsome Des! No wonder all the girls fell for him.

"You never remember anything and you're never grateful and you're hopeless!" she complained, and fell into his arms and was nearly smothered. Then he pushed her away, protesting, "I refuse to be seduced at seven fifteen a.m., so go and get the tea and behave yourself."

"You're one to talk! And it's seven twenty-five now and the tea's been ready for ten minutes."

"Well, make some more," said Desmond. He walked to the window and pulled up the Venetian blinds, letting in the delightful warmth of the Spring sunshine. He whistled. "Crikey, what a day! It'll be super up on the golf course."

She put some more water into the tea pot, poured out two cups and handed him one.

"Super. Out in the open all day — then the party tonight."

"Who's giving a party?"

"Honestly! You never remember anything," said Nira for the second time, "You've got such a ghastly memory. I've got to remember everything for everyone in this house including Susan, and I'm much older than she is."

"You don't look it," he said and threw an appreciative glance at Nira's graceful figure and the face that he used to tell her in their early days of wooing could easily have launched a thousand ships had she lived at the same time as Helen of Troy. He had a sincere admiration for his wife.

"Surely you remember it's Rob Bessiford's dinner."

"What, old Rob? What's he throwing the party for? I forget."

"*Comme toujours,*" said Nira whose French accent was poor but she made the foreign words sound withering.

Des was now in the bathroom. She could hear the whirr of his

11

electric razor. He called to her, "Okay—I remember now. It's for his birthday and it's at The Richmond."

Richmond Hall was one of the brightest spots in the otherwise unremarkable suburban town of Ponders Heath. Forty years ago, before the war, the Hall was private property—a beautiful Georgian building in a fine garden which nobody now could afford to keep up to anything like its old glory. But it made a superb hotel with the additional restaurant, dance room and a good bar which had been built on by the successful Brighton restaurateur who now ran the place.

They avoided ageing residents and catered for the general public. The gates opened on to what was now the main Ponders Heath Road from London to Brighton. There was much to attract passing trade, and the Saturday night dinner-dances at Richmond Hall Hotel had become very popular. There was a good band and the excellent cuisine encouraged the most elegant and monied among the local inhabitants.

"It is old Rob's birthday, isn't it?" Des called out to his wife.

"Yes, his forty-ninth, and he says it's the last he'll ever celebrate because he refuses to be fifty."

"You can't stop the march of time," came from Desmond, followed by a great splashing as he sponged his face.

Nira walked into the bathroom and grimaced at him.

"So speaks my thirty-year-old playboy."

"I wish I were a playboy, and I must say I've had a few chances of being one since I came here. I thought it was pretty ghastly, the life we led in Brighton. You never really got to know anybody. But they've all been very friendly in this little place. I suppose belonging to the local golf club has helped, and they've mostly turned out to be rather a smart go-ahead lot, haven't they?"

Nira began to brush her dark silky hair, shaking it back from her face. For the moment she was silent. She loved parties and good times and enjoyed everything with Des, but personally, she had rather liked Brighton. True, their flat had been far too small and once Renira was born they had simply had to find a house and garden. Besides, it was countrified in Ponders Heath — they thought it good for the kids, and they were not too far from Reigate where they could shop if they didn't find what they wanted here, but all kinds of new big stores and supermarkets were opening up in The Heath as they called it.

Brighton appealed only to Nira's love of culture, art and beauty.

There were good concerts, art exhibitions, and the Theatre Royal. She enjoyed all three. It was a part of her which had never really found response in the man she had married. They could get together — and did — in all kinds of other ways, but Des never wanted to stroll through the Lanes and look for treasures, or go to concerts or galleries. He only took her to the Theatre Royal to see the amusing shows. He didn't really like serious things. Because she was so much in love with him, and his influence over her was considerable, she did as he wished, and shrugged off the sad fact that her idol was fundamentally a selfish man. She loved him. It didn't matter that she was really much better educated than he. He was first and foremost a businessman. Because he was a gay companion and good lover when he was at home, she had so far felt he was all she needed.

They had had another important reason for wanting to leave Brighton — Des's mother. She lived in one of those attractive Regency squares near Black Rock. Since her husband, a chartered accountant, had died, she had devoted herself to charitable pursuits. She was a dedicated do-gooder. She spent most of her spare time helping the helpless, attending committee-meetings, opening bazaars and helping the Church. She had been left enough money to live in comfort. Although she loved her only son, she openly disapproved because he was not a churchgoer, and Nira had admitted that neither was she.

The only time the young couple entered a church these days was to attend a wedding, a christening or a funeral. While they lived in Brighton, Mrs. Curtis was too often on their backs, and had a genius for upsetting Des and making him irritable. Nira quite liked her mother-in-law but was relieved when Des decided to move to their present home in The Heath. Fortunately Nira was placid and tolerant enough to avoid falling out with her mother-in-law, but the one real point of contact between them now was the children. Gandy adored them. She was much better with them than she had been with her own son. Neither Nira nor Des could forget that they owed a lot to Gandy. She paid for Jonathan's and Renira's private school education, bought quite a lot of their clothes, and occasionally financed a special holiday for the whole family.

It was Nira who coaxed Des into going to see Mrs. Curtis more often than he would have done without her influence. Sometimes she accused him of lacking gratitude and affection for his mother.

But it was not her business, as she often told herself, and she had to admit that the rather smug little white-haired woman, now in her sixty-seventh year, could be very irritating. However, they had all been better friends since they put a few miles between them.

Des was successful in his business life but one had to have more salary than he could provide to run an establishment like this one in The Heath. It was a seven-roomed house with a small garden. They could only just afford Susan (Mrs. Curtis helped them to pay her wages). And whatever Des said or however much he clashed with his mother, he couldn't deny that the rather gay and free life they were leading now, they owed to her generosity.

Susan was Nira's greatest help and joy. Not only was she the baby-watcher, but dealt with all their washing, ironing and mending. Nira had had to do it herself in the old Brighton days. What a difference the allowance from Gandy had made! There remained the cooking. But Nira rather liked her kitchen, and trying out new dishes, and she watched the television chefs avidly. She shared the housework with Mrs. Tulk, a plump, cheerful daily who came three mornings a week to clean. Everything was organised. For the moment, Nira felt that she was so lucky—she feared something must go wrong.

2

They ran into Rob Bessiford as they walked into the golf club.

"Hi!" Des said cheerfully to the older man and grinned the schoolboy grin which Bessiford never felt was quite in character with the moustache, or the pseudo-American slang. Being essentially English and rather conventional, Rob returned with a more ordinary "Hello!" Then turning to Nira, he added, "And good morning to you, Nira. You're looking as fresh as the Spring morning, if I may say so."

"You may say so," said Nira happily. "I feel rather Springlike. It's quite warm. I shall shed my pullover any moment now."

"Don't forget you're my guests tonight."

Nira put the tips of her fingers against her lips.

"Oh, *of course*, it's your birthday. Many happy returns, dear Rob."

"Let's skip that," he smiled, "I'm only using the anniversary as an excuse to throw a party."

"Well, you can be sure we won't forget to come."

"And if I may add," put in Desmond, "you don't look a day over eighty, Rob!"

They all laughed. That sort of quip was typical of Des. It did in fact suddenly annoy Nira. She knew that Des meant to be just jolly, but she thought it rather a tactless joke. After all Rob was pretty well the oldest of them all in their circle.

"I *feel* eighty sometimes, my dear Desmond," he said. He was the one person who never shortened the name to Des. Some of Nira's friends thought Rob a bit on the staid and sober side. Des jeered and called Rob a flag-raiser, the type to get up and stand smartly to attention when The Queen was played; to do the right thing on all occasions; unfailingly courteous. The sort of chap Des wouldn't tell a dirty story to in front of the girls. He was interesting, well-informed and friendly to all. Worthy, of course. Nobody could possibly dislike Rob.

"I rather enjoy his old-fashioned manners," Nira had said on one occasion when she had heard Rob being criticised. "It's refreshing."

Des had qualified this by saying, "So are you at times. I don't know why you married a coarse brute like myself."

She had denied fiercely that he was either coarse or brutal. He was, she said, just—a devil at times. But she liked that. She adored him. Everyone had their little ways. Take Cricket Halling, who was tiny and looked fragile, but was never ill. She had huge limpid blue eyes and a silver-bell voice. That spurious air of innocence and childish laugh seemed to fascinate the men. But she was far from what she appeared to be. Nira had heard her tell a story in front of the boys which made her blush. Cricket prided herself on being with it, and frank about intimate subjects. Nobody could dislike her. She was as affectionate and cuddlesome as a kitten. There seemed to be no real malice in Cricket, but somehow Nira didn't trust her. She made her feel that although they were the same age, she, Nira, was a good deal older.

Nira had grown up in a rather dull conventional home—the kind that seemed to be rapidly disappearing. Undoubtedly it had left a mark on her. She had a reserved, dignified side, but fundamentally she was warm, impulsive and passionate. Her father had been a Regular Army Officer, killed in the last year of the War. A fine soldier, but not as strong a character as Nira's mother. The most important legacy he had left his daughter was his sense of humour and an honest approach to life.

This morning, Rob Bessiford looked down at Nira with greater pleasure than he knew he ought to feel.

He was in love with her.

He had fallen in love just like that, when they first met at a drinks party given by Anthony and Grace Conniston who lived at the Manor House—the oldest and most attractive place in Ponders Heath.

The Connistons—Anthony was a baronet—entertained on a large scale. He was at the head of all the Conservative activities. Her ladyship upheld the traditions. They had a teenage family. The eldest daughter, Vanessa, had become a model, which fact Grace Conniston was always trying to excuse. Grace was quite unable to cope with this permissive age. Vanessa seldom wore shoes and despite her parents' disapproval, appeared on most occasions wearing shorts and shirts (often her brother's), and with naked feet. Her beautiful face was usually half hidden behind two curtains of long red hair.

When Rob was first introduced to the Curtis family, he felt at once that Nira was different from the other young married women he met in Ponders Heath. Nira on her part, was impressed by Rob's exceptional height, and the attractive combination of suntanned face and silver hair. He had seemed old to her at first glance—then quite young—and Nira never again felt that he was elderly, in any sense of the word. His eyes were pure, piercing blue, but he had had trouble with his sight, and wore tinted glasses.

During the Conniston party they sat together, talking. She heard about his life in Nairobi and his subsequent illness. They talked animatedly. They were on the same mental wave-length. They discussed everything and everybody, including Vanessa, their host's daughter. She drank a lot of champagne and never left the side of a teenage youth whose fair hair was almost as long as hers, and who wore a crimson velvet suit.

It was a cold November day. The Connistons were celebrating their Silver Wedding. Desmond and Nira had been invited because when the Curtis family first came to the town, Lady Conniston's youngest — a boy of ten — had made friends with Jonathan who was at the same prep school. So the two mothers had met and liked each other, although Anthony, like Rob, admired Nira but was not particularly impressed by Desmond Curtis.

By the time the party ended, Nira felt she had known Rob all her life and decided to ask him to dinner.

She made him talk about himself.

He lived in The Hollies, an enormous Victorian double-fronted house, not far from the Curtis home. It backed on to the park which was also the local cricket ground. It was the sort of house that Rob secretly liked, although it was badly planned, rambling and draughty, but recently improved by the newly-installed central heating.

As a bachelor Rob might have been better in a flat, but the big house spelt home to him. It belonged to his eighty-nine-year-old aunt — Ida Bessiford — a maiden lady who had been part of Rob's life ever since he could remember. The oldest of his father's unmarried sisters and the only one left living, Aunt Ida was devoted to Rob and had made a will in favour of him. Not that she had much to leave now except The Hollies and its contents, but there was considerable value in the beautiful furniture, the Georgian silver, and one or two of the paintings. Rob had shared the house with her since his return from Kenya.

He told Nira that he had spent twenty-two years in Nairobi. He had become quite well known out there as a photographer of wild animal life. He even made money out of his movies, and regularly sold them in England, America and France. He had other business interests in East Africa but it all came to an end after Independence Day. Even then, because Rob adored Nairobi — the splendid rolling mountains and great lakes and rivers — the place had become dearer to him than England. He stayed out there until a sudden rare illness struck him down and finished his career. After a year in hospital, he was forced back to the old country. He could no longer go on safari nor lead the wandering life that had required so much stamina when living under difficult conditions.

The virus that struck him down had affected his eye-sight. During the last year his eyes had improved sufficiently to allow him to golf again, but he still suffered from headaches. It had all been a tragedy for him. He had given so much to his work in Kenya. He had hoped to end his days there. Now that he was rising fifty, the doctors had advised him to stay home in a more temperate climate. Fortunately he had saved enough money to make it possible for him to lead his present quiet but comfortable life without working other than for charity organisations in the locality.

He went away sometimes for weekends to friends. Talking to Nira he told her what a grand old lady his aunt was — marvellous for her age and with a mind still young. She was now almost totally crippled by arthritis, and spent most of the time in a wheelchair. When Nira herself first saw The Hollies, she was amused and interested by Rob's personal possessions — his elephant-foot table, his ivories, his leopard-skin rugs, and the other trophies he had added to Aunt Ida's collection.

Rob — the confirmed bachelor — from the first moment he had looked down into Nira's fine grey-blue eyes, knew she was the one woman he could have, and would have, married, if he had been given the chance. But it was far too late. She was Mrs. Desmond Curtis — very much so — and there were those two nice children — and that was that. As time went on and he saw more of her, he was determined that she should never guess he felt this way about her, and tried to be content with her friendship.

They got on very well. He hoped and believed that she liked him. He was usually included in her dinner parties, and often played bridge at Nylands, their home. He was glad, too, that he and Desmond were good friends, despite the fact that they had little in common save golf and bridge. Mentally, they were poles apart.

He tried to be grateful for the fact that he seemed welcome in Nira's home, and to stamp on more dangerous feelings. He was nearly twenty years her senior, and she must surely look on him as the children did — as an uncle, or elder brother. Nira was only just thirty.

He admired her when she was dressed up for occasions, but he found her even more attractive as she was in the Club this morning in that soft yellow pullover, grey ski-trousers and suède boots. Her grace and charm, as always, pulled at his heart-strings.

He was so tall that he stooped slightly. He made Nira feel short, but he gave her a curious feeling of security.

Rob and Desmond exchanged friendly comments. But Rob did

not particularly care for Desmond. He was not the type he could ever have made a close friend of — too boisterous and self-satisfied. But at least he seemed to keep Nira happy. That was important to Rob. They appeared a devoted couple. Obviously the sex side must be satisfactory between them. Rob's jealous eyes now and again noticed the way Nira stood close to her husband or how they suddenly held hands, or their eyes would meet in delightful appreciation of each other. But why she had fallen in love with him in the first place puzzled Rob. They were so different. She had been very young then — reserved — perhaps inexperienced, Desmond Curtis, so charming and self-assured must have swept her off her feet. He was immensely popular with all the females around here, Rob had to admit that. He definitely had what was called animal magnetism.

But for Rob, all the magnetism in the world lay in Nira's eyes. They fascinated him as she looked up at him this moment. Her lashes were dark like her hair, and luxuriant. Hers was an Irish type of beauty. The curve of her lips enchanted him. She used an attractive pink lipstick, and he had grown familiar with her perfume. He had asked her, once, what it was and she told him Pacco Rabanne's *Calandre*. Flower-fresh, like the graceful girl herself, he thought. Nira always seemed so well groomed and smelt so good. He had bought her a bottle of the *Calandre* for Christmas, and given it to her at the party the Curtis family always held on Boxing Day.

While Desmond chatted to another golfer in the bar, Rob and Nira walked out on to the verandah. There was a light breeze — cool but not cold. They gazed across the green course — it looked beautiful, with the fringe of dark fir trees on one side and a long row of hawthorn bushes, already in bud, warmed by the Spring sunshine. Nira loved it up here. One of the attractions that had led Des and herself to settle in Ponders Heath had been this eighteen-hole golf course, recommended in the first place by a business friend who had been a Ponders Heath resident for some years.

"How are the offspring?" Rob was asking Nira. She rewarded him with the bright proud smile which always lit up her face when her children were discussed. That was another thing he admired — her pride in these two children, and the way she handled them. Desmond was a permissive father, lavish with pocket-money and treats and it was not always because he loved to spoil them, but because it was the easy way of getting them out of his way when he wanted to be free of them. More than once Nira had argued that it was bad to spoil the children. She told Rob that she disliked what she saw going on around her. The way the young controlled their parents. It should be the other way round. Nira disliked pampered children and disobedient animals. Rob agreed.

"The babes are fine," she answered his question, "rather too energetic. I assure you I'm glad to have Susan."

"But you're with them a lot yourself."

"I used to be more so until we came here. We couldn't afford either Susan or a daily in the old days. I'm very lucky to have Des's mother to help with finance now."

Rob nodded. But he was not sure Nira was all that lucky. He could never bring himself to believe that Desmond Curtis was right for her. Physically, Nira was a splendid mature young woman, but Rob, who prided himself on being a psychologist, and also because he was so deeply attracted by her, had watched and listened and at times thought that she was immature in other ways. She was almost like a child in her frank enjoyment of things. She seemed to accept life as it was and ask no more. Just as she accepted that pretentious husband of hers. Women were wonderful, and a bit frightening to Rob. When they loved they seemed so blind to the man's faults, and even in these days of woman's liberation, still slavishly devoted to the one of their choice. Or did they accept what was really unacceptable and gloss it over? Whichever way it was with Nira, Rob found her touching and adorable. But he often worried about her.

Desmond was not worth her adoration, and Rob feared the day would come when Nira would wake up to this fact. She would, with her nature, expect fidelity from a man. *Did she get it from Des?*

Even during this short time that he had known the Curtises, Rob had heard a few things said at the Club about Des that he found disturbing. A week or two ago he had been having a drink at the bar and heard a man named Robinson — an estate agent who was a noted gossip — discussing Desmond with Lieut.-Col. Moffatt — a retired Army man now working for a Conservative organisation, and married to a nice dull woman. Typical Army wife, Des called her — tweed coat and hair-net, flag-waving, hearty and organising.

"Lover-Boy's going to upset old Boyce Halling soon if he doesn't watch out," Robinson had said, apropos of Desmond.

Someone else asked for an explanation of this. The answer was, "He's got this thing about Cricket."

"Hasn't everybody?" the plump and affable Colonel put in, laughing. "She's—what is the word they all use?—dishy!"

"Oh, definitely," said Robinson, "While Boyce was away on that business trip in the U.S.A. someone I know ran into the pair in town, and they were staying in some hotel together."

Rob had walked out feeling uneasy and suddenly troubled for Nira. Even more so when Robinson's rather loud voice, still gossiping with the Colonel, followed him.

"There's quite a bit of this and that going on in our little town, old boy. Ponders Heath will be in the wife-swopping class before long."

Laughter and a few mild protests followed, all in good fun no doubt, but Rob felt an active dislike of Desmond at that moment. Where there was such talk there was always a modicum of truth. Why did Desmond Curtis want to pursue Cricket Halling?

Afterwards Rob had thought a lot about the Robinson gossip. He was no prig. It was just that word *wife-swopping* that offended him. He might even have been amused by that if it hadn't been aimed at Des Curtis. Why should Des, with a wife like Nira, want another girl, even for a few hours' fun? As for Cricket Halling, Rob had no regard for her whatever. She and Boyce had long since seemed a bit too fond of that word permissive.

But of one thing he was certain—if Desmond was actually having fun with Cricket, Nira didn't know it. If she had done, there wouldn't be that contented glow in her eyes, nor would she be so vividly pleased with life—and Des.

Rob thought, *I hope to God she never hears what's being said.*

He felt fiercely protective and embarrassingly old. He was, of course, older than any of them in this young set. But Rob felt uneasy because he *minded* about Nira.

He heard her speaking now. He liked her voice. It was quiet and there was music in her laughter, unlike Cricket Halling's shrill squeals of delight.

"You've got a brooding sort of look this morning, Rob. Anything wrong?" she asked him.

He snapped out of the darkness of his thoughts and smiled down at her benevolently.

"Not a thing. How are we playing today? You and Desmond against Maggie and myself?"

"I imagine so," she nodded.

Here was Maggie now, coming towards them with her golf clubs slung over her shoulder and Desmond at her side. They were both laughing. They made rather a nice-looking pair, Nira thought, with the tiniest stab of jealousy which quickly passed. She despised jealous wives. If one loved a man, one must trust him. Still — Maggie was a very attractive creature. About Nira's age, she had been a widow for the last two years. Her husband was once a doctor in one of the local syndicates. Poor Bill Wilson — a general favourite — had been killed in a car smash, and Maggie's world had crashed, too. She lived now in a bungalow near the golf course with her mother and a small daughter of seven. She had been devoted to Bill, but everyone expected her to marry again. As she walked toward them, Nira generously admired the grace of the slim figure and the beauty of hair that held the bronze lights of beech leaves in the autumn sun. Her large red-brown eyes were beautiful. Nira knew that Maggie was one of Des's favourites. She was nice and at the same time fun. They had all been pleased here when she decided to stay on in the town. Recently she had taken up golf and proved herself exceptionally good. With a handicap now of twelve she was almost on a level with Nira, who had played much longer. Des was erratic, Rob was the best of them all. But they made a good foursome.

"Hi!" Maggie greeted them.

Her mother was American and Maggie had been brought up in Baltimore. As they discussed the fine weather and the approaching game, Des looked not at his wife but at Maggie. The creamy texture of her skin and her big sensual mouth usually excited him. As the conversation died, he put in, "Maggie's been telling me there's a film we must see, on next week, Nira my darling."

"What?" she asked, and linked her arm affectionately with his.

"What's it called, Maggie?" he asked the other girl.

"*The Virgin and The Gypsy.*"

"D. H. Lawrence," said Rob, and pulled a pipe from his pocket and began to fill it. "I'm in two minds about that fellow, you know. I was never a Chatterley fan but I admit he writes well at times."

"Mum and I saw this film in London," said Maggie. "I assure you it's worth a go, Rob. Lovely scenery — old-fashioned village scenes — lots of beautiful colour — I'm sure you'd like it."

"And what about the purple passion, you mentioned," Des asked with a laugh. "Plenty of that, isn't there?"

Maggie's creamy skin grew pink for a second but she laughed back.

"Yes, plenty of that, and awfully well done."

"Let's all go and see some purple passion next week," said Nira.

But suddenly for some unknown reason she moved away from Des and her eyes clouded very slightly. It was that sudden flush on Maggie's charming face that had troubled her. Maggie was not really a shy person. Nira had always found her rather sophisticated and with plenty of that free-thinking impetuous American blood running through her veins. She was not one to *blush*, and Nira had also caught the sudden swift glance that had passed between her and Des.

Then Nira reproached herself.

Don't be a fool, Nira, it didn't mean a thing. You're slipping.

As if she didn't know that Des was a born flirt. He was candid enough to admit it. But he loved *her*.

She forgot all about that exchange of glances and thoroughly enjoyed the game. But she played badly and disgraced herself at the eighteenth hole. She had taken five to deal with the little ball. She and Des lost the game to the other two.

While they were having drinks in the bar before lunch, the Hallings walked in.

Boyce was a man of medium height, on the thin side, his light brown hair growing rapidly back from a high forehead. He was not good-looking but all the women thought he had handsome eyes — hazel-green, magnetic, arresting. His movements were quick and nervous. He had definite charm. Personally, Nira had never really cared for him although she had to admit now and again that he was attractive. He was amusing, too, and she liked a witty man, more especially if he wasn't coarse. He had a son, Simon, the same age as Nira's boy, and the whole family was musical. Boyce played a guitar and was in great demand at parties. But there was just something about him that made Nira feel that she should be on her guard with him. As she put it to Des, "Those eyes of his are rather lecherous — like the way he looks at me."

To which Des had replied with his well-known flippancy, "Long live the lechers."

If she was ever cross with Des it was because she could so

rarely make him take her seriously especially when she showed a tendency to be prim.

Now Cricket rushed towards her and planted a kiss on her cheek. From this, Nira withdrew slightly. She didn't really like being kissed by other women and Cricket was always too lavish with embraces. Nevertheless, this morning Nira admitted that Boyce's wife was enchanting to look at in her cornflower blue trouser-suit. She used too much make-up, but pretty she certainly was, and only two things in Nira's opinion spoiled her. The too-full, petulant lips (that silvery glistening lipstick intensified their sensuality), and her high, almost falsetto, voice. But definitely she did not look her age, which was in the late twenties. They talked together, exchanged drinks and arranged to meet in the dining-room for lunch.

Rob had seated himself in a basket chair, alone. He was in what he called his looking-on mood. He didn't particularly want to join in the banter and general chatter. Through his tinted glasses, he watched when Cricket seized hold of Nira and kissed her. He puckered his lips, remembered what he had heard, and turning from Cricket to Desmond Curtis, he *wondered*.

It might have been the kiss of Judas or it might just all be malicious gossip that Rob had heard. Secretly, in defence of his beloved Nira, he continued to wonder.

During lunch he found himself still watching those two — Desmond and Cricket — but he gradually grew ashamed of his suspicions and began to feel that anything he had heard might be grossly exaggerated. Gerald Robinson himself, possibly had a thing about Cricket. So many men were amused and sexually excited by that wicked mixture of the adolescent and experienced female in Cricket. *Not me*, Rob thought grimly, *I'd run miles from our semi-demi-local Lolita.*

Added to this, all through lunch Rob saw that Desmond openly flirted with Cricket, quite careless of the fact that Boyce sat opposite and could hear and see it all. Desmond even put out a hand and caressed the silvery-blonde hair which Cricket had just had cut short. It used to hang like a curtain over her eyes.

"I'm all for the new styles," he said. "Put you in a cassock and surplice today and you'd look like a choirboy, dear."

Cricket giggled.

"Ah — men!" she intoned the words, and pressed pointed finger-tips together in mock supplication.

"We might ask the Vicar if he'd like you to replace one of his tribe at any time. What do you say, Boyce?"

Boyce cast an ironic glance at his wife and put his tongue in his cheek.

"Great! And I daresay she'd get away with it."

Rob thought, *I don't think he cares a damn what his wife does. And Desmond seems not to mind broadcasting his feelings, so why do I worry? Only about Nira, and perhaps none of it is important. They're all on the surface this lot. I mustn't start growing really old.*

He made an excuse to leave the Club early.

His ears might have burned if he had heard the few comments that were made after he left.

He returned home depressed—suddenly lonely.

The feeling of what's the good about anything, that had lately been attacking him, returned. His own fault, he thought moodily. What was the use of being in love with another man's wife?

As his tall thin figure disappeared from the club house, Nira looked at her husband and said, "Something's gnawing at our Rob. He seems very fed up—on his birthday, too. Have you noticed it?"

"No," answered Des, and nudged Cricket's knee with his very gently under the table. She had enchanting legs, and he knew all about the dimples in her knees which couldn't be seen at this moment, since she was wearing slacks. He was rewarded by a gentle answering pressure from her hand.

Boyce cut in, "I think Rob's beginning to show he's pushing fifty. These chaps who spend their lives in darkest Africa and such places, are seldom fit when they retire, do you think?"

"Well, I'd scarcely call Nairobi darkest Africa," Nira protested.

Boyce shrugged and pierced a cigar which he had just bought from the bar. He was rather partial to cigars, and being slightly health-conscious, believed they were better for the lungs than cigarettes. He was not a pipe-smoker. He adored women and he didn't think they on the whole cared for pipes. He could remember his mother saying how she loved to see Dad smoking his, but that was a bit outdated.

Returning to the question of Rob, Boyce gave Nira what she called his lecherous look. It made her feel uncomfortable. When he flicked that critical, smouldering gaze up and down her body it was so *obvious*. He said, "Well, didn't Rob go in for all that wild animal stuff—safaris and so on? They must have been de-energising. Then he had that session in hospital and his eye-operation and a lot of fever, hadn't he?"

"He's a hell of a nice chap. I like Rob," said Desmond suddenly.

Nira threw him a grateful look. She was so fond of Rob herself. She believed that she and Des had established a good sound friendship with him. Nira sometimes made a point of going to see Aunt Ida. The dear old lady was an awful bore because she always told the same story two or three times. But she loved to see young people and Nira was one of her great favourites.

Now Nira looked at her watch and decided that it was time to go home. They must fetch Renira and Jonathan from Brighton. Gandy would have had enough of them by now, little doubt. Nira clapped Des on the shoulder.

"Home, James!"

Reluctantly he drew his knee away from Cricket, whispered, "See you, pet," and drew smartly to attention, saluting his wife. "At the ready, ma'am."

They went off arm in arm.

"Nice pair," said Boyce.

"Isn't Des *handsome*?" Cricket sighed blissfully.

"Isn't Mrs. Des *lovely*?" said Boyce, mimicking her, and drew on his cigar, his eyes half closed, "There's something about our Nira that gets me right in here—" he tapped his chest.

Cricket burst out laughing.

"You and your lovely Nira!"

"Well, there's one thing, you're not the jealous type, my love."

"No," she said, "and neither are *you*, my love!" She mocked his voice.

"We see eye to eye, which makes for a happy marriage." He gave her a sidelong smile, then returned to his thoughts about Nira. He added, "Ring up the Curtises and arrange a nice little dinner with those two for next weekend. I won't stint the cash. We'll have champagne and you can play some of those new records, and we'll roll the rugs back in the lounge and dance. Not too many lights on either."

Cricket laughed again.

"I really do dig you, Boyce, when you start making arrangements for a big seduction. But go easy with the spending, *and* the showing off. You used to have a success with Maggie, but you seem to have lost her now. She's after Des. I won't let her get him. *I* want him and he's after *me*!"

"Is he indeed!" said Boyce and yawned and stretched his legs out. "I'll have to be careful, won't I?"

"What for, may I ask, if you're rooting for my boy-friend's wife?"

Boyce grinned at the rows of bottles behind the bar and at the bored face of the barman. It must be grim to be bored. He never was. He enjoyed his job, and although he had to be careful, now, he intended to make money in the future. But certainly he spent more than he should. Women were his downfall—any girl he made love to seemed to enjoy it and asked for more. And he wanted more. Cricket was, so far, the ideal wife for him because she had very few morals and liked to fool around with other men. That suited *him*. He knew all about her little sessions with Des and why should he care? Cricket no longer attracted him except as a sort of sister, and on occasions she was an amusing little companion. But she was damned bad-tempered. Let those who found her so alluring find that out in time. Once again, why should he care? He wanted Nira. He wanted to break down that aloofness, that cool poise. To make her soft and pliant in his arms.

He found her tall graceful body and exquisite camellia skin so maddeningly attractive. All the more so because she had never once shown him the green light. It had been the red, right from the start, as though she didn't really like him.

His thoughts travelled further while Cricket combed back her blonde curls and tied a chiffon scarf over her head. Boyce paid the bar bill. As he waited for his chit he turned his thoughts to his ten-year-old son, Simon. Rather a pathetic little boy who unfortunately had his mother's fragile limbs and baby-face. He didn't like games, preferred animals, and was Mum's pet. Boyce and Cricket were always fighting about the way Simon should be treated.

Boyce had wanted a daughter, but after Simon's birth, Cricket had decided that she would never what she called 'go through it again'. Simon had improved since he went to his prep school as a day-boy and it was satisfying to Boyce to know that he had chummed up rather thickly with Jonathan. Jonathan was big and strong for his age and promised to be a first-class soccer-player. He was good for Simon and the friendship between the two boys brought the parents into frequent contact.

Boyce was altogether satisfied with the charmed circle in which he moved nowadays. The golfing crowd were a bit stuffy but there were the others, particularly the stockbrokers — Boyce called them *the king commuters*. Boyce cultivated them. But greater than all other desires was his longing for Nira. *I'll make her respond to me,* he thought, with a maddening vision of those strangely beautiful eyes with their long silky lashes. *I'll make her somewhere — somehow — and soon.*

3

ROB'S BIRTHDAY PARTY at the Richmond Hall Hotel was a success. The dinner was specially ordered and excellent, and he did not stint the champagne. He was by no means a heavy drinker but he allowed himself as much as he could stand that evening, and was touched by the warmth of the applause that followed his few words after the guests had called for a speech.

"Good old Rob!" Robinson called out, raising his glass. Rob acknowledged these few words from his *bête noire* with a more friendly smile than usual, but he wasn't really happy as the evening wore on.

He couldn't quite cure himself of his habit of sitting back and being the looker-on. He didn't dance. An old accident out in East Africa when he was much younger, had left him with slight trouble in one foot. He disliked dancing, anyhow. He sat back and watched his adored Nira on the floor with the other men. God, she looked gorgeous this evening, he thought. That model-girl figure was perfect in the dark violet silky dress, high Russian collar embroidered with tiny pearls, long chiffon sleeves. Her waist was firm and small for a woman who had had two children. She had beautiful arms, and moved gracefully. He always admired the elegance of her clothes. On most occasions she stood out among the others. Tonight she wore pearl earrings and a small but beautiful pearl and gold brooch pinned against one shoulder. Des had had it made for her, shaped like an open fan.

Rob followed the slim violet figure with his hungry gaze through the glasses that magnified her beauty. He felt he could never see enough of it. She was trying to follow a new modern dance step with Boyce Halling. The band was playing a new T. Rex theme. The rhythm was stimulating. Cricket, glittering in a white and gold evening suit, was dancing with Desmond. Her movements were wild and skittish and she giggled loudly. Desmond seemed to be enjoying her antics and produced a few of his own.

Rob looked back at Nira and Boyce. The languorous movements of Nira's body made the blood rush to his head. He signalled the waiter and asked for more black coffee. *I've drunk too much*, he thought sombrely.

Boyce suddenly caught his partner round the waist and drew her nearer to him.

"What a pity we don't do this more often, Nira. You're a great partner."

"You don't do so badly yourself," she said, in the mood to be gay and totally unaware of Rob's unhappy gaze following her round the floor.

For her it had been a very gay party so far. It was rather fun behaving like a teenager—she, the mother of a ten-year-old son and a five-year-old daughter. Rob had done them well and this new band was good. Not that she cared much for the place. It had been spoilt by the new company that took it over last summer. This dance-room, built on recently, was ugly and ultra-modern—the lights too bright and the colour scheme too psychedelic.

Des called it amusing—but he and Nira didn't always share the same taste. He was, however, usually amenable and let her choose the things she wanted. But she had to admit there had been one ghastly moment when he had brought her a table as a present which she had disliked at sight. It wasn't even *nice* modern. It was new—varnished—and an ugly shape. She had tried to admire it and the words had stuck in her throat, then for the first time he had taken offence and said, "We never seem to agree on this sort of thing. I know you say your old home was marvellous, and I suppose your father was a collector and knew about antiques and all that, but I don't see anything wrong with my table or my taste."

She had tried to put things right by telling him that she loved him so she would love the table, but he had sulked. The table was still there in her room because she didn't want to offend him by not using it, but now and again she did feel that it spoiled her décor. She realised, of course, that it was not important. Just one of those small disputes that can arise between husband and wife and make them both suddenly conscious of certain discrepancies in taste. Anyhow, that had been years ago, before Jonathan was born, and forgiven — if not forgotten.

"Look at my wife and your husband. They're gyrating like tops," Boyce said suddenly, his lips rather close to her ear. She could feel his hot, wine-laden breath, and drew away. She glanced towards Des and Cricket.

"They're thoroughly enjoying themselves."

"Are you?"

"Of course."

"We make a good foursome, don't you think?" murmured Boyce. "You and Des and Cricket and me."

She hesitated. She didn't particularly admire Boyce. He wasn't her type but she was feminine enough to respond now and again to his flattery. He was never slow to show that he admired her. Des, in fact, had said the other night that old Boyce had a thing about her.

These *things*! she had thought at the time. She had never come across such a place as The Heath. Someone was always having *a thing* about someone else. Amusing, but she remained content with her own husband.

"Don't you agree — we make a good foursome?" repeated Boyce, and curved his fingers more tightly about her long slim hand.

"I'm sure we do," she said lightly. "Our golf, our bridge, our children."

"My trouble is that I never see you alone."

"You might get bored with me if you did. I'm not nearly as amusing as your wife."

Boyce looked slantway through the crowd at his wife's petite sparkling figure. He could hear her high-pitched laughter above the beat of the music and shuffle of feet.

"Cricket's a lot of fun — when she isn't nagging."

"All wives nag their husbands at times."

"I've never seen you out of tune with Des. He's a lucky guy."

"I'm lucky, too."

"You wouldn't mind if he was attracted by another girl?"

Now Nira opened her grey-blue eyes very widely, and flicked the long lashes that were darkened with mascara.

"If you mean do I mind his cavorting around with other girls—women—whatever they are—of course not! I'm not jealous and I don't think wives ought ever to chain their husbands. It's asking for trouble."

"Very wise. One of the things I admire about you, Nira, is your wisdom. I adore my wife but she's incredibly silly at times, and please don't think me disloyal for saying so."

Now a sudden impish wish to lash out at Boyce made her say, "I'm sure you *are* disloyal, Boyce dear, and discontented—a restless sort of man. I always feel that. You never sit still, and I've heard Cricket say you're always searching for fresh excitement."

"*She* can talk!" he protested.

"Well—do you look on yourself as a good loyal type of man?"

"Oh, I say!" Boyce protested again, laughing. "You're not being very complimentary. Anyhow, what about your own husband—I should have thought he was as restless as I am."

"Perhaps, but I know and understand him. I don't really know you, Boyce."

"That's because we're never alone and have never really communicated. I'd like us to get to know each other better. I won't deny that I find you very *very* attractive."

The red blood showed suddenly under the creamy skin of Nira's face.

"Boyce dear, *really*!"

He tightened his hold of her.

"I mean it. I know you're devoted to Des and I'm sure he is to you, but there are moments when I think he'd get on very well for an hour or two with Cricket. And wouldn't you—get on with me? Couldn't I meet you somewhere, sometime and take you out—or take you in," he added jokingly, and his eyes suddenly seemed to her to be more desirous than usual.

"Boyce, you're being an idiot. Let's stop dancing and have a drink."

Her voice was no longer friendly. He was astute enough to realise that he must be careful with Nira or he would get into her bad books and *that* he didn't want. But the blood was racing through his veins and he had to use all his control not to lean forward and kiss that wide sweet mouth of hers. He managed to release her—and to laugh.

"It's the champagne, dear, sorry."

"We've all had our quota," she said, relieved. "Let's join Rob. He's all alone."

"I'm not at all sure poor old Rob isn't your type really. He's always on his good behaviour."

"Well, not many people are, and it's rather nice for a change," said Nira a trifle coldly. "But I assure you, *Des* is my type."

Damn, Boyce thought, as he followed her off the dance floor, *I've boobed! I'll have to be much more subtle if I'm to get anywhere with her.*

He could see that the best thing he could do was to make it easier in future for Cricket to see more of Des. It might in time upset Nira. Then perhaps she'd turn to *him*.

Before they reached their table, he spoke lightly.

"Don't be cross with me. It's not my fault you're so attractive."

She melted and gave him one of her warm smiles.

"Okay. I'm not cross. Thanks for the dance. It was super."

But her thoughts ran in a different vein. *He's too blatantly sexy — the sort of man who thinks he can get any girl he wants. I don't really like him.*

He had nevertheless had one moment of truth — unconsciously — when he had said that Rob was her type. In his way, Rob was just that. But when she looked at Des who had just finished dancing with Cricket and sat down again, she caught his significant smile and the familiar droop of the eyelids — a habit of his when they exchanged glances — intimating that he was all hers and that he adored her. He said so — often. He was definitely attractive compared to the other men — her darling Des!

She reached his side and laid a hand on his shoulder.

"Hello, there!"

"Hello, there, honey —"

They mimicked American voices — another of their habits when the mood was festive and spirits high. It was fun being married to Des. Nira glowed.

Rob looked toward that glowing loveliness and was sad. He had never before known such acute loneliness as on this, his birthday. *Fifty next year*, he thought, *I'm middle-aged with a vengeance. I never imagined it would matter.*

Why did it? Just because Nira was so much younger — or because he was the old man of the party?

Boyce, who had moments of being generous-hearted, had asked

Joyce Moffatt to dance. He had an eye on Maggie but she was already on the floor with the Colonel.

Nira took the chair beside Rob.

He had half risen as she approached, then signalled to a waiter. "You'll want a drink."

"Yes, thanks, it is rather hot in here and I've been much too energetic," she laughed and fanned her flushed cheeks.

"I saw you and Halling doing fantastic steps. I rather envy you all. I wish I could dance."

"I wish you could," she said with that sweet sudden smile which narrowed her eyes and brought little creases around them.

"Don't sit here if you'd rather go on dancing, my dear. Where's your husband?"

"In the bar with Cricket. I must tell him to ask poor Joyce to dance. Boyce is the only one so far—except the Colonel—to ask her."

"I was talking to her just now," said Rob, "and she's really quite interesting. Everyone finds her unattractive just because she's a bit angular and dried-up, but she's spent a lot of time in the Far East when she was following the flag, and Army wives out there get like that."

"You're always kind to everyone," said Nira, and lifted the champagne which had just been poured out, towards him. "Cheers, Rob, and Happy Birthday again."

She isn't a bit jealous, he thought. *Doesn't seem to mind that that husband of hers has spent most of his time with Cricket this evening. Perhaps she feels invulnerable and safe, as well she might! He'd be crazy if he went after any other woman in the world.*

Aloud Rob said, "It's strange that we none of us really know much about the other people. How they live—what they are like in their private lives. You've got to get right under the skin in order to understand them."

"You're the sort of person people want to talk to," she said, and looked affectionately at the thin tanned face with its crown of thick silver hair. She understood exactly what little Renira had said to her the other day, "Uncle Rob's a *cosy* man, isn't he, Mummy? You sort of feel that when he talks to you."

Renira was perceptive. It was exactly what one did feel with Rob Bessiford—warm and secure. He was 'a cosy man'.

"Has poor old Joyce been confiding in you?"

"No special confidence, nothing one couldn't repeat, but did you know that the Moffats once had two children—twin girls? They died in an accident when they were stationed in Singapore—awful tragedy."

"Oh, how grim! No, I didn't know. I *am* sorry. She's never spoken about it to me. She's obviously the kind that doesn't talk a lot about herself."

"But I can see that it has affected her whole life. They're pretty lonely, that pair. Old Moffatt gasses a lot, and does the hearty Colonel stuff, but Joyce was telling me he's never been the same man since the accident. Now he smokes and drinks too much; she admits it."

"I must ask her round. I've never thought about it before."

He eyed Nira, his eyes tender behind the tinted glasses. "Typical of you to suggest it. I'm sure she'd be most appreciative. She was saying how much she admired you."

But he didn't add that Joyce had also said that she didn't trust Desmond Curtis one inch. He was much too good-looking and slick for her. She liked the more serious-minded and honest-to-God type. *And* she didn't think Des good enough for Nira.

Now Des came out of the bar, walked to Nira's chair, and laid a familiar hand against the back of her long slender neck.

"Nirry, would you mind if I leave you for ten minutes or quarter of an hour. Cricket's developed one of her migraines. I said I'd run her home. Boyce seems occupied with the Colonel's lady, and I wouldn't mind a spot of fresh air."

"But, of course, darling," said Nira happily. "How nice of you. Poor Cricket—she gets these migraine attacks quite often."

"Nasty things," put in Rob. "The medical profession doesn't seem to have got to the root of them."

Cricket appeared, looking in Rob's estimation, not at all ill, but she had put on her white fur jacket and was cuddling herself in it, pouting her full pink lips. She said to Nira, "Isn't it *sweet* of your Des, he's offered to take me home. I promise not to keep him."

"If you mean that, I won't take you home. I like to be kept," said Des with his usual sparkle.

Nira shook her head at her husband.

"The things you say!"

They moved away. Boyce, engrossed in trying to teach Joyce Moffatt to dance in modern style, did not even see his wife go.

Rob lit another cigar and looked at the ash speculatively. *I reckon she'll keep him longer than ten minutes,* he thought. *I wonder if she's got migraine at all. I wonder what Desmond is really up to.*

But if Nira didn't mind—why should anybody else?

He decided in any case to distract Nira's mind from her husband. He began to talk to her about the children, and the summer holidays.

"Are you going down to Cornwall, like you did last year, plus mama-in-law?"

"Not with Mrs. Curtis," Nira grimaced, and leaned forward to light her cigarette from the match Rob struck for her. "The weather was super and Cornwall gorgeous, but we had to mind our p's and q's because of Gandy who, poor soul, means so well. The children adore it. The sands and rocks are terrific and I love Mawgan Porth, but Gandy is not the best companion to have on a holiday. She loves the children but she narks at them if they do anything she doesn't think right. *Don't sit on the wet sand or you'll get cold, Renira. Jon, keep your hat on. The sun's so hot today.* And so on. She didn't like my bikini much. She likes to think she's modern but she's still shaken by the unclad bodies she sees around the beaches today."

Rob smiled.

"Some don't bear criticism, but I rather agree with your mother-in-law there's far too much nudity. A few more veils as there were in the old days, add to a girl's attraction, don't you think?"

Nira nodded. "Yes, but I do rather like my bikini when there's any sun."

Rob found himself picturing Nira in her bikini and was more than a little disturbed by his reaction to the thought. What the hell was he doing, letting this sort of note creep into their relationship which was a good and friendly one. He must never spoil things. He would be the loser.

"What are you going to do this year, then?" he asked her.

"Oh, we've made all sorts of plans. Des doesn't want to be away from the office too long so I am going to take the children down to Mawgan Porth again. We know it and they love the place and the surf-bathing and so on. That will be in July or August. Then we've got plans to take a proper holiday with the Hallings later in Majorca. They went last year to the Formentor Hotel and said it was super. It's expensive, but we all thought we'd be extravagant. So we've booked for the last week of August and the first week in September. I know everyone says it will be hot then and crowded, but we all like the heat and we'll have to put up with the crowds. The Formentor has its own little private beach, anyhow."

Rob smiled at her with the tenderness he found it hard to conceal. She really was such a darling. He wouldn't have minded a crowded beach and certainly not the heat; in fact he would give anything to go on that holiday with her. But why the Hallings? Cricket was pretty and engaging, but such a little *poseuse*, and Boyce irritated him. What did Nira see in them? Or was it Des who had arranged it?

Nira enlarged on her plans. She, herself, admitted that it wasn't the foursome she was really after. She would rather have gone away alone with Des, but he was so sociable and loved a party and got on well with Boyce *and* Cricket, she added laughing, they'd never been away in a foursome before and thought it would be nice to have someone they knew and could play bridge with if it rained.

Rob sighed quietly. God, he thought, he couldn't understand a fellow like Desmond Curtis wanting someone else on his holiday as well as this wonderful girl. But not for the first time he began to wonder if he was idiotic to think along these lines and not realise that the world was changing. Thousands of couples today liked crowds and fun and 'beating it up' and that sort of thing, whatever their walk of life. He, Rob, should have been born a hundred years ago. He was at heart a Victorian. Suddenly to his immense delight, Nira gave him a warm friendly look from her lovely eyes and asked him if he would like to join them on their holiday in Majorca.

"I don't know whether you know it, but the Hallings say Majorca offers such a lot and for so much less than you have to pay in the South of France. Do come with us, Rob. I'm sure the others would like you to. I know Des would."

"It's sweet of you both," Rob said, his cheeks colouring, "absolutely sweet. But I'd vaguely wondered if I could go up to Scotland for some fishing in June—"

"Well, do that," she broke in, "then join us later on for the Majorcan holiday. I'm sure it wouldn't be too late to get you a booking."

"I think it might be tricky. I've never been to Majorca but I hear it's absolutely top favourite, and some chap I met thought the Formentor pretty good."

"We could try for a room for you. Shall I phone our travel agent? Des goes to one in Town. He's on the ball."

She spoke quite eagerly.

Rob turned away from that beautiful face. He wanted to fall in with her suggestion and yet — he wondered if he could take the Hallings for a whole fortnight. Suddenly he spoke with frankness.

"Cricket and Boyce are all right, of course, but I'm not sure I want to spend a whole holiday with them. With you and Des — yes, indeed."

"You wouldn't have to be with the Hallings all that much. We shall all go our own ways, and I'm sure we'd find you a gorgeous girl," said Nira gaily.

"I don't want any gorgeous girls," Rob said shortly.

"Well, think it over, Rob."

"Thank you," he said, and now behind the tinted glasses his eyes were warm and grateful, "I'm very touched. I will indeed think it over. You must make sure first that the Hallings and your husband won't object. I'd be spoiling the foursome."

"You wouldn't!" she protested.

But they dropped the subject for the moment. Nira half forgot that she'd made the invitation. But Rob remembered it and was tempted.

4

"OH, GOD, THE kids are awake!" said Des.

He had just let Nira into the house. The light had been left on over the porch and there was one on in the hall. Nira slipped off her short fur jacket. Soft, brown, silky and rather like mink — but not mink, which was something that Des had promised but never been able to afford to buy her.

Now she saw what he saw — two small figures in dressing-gowns, sitting at the top of the staircase. Renira holding her best doll. Jonathan clutching a model aeroplane which he had just made and from which he refused to be parted.

Nira went to the foot of the stairs and called up rather crossly, "What *are* you two doing out of bed?"

They ran down the stairs. For all her crossness she opened her arms and gathered them to her. But she spoke severely.

"Go on — tell me why you aren't both fast asleep tucked up in your beds?"

Renira giggled. She had a slight lisp.

"My dollie couldn't thleep, either."

Jonathan, the beloved son who was the apple of Nira's eye, tall, rather grave-faced, with his father's chestnut, springing hair, and her soft grey-blue eyes, said, "I did go to sleep, Mummy, but I woke up, and Rennie came into my bed because she'd had a nightmare and she was crying."

Desmond, not waiting to listen to this, had walked into the dining-room and was pouring himself out a whisky and soda, which Nira noticed with disapproval. He had had quite enough champagne at the party — more than enough, and she wasn't at all sure she was feeling friendly towards him. She addressed her children, "Nightmare or no nightmare, do you realise that it's half-past two in the morning?"

"I know it's half-patht two," said Renira, "because I heard the grandfather clock and Jonnie told me what it said."

"Why didn't you call Susan? She's sleeping here tonight, you know it."

The children looked at each other. The mother, her thoughts wandering away from them because she was still looking through the open door at Des, drinking that whisky, tried to concentrate on the children again. Renira's blue woolly dressing-gown, with the white appliquéd rabbit on each pocket, was getting far too small. The child was growing fast — would be leggy and tall like her brother. All Des's family were tall. Renira wasn't as angelic as Jonathan, but very attractive with her *retroussé* nose, her enormous dark eyes, like Des's, and straight fair hair which in the daytime was tied back in a pony tail but at this time of night fell charmingly across her face.

Jonathan began to explain that they hadn't called Susan because they heard her snoring and decided not to wake her up. They then both giggled about the snoring, and suddenly Nira felt she couldn't cope with all this fun at such an hour. She felt cold and tired. She clapped her hands and ordered the children off to bed.

"This minute, the pair of you, up you go and not another word, or I'll tell Daddy no pocket money tomorrow."

"Oh, Mum!" Jonathan began to protest loudly. "He owes it to me. You told me you've always got to pay people what you owe them. Besides, Simon says we ought to have a union and strike if we don't get what we want."

"Yes, we'll stwike," said Renira, after which she became convulsed with laughter. But Nira felt that she had no sense of humour just for the moment. Unrelenting, she lectured and threatened, and finally the children went up to bed, grumbling. There was silence. Nira joined Des in the dining-room.

"Aren't *you* coming up?"

"Have a drink—" he began affably, and she thought he tottered very slightly and this so aggravated her that she spoke with more irritation than she had ever shown him before.

"I don't want a drink and you're not going to have another one either. You've had quite enough." She marched up to him, took away the whisky bottle and banged it down on the sideboard.

He laughed and rather thickly began to protest. "Steady on, ducky, it's two pound-something a bottle these days. Don't break it."

Nira stood glaring at him quite aware of the fact that he was taking not the slightest notice either of her attitude or tone of her voice. He even made an attempt to kiss her. Then she lost her temper, which was very rare because as a rule he could do no wrong, and it took a lot to upset her. She pushed him away.

"I've just had about enough of you for one night, Des. If you don't sober up and come to bed I'll—I'll—" she broke off, her face flushed, her eyes bright with angry tears.

"But darling, I'm not drunk. What's got into you?"

"Well, if you're not drunk, you're certainly not sober. You've been swilling champagne the whole evening, and—"

"Oh, rubbish," he broke in rather rudely, and his affability vanished. If she could glare at him, he could glare, too, and he did.

Her heart sank low. She could never remember them looking at each other like this before. In the past, the nearest they had ever come to a real row was when he had been particularly hard on Jonathan for not liking games and she had been up in arms on the side of her sweet, sensitive little son. Yes, they had been angry

39

with each other that day but not quite like this, and she had soon melted and they had been reconciled. But this was different and Nira, who did not like to keep anything locked away, and wanted to stay close to her husband, let loose the anger that had been consuming her since they left the party. She had taken great pains not to show it while they were still Rob's guests.

"And how much champagne did your friend Rob order anyhow?" Des spoke again, "I don't think any of us had more than we could take. It wasn't all that much of a party."

"How *could* you? It was a super party and he must have spent a fortune on the drinks. He's the last man on earth you'd call mean and he isn't all that rich."

Des shrugged. He kept a longing eye on the whisky bottle.

"Oh, I know he's your pet."

"You're being ridiculous! He's nobody's pet. He's not that sort of man. But what I'd like to know is how much Cricket gave *you* to drink once you got her home."

"I didn't go into the house."

Suddenly Nira felt frozen. It was as though a cold hand had been laid on her heart. *She didn't believe him.* Some strong intuition told her that he was not telling the truth.

"Des," she said, "whatever happens, don't let's start telling each other lies, *please*. I just couldn't bear it. I don't mind what you do but you *mustn't* lie to me. I didn't mind you taking Cricket home. You know I didn't. I've never been jealous, now have I?"

His eyes, not focusing very well, swivelled away from her. He gave a stupid laugh.

"No need to be, honey. You're my wife and —" he cast a glance upwards and added dramatically, "the mother of my children."

She could see that he was trying to be funny, and take the edge off their argument, but something drove her to continue it.

"Des — will you please sober up and tell me the truth. Did you or didn't you stay with Cricket and have drinks in her house? When you came back you were flushed and talking very loudly and *quite* unlike yourself."

Now he scowled.

"For God's sake don't start nagging me in the early hours of the morning. I couldn't take it."

"But you're going to tell me the truth," she persisted.

He put his hands in his coat pockets and swayed a very little from heel to toe.

"And what if I did spend a few minutes with Cricket? Is it a crime?"

Nira drew a breath. All her colour had gone. She looked suddenly very pale. The cold feeling of fear seemed to be clutching her heart a little more tightly.

"Des, I fully realise that you took her home because you wanted to be alone with her and not because she had a migraine or any such nonsense. Why don't you own up to it? You've got a thing about Cricket, haven't you? I've never taken it very seriously until tonight, but—"

"Well, if you take my advice you won't take it seriously now," he broke in and patted his lips to stifle a yawn. "Honestly, sweetie, I'm getting a bit bored with this. Let's go upstairs."

She said, "I thought it was very odd you offering to take her back like that—because she had a perfectly good husband of her own to look after her."

Des laughed.

"He'd had a ball all evening and was doing the good-boy act with Joyce Moffatt when Cricket folded. I wouldn't have disturbed him for worlds."

"That's nonsense."

"Anyhow, what are you so steamed up about? You were pretty engrossed with old Rob."

"I did not go home to Rob's house and have a drinking session alone with him," said Nira coldly.

"I wouldn't have bawled you out if you had."

She stared at him open-mouthed.

"Then *you* aren't at all jealous? You wouldn't mind what I did with other men?"

"Oh, really, Nira, you're being very dramatic. Why this attitude? Why the inquisition? You've always said you had no use for possessive wives."

"I've never been possessive, but there are limits."

He gave that stupid laugh again. Suddenly she found him singularly unattractive. She never remembered him being in this state before. What was happening to Des? Frantically she wondered where all the warmth and understanding that had existed between them had gone. What *had* happened tonight to make her feel so suspicious, so alarmed? Her eyes suddenly filled with tears which spilled over and rolled down her cheeks.

"I don't like possessive wives and I never wanted to be one, but

41

I do think you've got to be able to trust your husband," she said.

"So you don't trust me."

"I always have done."

"But not tonight."

Now the colour rose in her cheeks and she turned away and brushed the tears from her lashes.

"I didn't exactly say that. It's just that—oh, I don't know, forget it!" she added with sudden violence. "I'm being tired and silly. I am sure you did nothing more than crack a bottle of champagne with dear little Cricket."

Des turned from the alluring sight of the whisky. He was sobering up fast and he didn't like to see Nira's face stained with tears. It was such an unusual sight. Besides which, he had a very definite conscience. He knew perfectly well that it hadn't been just a question of 'cracking a bottle'. Cricket had been a little devil, and not for the first time if it came to that. There had been other occasions. She had a way with her; that flute-like voice and those big eyes; and the innocent nymphet-side she used as a cover-up for the sensual little cat she really was. Hell to it, a man was only flesh and blood, and he certainly was no saint. When she had turned her back to him and said archly, "Unzip me, darling— I'm going to bed as soon as you've gone," he had responded with alacrity—and didn't go. He found her an exciting change—with her petite curves and petal-soft rosy skin and dimples—a complete contrast to Nira's tall slenderness, her narrow hips and fine long legs.

Cricket played the little girl very prettily, and made him feel fine and strong. He was grateful too because she showed such blatant pleasure in him and kept saying, "You're *terrific*, Des— why can't we have fun like this more often?"

When he had asked her with some curiosity whether she had any qualms about being unfaithful to Boyce, she had laughed and said gaily why have a conscience when she knew Boyce was unfaithful to her. Then she had suggested that Des must find life a bit dreary at times because darling Nira was inclined to be serious and possessive—yes, she had used that word—and it had annoyed Des. He had told Cricket that he didn't want to discuss Nira, but it had all ended with more champagne and more passionate kisses and then he had left her and gone back to the hotel to rejoin Rob's party. He had been a bit sloshed by then and knew it. In his overheated imagination he looked back and thought it had all been a lot of fun with Cricket and could go on being so if he could get away with it. Cricket had quite convinced him that Boyce wouldn't mind and from what he had seen of old Boyce's behaviour, Des thought it true. But what about Nira? She was not the promiscuous type. He could hardly count on her to turn a blind eye to his conduct *if* she found out. It wasn't as though she fooled around with other men as Cricket or Maggie did or any of that lot. In one way it pleased him. He was proud of Nira. She had a damned fine character. But it would have been a bit more fun, perhaps, if she'd wanted fun and games now and then with, say, Boyce or even old Rob Bessiford. Of course Rob was a bit of a dry stick — she surely wouldn't fall for him, even for an hour or two. But she seemed to like him a lot. It could happen . . . here Des's thoughts broke off. All this was very much in his mind and he hadn't the least wish to crack up his marriage, or start anything awkward with his wife. They'd always been very pleased with each other. Why ask for trouble now? He loved her and his kids and his home. It was just, he told himself, that he hadn't got it in him to be as perfect as Nira might wish.

He was sufficiently sober now to review the whole evening's entertainment with more caution, and with a revival of the old tenderness for Nira. He walked up to her and pulled her into his arms.

"Hey! What's this all about, honey?" he asked, and put out a finger and touched the tear that was just rolling down her cheek. Then he kissed her like a lover. "This is ridiculous," he whispered. "I love you. Don't for God's sake jump to wrong conclusions just because I took Cricket home. I've never seen you so upset. You must be round the bend to be jealous of *her*, darling. Pull yourself together."

Nira responded quickly and with her whole heart. She relaxed in his arms and buried her face against his shoulder, hugging him tightly.

"Oh, I do love you, Des. I couldn't share you with anybody."

"Who's asked you to?" He laughed easily and brushed aside the memory of the exciting way Cricket had of driving a fellow crazy. He was content to hold Nira's cool loveliness and caress her, but without the same sort of passion. With one hand he stroked the bent dark head and kept telling her how much he loved her and that she wasn't to be so suspicious. Finally she apologised for her outburst and they went up the staircase with their arms around each other. Once in bed they almost at once fell into the sleep of sheer exhaustion.

In the morning neither of them made allusion to the Cricket incident. Des felt off-colour—Nira took him Alka-Seltzer, then left him to sleep it off and relieved Susan of the children. It was her Sunday off.

Nira couldn't quite forget last night, but she felt sure in the cold light of day that there was no need for her to have been so upset.

The sun was shining, Des suggested that if it stayed fine he'd drive them to Chanctonbury Ring. They'd climb up to the top of the Downs to see the beautiful Hammer Ponds. Then he'd give them lunch at Storrington.

All seemed right with Nira's world. Jonathan and Renira were in high spirits and had only one quarrel and that was about who should sit beside Daddy. Nira always let one of them do this while she sat at the back with the other child.

It appeared to be Renira's turn, which brought protests from Jonathan who was sure it was his. It ended as usual with Nira having to threaten to cancel the whole party unless they stopped quarrelling.

Nira knew she ought to be in great spirits and yet for some reason, which she had no intention of analysing, that cosy happy secure little world in which she had lived with Des and the children so long did not seem *quite* the same as it had done yesterday. A discordant note had crept into the song they usually sang together. The rhythm was spoilt. Des had denied that there was any cause for her jealousy and she had accepted his word. But she couldn't quite recapture the old sensation of complete trust. She even began to wonder if she was being silly and old-fashioned even to expect complete fidelity these days.

Bit by bit her fears settled down. By the time Des appeared and went out to the garage to fetch the car, she was happy again but one thing became apparent. She could not like Cricket any more. She might trust Des but she did not trust Cricket. They were all supposed to be going away together this summer. That seemed a pity now. She didn't want that foursome. Particularly as she was beginning to dislike Boyce. She wished she could work her way out of that little circle, and go away with Des alone.

Then she remembered that she had suggested that Rob might

join them. He hadn't seemed averse to the idea even though he had been afraid that he would make an unwanted fifth.

All the same, before that Sunday ended Nira had silently made up her mind to broach the Rob idea to Des, and if he didn't mind, she'd urge Rob to join them. She believed he'd enjoy it — lonely and bored as he was. And to her, somehow, he stood for safety (why she really didn't know) but she would like to have him along with them this summer. Perhaps his mere presence would put a brake on the flirtatious, and irrepressible Cricket — and, still more so, damp down Boyce!

On the bright warm April day the family enjoyed Chanctonbury Ring. It was windy, but sunny on the high Downs which gave them such a remarkable view of the Sussex Weald.

The children had fun. Des who had started out by complaining of a headache, felt better as the day wore on and was only short-tempered when the lunch turned out to be a failure. The food was half-cold and not as good as usual, and the service was poor. By the time they got home Jonathan and Renira, who had rushed madly over the Downs, were over-tired. Jonathan teased his little sister and made her cry. Des snapped and reduced his son to tears. In the end Nira was glad to get the children off to bed, then settle down to a quiet hour watching television with her husband.

Des went to sleep in the middle of the Sunday night play which rather annoyed Nira as she was enjoying it and liked to have someone to be observant and critical with her. She stared at Des who was slumped back in his chair and thought suddenly that he looked much older. The heavy drinking of last night seemed to have hit him harder than usual. Inevitably her thoughts returned to Cricket and the champagne Des had surely shared with her in her house.

Nira tried to concentrate on the television again, but once Des stirred and yawned and exhibited some signs of life, she brought up the subject of the forthcoming holiday in Majorca.

She drew a tapestried stool close to his chair and sat there smoking a cigarette. She was not a dedicated smoker but liked one after her meals, and one last thing at night. Turning her head, she looked at Des with the warm smile that narrowed her eyes, and which most people found so delightful.

"Des — I want to talk to you about Majorca."

He ran his fingers through his hair, gave her a sleepy smile, and looked down at the hand she had laid on his knee. It was rather long, fine-boned and slightly tanned. He had always admired her beautiful nails. She was careful of them and wore rubber gloves when she washed up. Tonight they were especially attractive because she had had a manicure for the party. They were varnished a deep rose. He patted the lovely hand and tried not to yawn. He was still feeling the worse for last night.

"What about it?"

"If we could get a room for Rob, would you object to him coming along with us?"

Now Des felt more wide awake. He sat up and reached for a cigarette. She lit it for him. His immediate reaction to her suggestion was to reject it.

"What on earth do we want him for? There are the four of us — the Hallings and us — why a fifth?"

"Darling, we can still play our bridge or cut in if Rob wants to play, and quite frankly we're not going to the Formentor to play cards. We only said it would be useful to have a bridge-four in case it was bad weather, but everyone says it should be gorgeous in Majorca in early September."

He frowned slightly. "Why ask old Rob? He doesn't sort of fit in, does he?"

"Oh, I don't see why not. Everybody likes him. Even Cricket said the other day that he was very good-looking really, and had a lot of charm in his quiet funny way."

"Darling, we don't really need quiet charm, do we? I mean, it will spoil the foursome," Des grumbled again.

Suddenly Nira drew her hand away from his knee. She found that she wanted in a stubborn way to defeat Des on this issue.

"I think it would be a great kindness to Rob. He was the first to say that surely he wouldn't be wanted, but I don't agree. He's always so amiable. Everybody likes him. The kids adore him, and he *is* a bachelor."

"So you've often said. I like old Rob too — but I don't see why we should suddenly include him in our foursome. Besides, we mightn't even be able to get a room for him."

"Okay — if we don't, he can't come."

She was smiling at him again, but it struck him suddenly that Nira really *wanted* Rob on this holiday. He ruffled her hair and laughed — his humour restored.

"Sweetie—is this just because you're sorry for the lone bachelor, or because you've suddenly got a bit sentimental about him and want him to cherish yourself?"

"Don't be silly. I don't want to cherish any man but you."

"You're a darling," said Des, but he said it rather mechanically, and was finding it difficult to control that desire to yawn. He didn't really mind if Rob did join them in Majorca. It just seemed an odd idea. But he knew his wife. She was always particularly nice to lame dogs, and Rob in his opinion was one. To his mind the friendship between his wife and Rob was just that.

"What would the Hallings say?" he asked.

"I don't think they can say anything. It's really our party. We asked them to join us and *I* booked the rooms."

"Have you any particular reason for altering the plans, honey? Of course I'm only teasing you about old Rob. I expect you find him a bore really."

She didn't and was honest enough to say so, but now that innate honesty led her to add something that she had been wanting to say for a long time.

"If you want to know, Des darling, I just can't take Boyce the whole time. I mean, quite frankly, *you* enjoy Cricket's company; most men do, and she's attractive and amusing, but Boyce—well—I don't know what it is about him but there's something which rather shakes me at times."

"Has he tried anything on with you?"

"Not definitely, but when he dances with me he gets as close as he can and he flatters me all the time and—oh, I don't know, he just makes me feel that he's wanting to sort of get-together with me, and I just don't want it."

Des got up, moved away from her, walked to the mantelpiece and looked at his reflection in the gilt-framed antique mirror. He scowled, put out his tongue, didn't like what he saw, and put it back. He was slightly worried by what Nira had just told him. He knew Boyce was a bit of a bastard, but he had half hoped that Nira liked him sufficiently to enjoy being paired off with him on this holiday. It would have left him, Des, more time and freedom for pretty Cricket. He ought to be ashamed of himself for having such ideas and he adored Nira, but dammit, a man did sometimes need the stimulus of a new face, a fresh passion, after eleven years of marriage.

He liked to believe he'd been a devoted husband because his wife was ignorant of his lapses from fidelity. Then Cricket fell for him. He found her irresistible—she roused all that was most sensual in him. He knew that he would get tired of her as he had done of other promiscuous love affairs. He would have been alarmed at the mere idea of Nira finding out, and wanting to leave him, or any such thing. Nothing was further from his mind. He just wanted to eat his cake and have it. He knew a lot of other men who managed to do that. He wasn't the only one. But he did think it a pity, perhaps, that Nira was quite so single-minded about him, and so disinclined to enter into any kind of flirtation with any other man, no matter how light or meaningless it would be. He wouldn't of course, want her to be actually unfaithful to him, but it was a pity she was quite so reserved. It would just have fitted in with his schemes a bit more, for instance, if she had found Boyce attractive. He had been mistaken in imagining that was so. She had made it quite obvious tonight that Boyce annoyed and even alarmed her.

"You do understand what I have been telling you, don't you darling?" Nira asked him.

"Of course, of course. Why not cancel the whole holiday if Boyce upsets you? I don't want you upset."

"I don't want to cancel Majorca, darling. That's absurd. Don't let's exaggerate the situation. It's just that I know you could have a lot of fun with Cricket, but I don't want to have fun with Boyce."

"Of course not," said Des with a heartiness he was far from feeling. "And you needn't think I'm out to spend all my time with Cricket, either."

Now Nira blew a ring of smoke into the air and gave him an impish look.

"No, dear, I'm sure you're not!" Her friendly laughter redeemed the sarcasm but it was not lost on him, and he began to feel that he would have to be more careful. He remembered the little devil Cricket had told him last night that she was going to make him take her to some lonely uninhabited beach, right away from the others, *and* she had enlarged on what could happen on the lovely lonely beach!

"Darling," Nira's voice interrupted his thoughts. "Let's forget about Rob. We'll stick to our old plan and I'm not all that averse to Boyce so long as he's sensible, otherwise I wouldn't have agreed to it in the first place. We've always got on well together—all four of us. I even find Cricket fun when she doesn't drink too much or be so coquettish. Our kids like each other—I don't know what Jonathan would do without Simon. They're going to have a big get-together while the parents are away. We mustn't cause ill-feeling. It would be wrong. Besides, it's all arranged. Don't let's give it another thought."

But this was where Des changed his mind. Why not let old Rob be included in the party? At least he knew that Nira was fond of him. He'd distract her attention a bit from Cricket, per-haps. As for Boyce, there were sure to be one or two unattached dolly-birds in a big hotel like The Formentor, and once he found Nira engrossed with Rob, Boyce would soon seek an alternative.

"I think I was wrong about old Rob," Des said briskly. "By all means let's include him in the party. Ring up the agents in the morning and see if you can get him a room."

Nira was pleased though anxious not to get her own way at the cost of annoying her husband. But when he made it clear that he really didn't object and even agreed that it might be doing a great kindness to Rob, Nira stopped talking. It was all fixed.

Once in bed, Des, who was nothing if not greedy, decided that he had better pull himself together and stop thinking about Cricket. He made love to his wife with a sudden hot flash of passion that took her breath away, and left her completely satisfied.

All was well again between them. She told herself that nothing was of real importance except the fact that they loved each other. They always would.

Des accepted his wife's total surrender and response—without conscience. After all, he decided yet again that the average man needed not one woman in his life, but two. That being so, he excused his attitude of mind and was as pleased with Nira's devotion as with Cricket's attentions. He could manage them both. He was nothing if not a diplomat, he told himself gaily and went to sleep holding a happy and contented Nira in his arms.

5

BOYCE AND CRICKET had a row about Rob's inclusion in the summer holiday.

With vast indignation Cricket broke the news to her husband when he came home from the office a week after Rob's birthday party.

"I think it's the end. When I saw Nira this morning — we both happened to be in Sainsbury's — she told me she'd suggested that Rob should go with us, and said Des didn't mind and they were hoping to get a room for Rob at The Formentor. That means there'll be *five* of us. Don't you think it's an absolute bore?"

Boyce privately thought rather more than that. He actually changed colour, and poured himself out a stronger gin than usual. Everything had gone wrong for him at the office today. One of the projects they were working on had proved unsuccessful. His partner's blonde secretary, whom he had rather stupidly kissed one day, had taken him more seriously than he intended. She was now writing amorous notes and he really didn't want her on his hands. He had certain money problems — he was always spending above his income and although he was making more money these days, there was Cricket with her overdraft and constant extravagances and the general rising cost of living. *And* that new petulant cry from her: "Everything's going up. You ought to give me more for housekeeping."

Now his little schemes for softening Nira up while they were abroad looked like being thwarted. Rob was a first-rate fellow but he wasn't, in Boyce's opinion, quite one of the Ponders Heath charmed circle. Somehow he always stood outside it, and he'd be outside it in Majorca. How were they going to pair off as Boyce had pleasurably anticipated with Rob as a fifth.

Rather viciously, Boyce poured a half-bottle of tonic into his gin, then banged it down on the table.

"Really! I've never heard of such a thing. It's a god-damned silly idea. Is it a certainty?"

"Yes, if the agency can get him a room and I bet just because we don't want them to, they will."

"Who engineered this? You? I thought you were all out for moonlight on the seashore alone with our Des."

"So I am," said Cricket frankly. "Meanwhile you might be polite enough to offer me a drink."

"Help yourself."

"You wouldn't say that to Nira."

"Oh, don't be silly," Boyce said, his eyes dark and angry. He really couldn't be bothered with his exacting wife tonight, but he got up and poured her gin. "It's Nira who wants Rob on the holiday, I suppose," he grunted.

Cricket looked at him through her lashes. She felt suddenly spiteful.

"Well, she never does behave as though she is all out for moonlight shores *toute seule* with you, dear. Maybe she wants to initiate dear innocent old Rob into the sweet mysteries of life and love."

"Oh, shut up," said Boyce rudely.

"Diddums want his Nirry all to himself," cooed Cricket, who was feeling rather pleased with life, and still confident that she was going to have a good innings with Des out in Majorca—Rob or no Rob. It would amuse her to see Boyce fighting Rob desperately for pride of place with Nira. She admitted that Nira had a gorgeous figure and was very dignified and charming, but she didn't see what the men were so mad about. All that virtue! In Cricket's opinion—and she considered herself an expert in the matter—men wanted a bit more fire and excitement than Nira Curtis offered. A bit of holding back before the final surrender—yes. But in the long run Nira would be far too gentle and mild. However, although Cricket was bored with her own husband and mad about Des, she was maliciously pleased because Boyce was not getting all he wanted.

"Did Nira guess that we mightn't want Rob in the party?" asked Boyce in a sulky voice.

"Oh, she sort of suggested that if we objected she'd fob him off, but of course I couldn't say we did. The Curtises originally organised the holiday and I don't really mind old Rob. I think he's quite sweet in his way."

"There's too much sweetness being poured around here," said

Boyce with an acidity he had been storing up all day. "You make me tired."

"Don't be stupid. I didn't say I wanted Rob on the party. I told you I was cross about it. Why don't you tell your darling Nira how you feel?"

"I can't very well. It's too late anyhow."

They wrangled until dinner time when their son joined them. Then Boyce complained of the meal—Cricket never had been a good cook. The beef was overdone, which Boyce disliked, and the roast potatoes were soft. He liked them crisp.

Simon seized his plateful and went back to the lounge to sit in front of the television in order to see a special crime play. Husband and wife started to bicker again, and this time Cricket had to climb down, Boyce held the financial reins. She wanted some extra cash for new holiday clothes. She knew she had to be careful to keep on Boyce's right side. She wanted to look particularly alluring in Majorca—for Des.

Finally she pretended to be on Boyce's side and to sympathise about the Rob affair. But if she wanted fun with Des she'd better ensure that Boyce found some distraction. She, Cricket, would no doubt take Rob off all their hands sometimes. There was a band in The Formentor and a dance every night. Rob couldn't dance, so Boyce would keep his dear Nira for his partner. And Cricket didn't think Nira particularly wanted to chum up with Rob, anyway. It was just that she was sorry for him being so lonely, she told Boyce soothingly.

"Don't let's worry about it any more. I was angry at first but I'm not now. Give Cricket a kiss," and she went up to his chair and put her arms around his neck.

Boyce's humour was restored. He returned the kiss but his thoughts were still on Nira. Her continual cool rejection of him—unspoken but obvious—was getting on his nerves.

That very next evening he and Cricket went to dinner and bridge at the Curtises' house. The first thing Nira had to tell them was that Boyce's fears had been realised. There'd been a single-room cancellation at The Formentor and Rob had got it.

Cricket, her big blue eyes dancing, looked wickedly at her husband.

"Isn't that nice, Boyce?"

"It's okay by me," he said icily.

Nira, who felt relaxed and happy this evening, said, "I think

Rob feels rather embarrassed about it all but I persuaded him we're pleased. I do think it'll be a real break for him. He must get terribly fed up with life at The Hollies with his old aunt."

"Yes," said Cricket, "after that wonderful life he led in Kenya. It was a sweet idea of yours, Nira."

Here Des cut in. "I was a bit worried that you two might mind," he said, looking from Boyce to Cricket.

"Of course we don't," said Cricket and gave him a look that set his pulses racing. She had a frightful effect on him, he reflected.

"Why should we?" asked Boyce, but he looked at Nira. She didn't notice it. She was busy with her entertaining. *Beautiful as ever*, Boyce thought moodily, *too damned superior and unattainable*. It drove him mad—with a longing of which he was far too conscious. It wasn't like him to be so serious about girls. Most of them fell for him. Why must Nira be the exception?

He began to feel that Rob's presence in Majorca wouldn't really make the slightest difference. He wasn't in the running for Nira anyhow. He wouldn't need to battle with Rob. It was Nira, herself, he would have to fight.

He didn't get a chance to speak to her alone that evening. The bridge party went off as well as usual, although once or twice Boyce's cold shrewd mind became alive to the fact that Desmond was beginning to drink rather a lot. It reddened his face, made his voice louder. He blared, and he laughed a lot. Looking from him to Nira, Boyce also thought that he saw a slight look of disapproval in those wonderful eyes. He couldn't blame her. Boyce had a fondness for women but not for wine. He didn't think the two went well together and he preferred women.

Yes, he was sure Des was not only downing the whisky but throwing too many sidelong glances at Cricket. He wondered if Nira was conscious of this. She gave no sign of being the least upset so far as *that* was concerned, although she did at one juncture put a slim hand over Des's glass and say, "Easy, darling. You'll be trumping my aces in a moment." To which Des responded with one of his hearty laughs and promptly poured himself out another whisky.

The result was inevitable. Des began to play carelessly. As a rule he and Nira were the superior pair. Cricket was erratic and sometimes rather stupid about cards. Boyce was used to losing when he played in this house. Tonight Des overcalled and went down, doubled and vulnerable, on two occasions. He paid his losses—and Nira's—with his usual good humour, apologised to her, ruffled her hair gaily and said, "I don't think I was playing up to form, do you sweetie?"

The watchful Boyce now for the first time saw Nira's mouth tighten, and although she smiled, her voice was hard. "You weren't, were you?"

That was all but Boyce could sense the reproach behind it. He really had to admire Nira as much for her character as for her extreme beauty. She was so controlled. Cricket would have stormed at him and called him an 'old boozer', or any other name she could think of. Some of the women he played bridge with held post-mortems and liked to prove that the heavy loss was all their husband's fault. Nira said absolutely nothing to Des while she collected the cards and tore up the used markers. On the way home, Boyce mentioned this to his wife. Cricket giggled.

"I bet there's a super post-mortem going on now. Des really did play badly tonight. Did you think he was drinking a teeny-weeny bit too much?"

"Teeny-weeny is a masterly understatement," said Boyce.

"Well, I don't blame him. Nira's gorgeous but she does rather expect a lot of a man, don't you think?"

Boyce put his tongue in his cheek. It wasn't unusual for Cricket to try and disparage Nira. He held his peace. But as they turned into the drive of their own house he had one more thing to say on the subject of Des and Nira.

"You're wrong about a post-mortem going on back in the Curtises' home. I'll lay you a wager she won't say a word to him about the game. She's a very diplomatic sort of girl."

Cricket's blue eyes widened. She giggled again. Who cared? Des could drink as much as he liked, so far as she was concerned. She just doted on him. He was such fun and so *passionate*. Boyce left her cold these days. And as for Nira, let Boyce think her an angel. Who cared? She, Cricket, didn't. And as Boyce fancied Nira, Cricket didn't feel she need have much conscience about taking Des as a lover.

Her parting shots were to make further disparaging remarks about Nira. She couldn't cure herself of that habit she had of pecking in a nasty little way at the other women in the neighbourhood whom she thought too attractive to men.

"I've never met a real angel, but I've a horrid suspicion that if I

54

did, I'd find her an awful bore. Maybe Des's drinking because he's bored with his angelic Nira."

Boyce continued to hold his peace. He let himself into the house with a cynical smile on his thin lips.

As he so rightly predicted, in the Curtis home; Nira was not reproaching her husband although she felt, for the first time during her marriage, the horrid sensation of having been let down.

Her love for her big, handsome, genial husband had always been so entire. She had never once doubted that it was deserved — and returned. He had his faults. She was not so stupid as to think that any man could be perfect. But Des had supplied all her needs so far.

She had perhaps always known in the depths of her heart that he was a little shallow and that there was something deeper in her own nature. He was a Philistine. She from her schooldays had been interested in art and philosophy, but after her marriage these things had taken second place to her love for Des and their children and the home.

She did not want her trust and happiness to subside in the smallest way. It must always be kept up to standard.

There was a stubborn streak in Nira and without being of a combative disposition, she was prepared to fight for things she believed in. However, there was going to be no open fight with Des on this question of drinking.

She remembered how, when she was a teenager, an uncle on her mother's side had come to live with them for a time, and was rarely sober. Her mother had reluctantly admitted that he drank too much.

Fresh, innocent, idealistic, the young Nira had expressed her indignation and announced that she couldn't understand why neither of her parents ever stopped Uncle Bill from drinking. When he wanted a whisky, they gave it to him. They should have made him take soft drinks, Nira said. She had then received her first lesson in how to deal with this human weakness. First and foremost, never to nag. Her mother told Nira that Aunt Jean, Uncle Bill's Scot's wife, had done too much of that. She hid the whisky — nagged at Bill every time he brought home a bottle — and this only drove him to drink more. He had been going through a bad time in the City and was harassed and very tired. Possibly he needed the extra stimulant, and if Jean had been sensible and not denied it to him, he might have got over the bad phase and settled down to the usual harmless glass or two, which the average man needed.

Nira had seen the wisdom in this, but she remembered telling her mother about a girl friend whose father never drank at all and was a teetotaller. Didn't Mummy believe that was best? Mummy had smiled and patted Nira's cheek and told her that she must learn to accept all kinds of people with all kinds of different ideas and principles. The great word—the operative word—to adhere to through life she declared was *tolerance*.

Nira never forgot that lesson. She could see for herself that Aunt Jean had been an intolerant woman. The young Nira had made a vow that she would never be like that. So now when it came to the test, and she had to face the fact that Des, for some reason best known to himself, was exceeding his ordinary quota of alcohol, she behaved with the diplomacy Boyce had attributed to her. It was Des, not Nira, who mentioned the alcoholic evening. First in bed, he watched Nira brush her long silky hair and in a mumbling voice suggested that she should hurry up and join him. It was midnight and he was sleepy, he said.

She put down her brush and turned to him smiling.

"Then go to sleep, darling. I'm not ready."

He blinked at her and held out a hand.

"Oh, come on—and while you're about it—how about getting me a drink? I'm damned thirsty."

Now she went back a little on her own philosophy.

"Haven't you had enough?"

"Possibly. But I like it. Don't try and ration me."

That stung her. She didn't think she deserved it. Her cheeks went hot and pink. She turned from him and continued to brush her hair.

The next thing she heard was a loud snore. When she looked at her husband again he was fast asleep. Mouth open, grunting, he didn't really look as handsome or attractive as usual. Her heart suddenly sank low. She slipped into bed beside him and switched off the light. The sound of his snoring was not conducive to sleep. He did snore sometimes and she usually managed to ignore it; snuggled up to him, warm and content. Tonight she felt chilled and lonely. Contentment was far from her heart. This Des was a stranger. With all her heart she loved him but her idol was toppling a little on its plinth, and she was horrified at the prospect of it crashing to the ground.

She could not bear the isolation. She put out a hand and shook him, hot tears in her eyes.

"Des, Des, wake up. You haven't kissed me good night."

He made no answer but edged away from her grunting again. The snores intensified.

For a moment she thought she was going to cry. On second thoughts she decided that she was being stupid. He had done nothing frightful. Let him have a few extra drinks if he wanted. Everything would be all right in the morning. She mustn't lose her sense of humour or expect too much. After a sleepless hour she was not very happy and she put on a dressing-gown and retreated to the spare bedroom where she curled up in a blanket and soon was sound asleep.

As usual she was the first to get up. She woke Desmond with a cup of tea. He looked livery and obviously had a hangover, but he was full of remorse.

"I drank too much, didn't I? Darling, I'm frightfully sorry. I played ghastly bridge, too, I remember. I don't know what came over me. And you had to go into the spare room, poor sweet! I suppose I was snoring like hell."

Nira gave him a faint smile.

"You were, and it's time you got going, darling, or you'll miss your train."

He ate no breakfast but drank two large cups of coffee. Shaven and spruce, in his city suit, his thick brown hair brushed and shining, he was her Des again, treating her with the usual consideration and begging her to forgive him.

The unhappiness of the night was forgotten. They embraced happily—close and normal again. Nira drove the children to school and began to tackle the day's work as usual. Only one awkward thought of last night's bridge party troubled her. She hoped it wasn't going to be repeated—at least not so that anyone would notice it. If Des were to start to drink heavily, it would be too awful, she reflected. She *couldn't* love a drunk. There was something so repellent about being close and intimate with a man who was full of alcohol and whose breath smelled and who didn't even behave in a civilised manner. The blaring voice, the boastful manner, the rather idiotic grin, then the sudden aggressiveness— all this would become unbearable. But at least he had assured her it wouldn't happen again.

That next evening, he took her out to a film they had both

marked down as being worth seeing. They had a pleasant time and he was once more the Des she knew and was so dear to her. She went to sleep happily with his arm around her in what she called their 'spoon and fork' position—homely, comforting, married bliss.

During the few weeks that followed all seemed well. Des certainly didn't disgrace himself by drinking over-much, nor had Nira anything to complain of except that once or twice, as the summer approached, he rang up from the office at the last moment to say he couldn't be home for dinner. As he never seemed able to let her know his movements in advance, she couldn't make her own plans so was left to spend the evenings alone. When she asked him if it was going to be like this often, he said that he didn't get any warning himself. It was only when the senior partner asked him to stay on for some conference connected with their business, that as an executive in a big firm he couldn't very well say no. Nira was determined to be patient and co-operative, and tried not to grumble. If Des was working so hard for her and the children, it was up to her to make things easy for him.

Then one day early in June he phoned her from the office just before five and told her it was going to be another late night in the office and suggested she asked someone to spend the evening with her, watch television or something.

"I shall begin to believe you've got a blonde up there," she teased him.

He gave one of his hearty laughs.

"I'm too busy and tired for lovely blondes, my darling. Look—why don't you ring up old Rob and get him to come round and have a chat with you? I won't be jealous."

"You don't have to be jealous of any man, and I'm quite sure I don't have to be jealous of any woman, joking apart."

"You couldn't be more right."

"I'll ring Rob. As a matter of fact I'd quite enjoy a chat with him and I know he gets enough of Aunt Ida."

Rob accepted Nira's invitation with alacrity. It would be a great treat, he said, to spend an evening with her and charming of her to think of asking him.

"Des is terribly busy these days," she sighed.

"Well, his misfortune is my good luck," came Rob's quiet friendly voice, "I'll be with you within the next half hour."

6

Rob brought her a large box of chocolates and she gave him coffee and a drink. They settled down in the drawing-room. But neither of them wanted to watch television. They were both good conversationalists and Nira, having got over her disappointment of having to spend another evening without Des, found herself well entertained by Rob. Not only was he a good talker, but a sympathetic listener. She could discuss almost anything with him.

She had always known that he was like that, and although she felt a small twinge of disloyalty, she had to admit that he was, strictly speaking, a man with more understanding than her dear Des. Of course Rob was older—more mature—Des was the eternal schoolboy. There was always a touch of sadness, too, about Rob which made her feel more warmth towards him than the average man she came across.

They only stopped talking to turn on the nine o'clock news. It was while they were listening to the latest story of the American astronauts soaring towards the moon, that the telephone bell rang.

Nira answered the call in the hall. To her surprise—and some irritation—it was Boyce.

"I really wanted to say a word to old Des—" he began, but Nira cut him short.

"He isn't here. He's working late tonight."

"In that case, would you be very bored if I ran round to see you?"

"I'm sorry, Boyce, I've already got a friend here—do forgive me." Then she added on a lighter note in order not to appear hostile, "What's Cricket doing?"

"Oh, I'm a grass-widower. She's away for the night in town staying with her aunt. She planned to do a day's shopping to-morrow and Aunty's off to South Africa. She wanted to see Cricket before she went."

"Oh!" said Nira, disinterested.

Boyce tried to keep her on the line, but she managed to make it clear that she was in a hurry to get away so he said goodbye, not forgetting to add that he was very disappointed.

She put down the receiver and stood for a moment, frowning, thinking.

Des and Cricket—both up in London tonight. Oh, but why not? There couldn't possibly be any sinister connection there.

She went back to Rob, who stood up in his courteous old-fashioned way as she entered the room.

"I've switched off the news. There was nothing interesting," he said smiling. "Let's go on with our chat. I am having such a lovely evening."

She warmed to the flattery in those words and knew that he really was enjoying himself. She could see it. She enjoyed having him there, too. He couldn't be nicer.

She forgot about Des and Cricket, and made fresh coffee for Rob and herself. They were still discussing life and the age they lived in when Rob suddenly looked at his watch and said, "Good lord—I must go! I do apologise for keeping you up so late. It's half-past eleven."

She found herself quick to suggest that he should stay.

"I don't want to go to bed early unless you do."

He gave her that charming smile that crinkled the corners of his eyes, and lent that fleeting glow of youthful happiness to a tired face.

"Not in the least," he said.

"Are you hungry? Can I make you a sandwich?" she asked.

He found her, as usual, completely disarming. She was married with two children, but she seemed to him so young at times, yet such a real woman. There was nothing silly or coy about her. She had a genius for friendship—for putting a man completely at his ease.

Tonight, looking at her, he realised to the full that she had become an essential part of his life. It was wrong and sometimes he wondered whether he ought to go on seeing her. But he could not tolerate the idea of cutting her out. He could not do without her. That he was fashioning a sword for his own heart, he could well imagine. But even that fear could not turn him away. And thinking of Des he wished Nira's husband was a better type —a bit more worthy of the quite extraordinary love and devotion that she squandered on him.

Des was gay and amusing, a man's man, and very attractive to women. But Nira was serious-minded, and in Rob's opinion, Des was shallow. Just how long it would be before she was dis-illusioned and the marriage deteriorated, Rob did not know. At the moment he did not want to think about it. It would hurt her too deeply. But it remained stubbornly at the back of his mind.

He stayed with her another hour, enjoying the ham sandwiches she brought him, and drinking one more whisky.

Reluctantly but inevitably, Nira compared her husband with this man who was strong-minded enough to stop her pouring a strong drink into his glass. "Only a weak one," he said. Why couldn't Des be as moderate? Deep down she was still sore about that unpleasant episode with Des on the night of Rob's party when he had taken Cricket home.

Just before Rob left, Nira remembered that she had some new photographs of the children. She delayed him in order to show them to him. He found them charming and remarked on the likeness between Jonathan and herself.

She said, "He has Des's gorgeous chestnut hair, but my eyes. I reckon he'll be just as handsome as his dad."

Rob smiled and laid the prints down.

"You're really very fond of that husband of yours, aren't you?"

"Very." Then she made him admire little Renira's photograph.

"She's a poppet," he nodded.

"She loves Uncle Rob. So does Jon. You're awfully good with children. You know, Rob, you ought to have been married."

Now he hastily said good night. She didn't notice the sudden look of pain that darkened his eyes, nor the fact that he made no comment on her remark. She was feeling relaxed and happy after a most pleasant evening. It was only when she put out a hand to say good night and he took it and kissed it, that she became aware not for the first time, how much she liked this man. Neither could she be blind to the fact that he more than liked her.

"We must have another evening together sometime when Desmond is away," she said involuntarily.

"I'd like that," said Rob, and turned away because he was suddenly sorely tempted to do more than kiss Nira's slim, friendly hand. He wanted with all his heart to take her in his arms and hold her against his heart, tell her that she was the sweetest thing on earth and that he worshipped her.

The idea of the holiday in Majorca began to assume tremendous proportions. To be able to see and talk to *her*, every day — what a dazzling prospect! He hadn't looked forward to anything so much since he left East Africa. He couldn't wait for it.

It was only when Nira was in bed winding up her little clock, that the lateness of the hour struck her. Surely by now Desmond ought to be home. Why on earth was he so late? She felt almost guilty because she had enjoyed herself so much talking to Rob and she had hardly noticed the time till now.

Rob had been very helpful about Jonathan. Des adored his son but he was not very scholastic and never went deeply into the question of Jonathan's schooling and future education. He knew that his mother would give him the money for the fees when the time came to send Jonathan to his public school. They had him down for Shrewsbury because that was where Des was educated, but it would have been much too expensive for them to send a boy there in these days without Gandy's help. Des as a child had not been too keen on his work; it had always been *games* with him. Although Nira tried to shut her eyes to the fact, Des could at times be rather stupid. He would never be much help to Jonathan, who even at ten was showing remarkable signs of being a brainy boy. Top of his class in quite a lot of subjects — particularly keen on history. Already he had acquired an astonishing fund of knowledge. History happened to be Rob's subject. He also had a very fine library of historical novels. He had mentioned more than once to Nira that as soon as Jonathan was a little older he could go and borrow any book that would help him, in whatever period he was studying at the time.

"I wish you had been his godfather," Nira had said one day, and then out of her innate loyalty to Des, added that of course Jonathan's own godfather was a terribly nice man — but he had unfortunately died not long ago on a racing-track, trying out a new car. While he had lived Jack had never talked to Jonathan about school — only about cars. Jonathan was mildly interested, but confided in his mother that he wished Uncle Jack had been interested in history. He hadn't seemed at all impressed when Jonathan told him about the essay he had written on Henry VIII. Jonathan had read it aloud to the whole school and was proud of the fact. But Uncle Jack (and Daddy) guffawed with laughter and just made silly jokes about the Merry Monarch and his wives.

Rob had won Jonathan's heart by doing exactly the opposite. He had asked to be allowed to read Jonathan's essay and commented on its excellence and originality.

Later Jonathan said to his mother, "Uncle Rob is super to talk to, isn't he, Mum? I think he's super altogether."

That was exactly what Nira felt while she waited for Des to come home. She even felt a trifle aggrieved because Des had become slightly scathing in his various comments on poor old Rob. He was neither poor nor old. The last person on earth who would wish to be pitied.

She read until her eyes blinked and she had to turn out her bedside lamp and sleep. She had given up waiting for Des. She began to wonder if he would come home at all. He could always, of course, find a bed in an emergency with Morris Fairway. Morris was one of Des's old school-friends, and the one whom Nira liked least. *He* certainly drank too much and seemed to think of and talk of nothing but girl-friends. He was still a bachelor and likely to remain one. The last time Nira saw him he annoyed her by openly denouncing marriage as a trap and jokingly sympathising with Des's position. Nira hadn't found it very funny. Still less had she liked it when Morris tried his wiles on her as the evening wore on. He was really a type she couldn't stand, but she supposed that Des liked him for old times' sake. And after all Morris's flat was a boon.

After this evening with Rob, feeling so cherished, Nira decided not to worry any more about her husband.

When she next opened her eyes it was to hear the two children outside her door asking to be allowed to come in, and to see broad daylight. Rubbing the sleep from her eyes, she realised with a shock that it was seven o'clock. The pillow beside hers was untouched. Des had never come home.

Renira and Jonathan flung themselves on the bed and asked where Daddy was. Nira said, "You may well ask. Your dear Dad has deserted us. He's been up in London all night."

"Ooh!" exclaimed Renira.

"Jolly lucky!" said Jonathan.

Nira kissed them both and told them to go off and get dressed.

In the bath she was no longer smiling or joking. She felt thoroughly disturbed. Even if the business dinner had been prolonged against Des's will, he might at least have rung her up and let her know that he would be staying in town. Her feelings changed somewhat when by ten o'clock he had still neither telephoned nor come back. Aggravation gave place to anxiety. She telephoned

Des's office. The telephonist, whom she knew, told her that Mr. Curtis hadn't yet arrived.

Nira's pulse-rate quickened and some of her colour faded. There must have been an accident. Whatever Des did, he never failed to turn up at the office at half-past nine. He had a conscience about that, because as he so often said, the young had no sense of time or discipline so it was up to men of his age to set an example. One of Des's good qualities was his punctuality.

Nira left a message with the telephonist for Des to call his wife as soon as he arrived. For the next hour she tried to busy herself in the house. She was definitely worried now. She set to work to make a steak-and-kidney pudding which was one of Des's favourite dishes. Just as she was tying it up in the cloth, she heard a car in the drive. She wiped her hands and rushed to open the door.

At first she saw only Des's back. He was paying a taxi. She supposed he had come from the station. But why hadn't he gone straight to his office?

A shock awaited her when Des turned round and walked slowly towards her — very slowly. He was limping and he had a piece of sticking plaster over his right eyebrow. The whole of the right side of his face looked red and bruised.

She felt sick. So there *had* been an accident. All her love and deep feeling for him surged up. She led him into the house.

"Des, my *darling*, what in God's name has happened?"

"Sorry if I've given you a fright," he mumbled the words. "I — let me sit down, sweetie, will you? And bring me a drink. I need one."

She helped him to an armchair in the lounge and threw open one of the windows to let in the air. She ran to fetch whisky bottle and glass without questioning his need for it.

He drank thirstily, then leaned back, closing his eyes.

"God, I feel lousy!"

"What's happened? For God's sake, tell me, Des. Why didn't you ring up? Why didn't you let me know? I'd have come up in the car to fetch you. Oh, Des, what *did* happen?"

He looked away from her.

"I was nearly run over coming out of the restaurant with old Steadman."

"But how? Where? *When*?"

"Just let me get my breath," he muttered, "I feel a bit sickish."

64

"The whisky will settle your stomach, my poor darling," she said tenderly, and filled his glass again.

He took it but he did not meet her gaze. He had too much on his conscience. He let her fuss over him. Talk about the whisky settling him, he reflected, he had nearly been settled for good and all last night, and he hadn't been with the senior partner when it happened, either. He had left old Steadman outside The Mirabelle where they had dined. After that he had gone on to Morris's flat where Cricket was waiting for him. Oh, it had all been so well organised and things had gone swimmingly. Boyce supposed that *she* was with her aunt and Des had meant just to borrow old Morris's flat for an hour or two in order to spend a few glamorous hours with Cricket. Then he meant to catch the last train home. But his plans had gone awry. His own fault, of course; he wouldn't deny it. Not that he had any intention of letting Nira know a thing.

After the second drink he opened his bloodshot eyes and gingerly touched the cut on his forehead. He began then to tell her a cock-and-bull story about Steadman dropping him outside Victoria Station and how, just as he was crossing the road, a car had backed into him and he had fallen down heavily. Hence the injured face and bruised shin.

"But how awful!" exclaimed Nira. "Oh, why didn't you let me *know*? What time was it?"

"It was only ten o'clock, but I was knocked unconscious. They took me to St. George's Casualty."

He had stayed there until he came out of his stupor this morning. The doctor had let him go in time for him to get the nine-ten train home. Des hadn't phoned her because he didn't want her to be worried.

"You'd have had a fit if you had heard I was in a hospital," he ended.

She knelt by his side, looking at him with lovely tender eyes, the colour gradually coming back into her face. She felt brimful of love and pity, and also of remorse, because she had been so suspicious and thought he had deliberately stayed away, or done something that he shouldn't do.

"I hope you took the name and address of the man who knocked you down," she said hotly.

Des ignored this.

"But why didn't the hospital let me know?" she persisted.

He continued to lie.

"My wallet dropped out of my pocket, when I fell, I suppose. Somebody pinched it, so there was nothing to identify me when they put me to bed. Don't look so tragic, darling. As you see, I am alive and kicking. Luckily no bones were broken. It was just that I fell on the side of my face and one leg and so you see me now — looking *ever* so handsome!" He uttered the last words in an attempt to be jocular.

She took one of his hands and pressed it against her cheek.

"Oh, thank God you're all right, Des. I don't know what I'd have done if you'd been badly hurt!"

"You're sweet," he said mechanically. "And I'm sorry I couldn't contact you. Now be a good girl and help me up to bed. I feel a bit dizzy still and I could do with a sleep."

"Would you like another drink?"

"Hey! Who's encouraging me to take to the bottle? I thought you were on the war path about my boozing."

As he got up, she looked up at him with that tender and trusting gaze which he found rather awkward to accept.

"Under these circumstances, darling, of *course* you need a drink."

He didn't refuse. The whole bloody affair had resulted from too much champagne with Cricket. Damn Cricket *and* her sensuous little body. She bewitched him. She knew just how to drive a fellow wild, and she laced her kisses with alcohol, then the cycle started all over again.

After he put her in a taxi to go back to her aunt's house, he felt suddenly dizzy in the cool night air and the world had spun around him. He'd tripped and fallen into the gutter, hitting the side of his face and one leg against the kerb.

A passing policeman had helped him up and taken him back into the flat.

"Better get that cut over your eye seen to, sir," he had said.

Des had been just sober enough to make light of the affair and to assure the man that he had Elastoplast in the bathroom cupboard and he'd use that and some disinfectant and it would be okay. The whole story of his night in the hospital had been a fabrication but he didn't want Nira to know that he had spent those hectic hours in Morris's flat.

Nira was being particularly sweet and attentive but all he felt was a desire for sleep. His head hurt damnably and he was suffering as much from an appalling hangover as the effects of his fall. He was no lightweight and he had come down on that tarmac with one hell of a plonk, he recalled.

He was barely conscious once he got up to bed, but he heard Nira say, "I must get something to put on your eyebrow. It's swelling."

That irritated him and he couldn't stand one minute more of her tenderness and coddling. He wanted to be left alone.

"Oh, don't fuss so!" he muttered.

Hurt, she drew back from him. Then he was out like a light. She stood a moment staring down at the disfigured face and listening to a snoring that was becoming rather too familiar. All her tremendous feeling for him—the shock of his accident—the fear that he was really hurt—gradually diminished.

She pulled the curtains in order to darken the room and left him lying there, still dressed, having only taken off his collar and tie.

As she tiptoed from the darkened room the sound of his noisy breathing followed her. She went downstairs, a hollow sort of feeling inside. She was beginning to suspect that Des was stale drunk and that the whisky she had given him with so much sympathy had been little more than the 'hair of the dog that had bitten him'.

Later, after making the children's beds, she tidied up downstairs. When she looked in on Des, she found him still snoring. He had taken off his coat. On the carpet half under the bed, she suddenly saw his pocket-book. It must have fallen out of the pocket. Slowly she picked it up. There wasn't much money in it, only his driving licence, a bank credit-card, and a small black book of telephone numbers which she did not bother to investigate. Her mind concentrated on the fact that he had lied to her. He had told her that someone had pinched his wallet but he had had it all the time. Having lost the wallet was his explanation of why the hospital had not been able to contact her. But why? *Why?* Had he been with Steadman at all? *Or with Cricket?*

Once more Nira was tortured by doubt. But her practical side reminded her that she *must* get out and shop as it was early closing day in Ponders Heath. Des would sleep for at least another couple of hours. She had promised the children strawberry mousse for afters and she had only just discovered they were running out of cornflakes. She had to go now, at once. To add to her depression rain was beginning to pelt down. She found her waterproof jacket and an umbrella and tied a scarf over her hair.

Just as she was leaving the house the telephone-bell rang. Hastily she ran back and lifted the receiver. Rob's voice; thanking her for a lovely evening.

"You don't know how much I enjoyed it."

"I did, too," she said. But the sight of her own face in the hall mirror almost scared her, it was so grim. She had never seen herself look quite like that before.

Rob started to tell her something—she really couldn't concentrate and interrupted him.

"Do forgive me, Rob, I've got to go out before the shops shut."

The man at the other end of the wire was suddenly alive to the fact that all was not well with his Nira. Her voice sounded strange.

"Are you all right?"

"Yes, of course," she bit her lip and laughed. But the laugh did not convince him.

"You don't sound yourself this morning."

"Perhaps I'm not." She laughed again, a trifle too loudly.

"What time did Desmond get back?"

"He didn't. He stayed in town."

Silence. He waited for her to speak again.

She added, "He—he had a lot of work and he stayed the night with a friend."

"H'm," said Rob. But he didn't believe a thing about that work. "Well, well—let me know when you can have some lunch, or a game of golf," he added, "I won't keep you, my dear. Goodbye."

"Thanks awfully. Goodbye, Rob."

She turned from the telephone. Her lips were trembling. There were tears in her eyes. She felt somehow that her world was falling apart. Her faith in Des had been absolute during the eleven years of their marriage. But now—she wondered. Yet was she being unreasonable? What had he done except drink too much and stop the night in town? There was that stupid lie about his stolen wallet and not being able to get in touch with her. Why all *that*? She'd have to have it out with him.

She seized umbrella and shopping bag and hurried out into the pouring rain. Once in the High Street she had to dive suddenly into one or two shops to avoid meeting neighbours—women she knew. She was unwilling in her present state of mind to be forced into gossiping.

She bought what she wanted in the new big supermarket which had recently opened, then turned down Heath Hill which led to Nylands. Nylands—her home, the attractive house she loved so much and where she had been so happy. As she put the key in the front door this morning, she felt unbearably sad. She found herself wishing that the Bessifords' home was nearer so that she could run in and tell Rob all about things. He was wise and kind. She could confide in him and his advice would be good. Then she dismissed the idea.

The telephone-bell was ringing as she let herself into Nylands. She felt so tired she wished she did not have to answer it. This time it was Boyce.

"Hello, Beautiful," he said in the caressing voice which she was beginning to dislike, "I'm speaking from the office. I just felt I must have a word with you."

"Forgive me, I'm terribly busy this morning," she said coldly.

"I won't keep you a second. I just want to know what's wrong with old Des?"

"What should be?" she asked, startled.

"Well, I saw him getting off the London train just as I was leaving the Heath this morning. He was limping."

Nira tried to calm down and collect her thoughts. She had to be careful what she said but she was not good at covering up—Des often said she was too honest. She had never found it easy to lie.

"Hello—are you there, Nira?"

"Yes. Nothing's wrong with Des except he hurt his leg slightly. He stayed the night with his friend Morris. He woke up with a ghastly headache and decided to come home instead of going to the office."

A little meaning laugh from Boyce.

"You and I are in the same boat. My dear wife was supposed to be staying with her aunt last night."

Nira snapped at him, "What's that meant to imply?"

"Well—she rang me first thing this morning and sounded as though she'd swallowed a magnum of champagne. She'd been out on a party and *not* with aunty. She even forgot she was supposed to take Simon to the dentist after lunch today. I can see I'll have to take a firm hand with her," Boyce ended with a laugh. "And you must do the same with old Des."

But Nira was not amused. Her face was hot, her thoughts confused.

"I don't get you, Boyce."

He ignored this.

"Cricket also complained of a frightful headache. Our better halves seem to have hangovers — the pair of them."

"*Really*, Boyce," Nira protested furiously.

He said, "Nira, my pet, aren't you thinking what *I* am thinking? Aren't we innocent victims of a great betrayal? Don't you twig that our devoted spouses were by some chance imbibing champagne *together*?"

Nira gasped. This was plain speaking now.

"I don't like your suggestions, Boyce." Her voice trembled.

He laughed. "Don't take me too seriously. But why didn't you let me come over and see you last night? You know I wanted to very much."

With her nerves in shreds, Nira was afraid she would break down unless she could get away from this man and his insinuations. She felt almost certain now that he was right. His wife and her husband had been together last night. Everything pointed to it. They had shared that champagne, and they both had hangovers this morning. Cricket had been away — with whom, if not with Des?

Nira put down the phone without even saying goodbye to Boyce. Her breathing was quick, her throat dry. She made up her mind then and there she must get the truth from Des. And another thing — she was determined now to make him cancel that party for Majorca. Nothing would induce her to face two weeks of Boyce, and his unwelcome attentions — not even though Rob was supposed to be with them. Neither would she stand by and watch Cricket's brazen attempts to seduce Des (or vice-versa, for all she knew).

It was no longer a compassionate loving wife but a jealous, angry woman who marched into the bedroom and roused her sleeping husband.

7

"THE WHOLE THING is ridiculous. Why the hell should you take it for granted that Cricket and I spent a night together just because we'd both been to a champagne party. As for Boyce suggesting I'm having an affair with his wife — I've a good mind to go round and have it out with him."

Des spoke in a loud hectoring voice. Nira stood at the bottom of the bed looking at him. He was drinking a cup of strong black coffee that she had just made for him. She noted how the hand that held the cup was shaking. He didn't look very nice this morning. There was a bluish tinge to his unshaven chin. His eyes were red-rimmed and when she had bent over him she had to draw back quickly, repelled by his breath.

For the last half-hour they had been wrangling. Quarrels were something they had never before indulged in so long and so bitterly. She had had a few words with him over his drinking on the night the Hallings came to dinner but she had reproached herself after that for being intolerant and for nagging and all had been forgiven and forgotten.

This was different.

Des was trembling with temper and alcoholic excess. Nira was trembling because her whole nervous system was keyed up to a pitch she could hardly control. This was the husband she had always adored and believed in. It was ghastly to suspect that he had spent last night with Cricket — or any other woman. Over and over again he had fiercely denied it. He brushed off the incident of the wallet.

"I actually did think someone had whipped it," he said. "If it's still here so much the better. I admit I was drunk last night and that's why I fell down. It's the only thing I've been lying about. I just didn't want them to send for you from the hospital in case you saw me in that condition. I happen to love my wife and want to keep in her good books. Is that such a crime?"

Now Nira turned from the sight of his spoiled face and walked to the window. She opened it. The rain had stopped. The odours from the garden were sweet and fresh and the scent from the jasmine strong. The birds were singing madly and happily. The tears rushed to her eyes and she put her hands up to her face. She had been so madly happy, too. Was she really wronging Des by suspecting him? Was it just jealousy on her part? Was it coincidence that Cricket had been out all night drinking champagne as well as Des? She really had nothing concrete to confirm her suspicions. As for Boyce—she was fast coming to the conclusion that he was a nasty piece of work and no real friend either to Des or herself. He was also disgracefully disloyal to his wife. Of course he had a motive for wanting to link Des and Cricket. It was because *he* wanted to justify his pursuit of her, Nira.

He'd never get her—never as long as he lived. She wouldn't want to be touched by him—not if they were on a desert island and he the last man alive. She used once to think him quite attractive but now he stood for complete lack of moral scruple, for lies, for everything she disliked.

Des had never been like that. *Oh, Des, you couldn't have betrayed me!* Yet even as her mind dwelt on the word *betrayed* she wondered if she was an old-fashioned prig. She certainly wasn't 'with it'. So many couples were unfaithful to each other these days and thought nothing of it.

When she turned back to Des she was weeping.

"I don't want to think the worst. If you swear that all this was— was just because you were drunk, and you weren't with Cricket, I'll believe you."

The man in the bed put down his coffee cup and flung himself back on his pillow. His head ached abominably. He had never felt worse after any night out, and quite genuinely he was sorry about the whole thing. He was weak and he knew it. He'd let that little so-and-so, Cricket, get round him. Very exciting it had all been at the time, but he genuinely loved his wife. *In my fashion,* he thought. *Isn't there a song about it somewhere? I've been faithful in my fashion.*

He hated to hear Nira crying and to see the anguish on the face he had always found so sweet and lovable as well as lovely. He'd behaved vilely and he had been found out. That was the major crime—to be found out. But he had never had any intention of upsetting his marriage because of an affair with Cricket. He knew her—and himself—only too well. He soon tired of his girl-friends. There'd been a good many in his life. The only person he'd ever stood by and been faithful to (except for the few odd kisses and caresses in the corner) was Nira. And thinking over the last eleven years he began suddenly to admire his own fidelity. Eleven years of just making love to the odd girl or two! And until now he had kept Nira happy. Crikey! Not bad! He was really quite a fine fellow. There were lots worse including that ruddy fellow Boyce. He bet Boyce had not been as decent to Cricket. If only his head did not ache so badly, he'd get out of bed and take Nira in his arms and show her he still loved her. But there was no desire in him this morning for any woman, and all he could do was to stretch out a hand and say, "Nirry, my darling, come here."

She went over to her dressing-table, pulled out a couple of tissues, pressed them to her lips and wiped her streaming eyes. She felt dreadfully unhappy and still uncertain about the whole thing.

"Nirry," Des repeated, "come here, my pet. You can't just stand there howling like a kid. I won't have it. I can't bear you to be unhappy. You know I love you. You *know*."

All her old affection welled up. She rushed to the bed, sat down and buried her face against his shoulder. She sobbed, "I've never stopped loving *you*. I never thought anyone could come between us."

"They haven't. No one ever will. You're barking up the wrong tree, my angel." His fingers threaded through her hair and he caressed her neck and shoulders. "I swear I haven't been unfaithful to you, Nira. Now will you accept my word or do you *want* to go on believing the worst? If so, you're just a horrid jealous little thing!"

She sobbed and laughed in turn. His attempt to be jocular and the familiar touch of his big strong fingers began to reassure her. The ice round her heart cracked into a million pieces. The warmth seeped back. She was in the right place — in the circle of his arms — confident, secure again.

"If you give me your word of course I'll take it, Des," she whispered. "Forgive me for being so jealous and for accusing you, but it did all seem rather odd, didn't it?"

He agreed. "Certainly it seemed to add up to something against me and I'm the one who ought to ask for forgiveness — not you. I'm sorry I upset you so badly, darling."

He began to feel better now that she had said she believed him. He even began to believe in himself. He cut out the memory of that night's passion with Cricket. He went on stroking his wife's silky hair and dropping little kisses on her head. She must never suspect him again, he said. "And I won't drink or have any other woman in my life but you, which is as it has always been," he ended grandly.

Comforted, she pressed her cheek to his.

"Okay, Des, let's forget it. I'll run a bath for you, and, darling, do you feel fit enough to get up and dress and take me out in the car? Why don't we have lunch together somewhere? At The Rifleman where they have such good sandwiches, don't you think?"

He lied with a swagger. "I'd adore it—great idea. I'll feel myself again after a bath. They'll have to do without me in the office until tomorrow. I've still got a cracking head, you know."

"Are you sure you want to come out? Does the cut still hurt?"

"It's nothing," he lied again, thinking it best to do exactly as she wanted, and to make light of his accident. He'd had a nasty fall all right. But he was anxious to wipe this 'unfaithful with Cricket' fear right out of Nira's mind. He'd do anything to get back into her good books. As for Cricket, he'd tell the little devil as soon as he could get in touch with her, that their affair must stop. She was growing far too possessive and he knew that the next time—if he gave her cause—Nira would not only suspect but condemn him. Then the fat *would* be in the fire. It wasn't any use him wishing his wife was a bit less loyal and full of high principles. It wouldn't, of course, be Nira if she behaved like Cricket—or Maggie Wilson, whom he knew he could have an affair with any time he wanted. He honestly liked being married to Nira and adored the kids. They'd always had fun together. Better keep it that way.

So he bathed and dressed and after nailing down a horrid wish to take another drink in order to bolster himself up, he went out in the car with Nira.

She was happy again and ready to chat in the old gay friendly way, but he barely listened to all the things she had to tell him about the children. He wasn't in the mood. The sun hurt his eyes. His leg ached. He put on dark glasses. Because he knew she liked it, he kept his hand on Nira's knee, pressed it now and again and gave her one or two of the long sidelong looks which had always thrilled her and made her feel they were still lovers.

The difficult moment came when they were seated up at the

bar in the charming little pub ten miles out of Brighton eating cold turkey and salad. Once again Des closed his eyes to the sight of the bottles behind the bar.

"I want to discuss our holiday, darling," she said suddenly. "I know we're all booked up and so on, but I just *don't* want to go away with the Hallings now. I've *had* Boyce—and I don't think I could take two full weeks of watching Cricket flick her eyelashes at you."

"Darling, I thought you'd told me you weren't going to be jealous any more."

Nira flushed.

"I'm not. I just don't like her or her attitude to men and the way she behaves to other women's husbands. I can think of lots of other couples I'd rather we went away with. I made a bad mistake in ever thinking otherwise."

Des took off his dark glasses and put a tentative finger up to the sticking plaster. It was pretty obvious that Boyce had offended Nira, and he, Des, had decided to cut loose from Cricket; okay, but how were they going to get out of their commitments, when they were all supposed to go to Majorca together?

"Everything's booked, Nira darling," he reminded her.

"It can be cancelled. Anyhow, *they* can go if they still want to."

"What about Rob?"

"I'll be sorry about Rob, and he'll be disappointed but he'll understand."

The throbbing pain over Des's eyes added to a strong urge to get back to bed and sleep for another few hours began to make him feel irritable—despite his desire to placate his wife and get back on normal terms with her.

"I honestly don't see how you are going to explain it away. Rob will imagine all kinds of odd things. We don't want to start any sort of scandal."

Nira bit her lip.

"Of course it will be awkward. Can't we just say we've had a change of heart about our holiday and don't really want to go with Boyce and Cricket? That we don't want a communal holiday? Lots of things I could say. Rob doesn't like the Hallings anyhow, so he will sympathise, and I'll make it plain that it's best to cancel the plans," she ended rather sadly, thinking of Rob.

"Well, of course, as long as he doesn't get the wrong impression and think I am worried about you and Boyce—"

"Don't be funny!" Nira interrupted Des with a short laugh.

She was beginning to be impatient with her husband. Why didn't he see for himself that in the present circumstances it would be far too difficult for them all to go on holiday together — especially living in such close quarters, in the same hotel. As for what he had just said about Boyce and herself — her cheeks burned and she gave Des a reproachful look.

"Really! Why should Rob think there has been anything unusual between Boyce and me? Surely the boot is on the other foot. Quite a lot of people have probably seen you and Cricket dancing cheek to cheek in the Club and — and — all that," she finished lamely. Des quickly picked up the cudgels.

"My dear sweet Nira, when do people think the worst because they see a couple dancing cheek to cheek? You're being ante-diluvian."

"Well, anyhow," said Nira, "I refuse to have this crisis blamed on anything that has been going on between Boyce and myself because nothing *has* — as well you know."

"Don't you admit that he has got a thing about you?"

She waved a hand.

"Okay — so he has, but it is not serious and I don't take any notice — as you know."

"Well, I don't take much notice of Cricket," said Des blandly and pulled a packet of cigarettes out of his pocket.

"You're smoking too much," said Nira mechanically.

"And you're nagging."

She stared behind the bar at the shining glass case of lobsters — pink and inviting, on a nest of green salad. The little glow of happiness that had been warming her heart since her reconciliation with Des was rapidly fading. She looked around the attractive room. It was full of people. She always liked The Rifleman; the charming décor, yellow-buttoned sofas; the gay painting of a Victorian Rifleman in action; and the excellent cold buffet. This was one of their favourite places. But today it had lost all charm for Nira and the big handsome man beside her with his bruised face and cut eyebrow did not seem like her adored husband. He was a stranger and they were quarrelling again.

She didn't want to talk about the holiday any more. She slid off the stool and said, "Let's go."

Des paid the bill. They walked out to their car. The sun was shining. Several people were sitting at the little tables on the terrace. Taped music provided a suitable background and added to the clinking of glasses, gay voices and laughter. But Nira had seldom felt more depressed.

Neither one of them spoke until they had passed through the village of Warninglid and were well on the way back to Ponders Heath. Then Des pulled up the car, opened the door and got out.

"Drive the rest of the way, will you?" he asked. "I can hardly see out of my one good eye."

"I'm sorry," she said, and took his place.

For the rest of the way home Des folded his arms over his chest and stared gloomily ahead. He didn't much like this state of affairs. Her cool unfriendly attitude quite alarmed him. He was too used to her being the starry-eyed, tender-hearted girl who liked to say yes to everything he wanted. He supposed that he had only himself to blame, but he was going to stick to his role of injured innocence. He decided that he had a grudge against Nira.

"I don't know what all this bickering is about," he said, "but I wouldn't have bothered to get up and take you out to lunch if I'd thought you were going to start picking on me. Besides, you told me categorically that you had nothing against me and that you had been silly. Honestly, Nira, I don't think you are behaving very prettily."

She kept her eye on the road. Her lips were set and there was an expression on her face he had seen before — a stubborn look. Of course, Des reflected, he had always known his wife could be stubborn when she chose. He hated being criticised or frustrated. Damn it, Nira needed shaking sometimes. She was oddly old-fashioned in many ways — too set in her ideas.

They'd been happy and got on very well all these years but of course he reminded himself, she'd never had occasion to suspect him of infidelity. She'd only jokingly accused him of being a bit too keen on some girl or other. But up till now he hadn't felt such a strong craving for new excitement as he had experienced lately. Marriage was a trap, he told himself crossly. Men were different from women. They didn't always want to be pinned down to one woman, and most of them — most of the fellows he knew, anyhow — let their fancy stray now and again. He had better take a strong line with Nira or she'd take a new line with him and try to become the boss of the house, want to organise his whole life. That was something he wouldn't tolerate, even from her. Apart from her beauty, her sweetness, one of the reasons why he had been so fond of her in the past was because she seemed so pliant—easily taken in by him—so affectionate! He wouldn't enjoy married life if she started being a difficult wife.

He half decided to put her in coventry once they got home. Perhaps if he didn't speak to her for an hour or two, she would come to heel. And all he really wanted, anyhow, was to be allowed to go back to bed and sleep.

As they reached their home they saw Rob. He was standing beside his car which was parked in front of Nylands. What the hell was *he* doing here at this hour of the day, Des wondered fretfully.

Nira pulled up.

"Did you ask your boy-friend round?" Des growled in her ear. "If so you can send him away because I'm not in the mood for visitors, my dear."

Nira's colour rose.

"He's not my boy-friend," she whispered fiercely, "and I *didn't* invite him. And I'm not going to be rude to him now, even for you."

"Charming!" muttered Des.

Nira felt quite distraught. She was totally unused to such an atmosphere between her husband and herself. It destroyed her self-confidence. She didn't know who was in the wrong now—or how she was going to explain to Rob about cancelling the Majorcan holiday.

Before she could say anything, Rob walked up to them smiling. The very sight of his nice friendly face and those extremely kind eyes behind the tinted glasses warmed her heart. Her spirits rose a little.

"Oh, hello!" she said with a faint smile. "Have you been ringing the bell? Sorry we were out, Rob."

"No, I've only just got here," he said, and looked at Des who was edging himself stiffly out of the car. Des felt that his whole body hurt after last night's episode. He was in a poor temper. But he, too, tried to force a smile.

"Hi, Rob! Sorry we weren't at home."

"I didn't expect *you* to be," said Rob. "Is the commuter taking a day off?"

"No, I've had an accident," said Des briefly.

Rob now noticed the sticking plaster, the bruises, the limp and Desmond's generally poor condition. Quite unlike his usual hearty self.

Before Rob could sympathise, Nira said, "Do come in, please."

"No. I actually only came to ask if you had a brochure about that Majorcan hotel we are going to. Aunt Ida wanted to see one."

"Is she thinking of coming with us, too?" Des asked with an icy smile.

Nira felt that she was going to drop through the road. How *could* he? But Rob only laughed—charming and easy as ever.

"That I doubt. She wouldn't get much farther than the front door. The old lady never goes out, but she likes to see what's doing and where I'm going, and that sort of thing. But please don't worry about the brochure now. Any time will do."

"Well, I'm off to my bed. I'm not feeling so good," Des said. "Nira will look after you, Rob. Excuse me."

Rob and Nira were left alone on the pavement. Rob was now aware that something was very wrong. There was a distinct atmosphere between husband and wife. He said, "I've come at the wrong moment, do forgive me, Nira. Any time will do about the brochure, really."

But Nira had other ideas. She thought that this would be as good a time as any to try and tell Rob that their plans for the summer holiday must be cancelled.

"Please do come in, Rob. It's past three. I'll be making a cup of tea in a second. Des and I've just come back from The Rifleman. You've been there, haven't you? It's such good food."

She started to lead the way to the front door. Rob followed but with some reluctance.

"I don't want to intrude. I can come back any time and—"

"No, please come in. As Des said—he's going to lie down. He had an accident in town last night."

Rob said no more but he wondered very much what this was all about. He didn't remember ever having seen his lovely Nira look so grim.

"Go out in the garden and sit down by the pond," she added, "I'll join you in a moment."

Familiar with the house, Rob walked into the small study at the back and through the french windows into the small but attractive walled garden which Nira adored. She was only an amateur gardener and hadn't much time, busy as she was with her household chores and family, but she managed to produce some beautiful roses.

The sun was warm after the rainfall. The long bed beside the goldfish pool was brilliant with early roses. Rob stood looking down at the little golden fish darting in and out through the stones and green weeds in the cloudy water. As he knew, these fish were the children's pride and joy. Desmond had made the pool for them. He could be quite a useful chap when in the mood. Rob knew that too. What was happening between those two? She looked so pale, so strained.

When she joined him a minute later she had a cigarette between her fingers and she smiled. But he didn't think it was an easy smile.

He pulled up a canvas chair for her.

"Shall we sit?"

"Yes," she said, and looked down at the goldfish. They were coming up to the surface, mouths gaping, looking for food. She had forgotten to feed them this morning.

She felt so heavy-hearted and embarrassed about what she had to say to Rob, she didn't know how to begin. She fed the goldfish.

Once back with Rob, they both lit their cigarettes and she began to talk. He sat silent, listening. She stumbled over her first few words. "I—I don't know what—what you'll think—I'm so sorry—s-something has happened. I've got to ask you to cancel going to Majorca with us."

He looked at her. She was flushed and obviously disturbed. Just how bitterly disappointed he was, he had no intention of telling her, but he had begun to look forward very much—too much—to the prospect of a fortnight in Majorca with the Curtis family and particularly to being with *her*. Aunt Ida, only last night, had remarked that she hadn't for years seen him so keen on taking a holiday. Now *this* blow!

"What's happened, Nira?" he asked. His quiet voice gave her confidence, as it always did.

"Well, you know we were going with the Hallings?"

"Yes."

"Well, I—Des—there's been a sort of row with Cricket—I can't really explain—I mean we all still talk and that sort of thing but I—Des and I have decided we don't want to go away with them. They may go—if you'd like to join them, please don't feel—"

Rob interrupted, "I wouldn't dream of it. I assure you I was only going so as to be with you and Desmond."

"That's nice of you, but—"

"No buts. I'll just fade out—as you've done. After all I only booked my ticket over the phone and I can ring up and cancel it, as soon as I get home."

She did not look at him but stared at the water blindly, watching the little goldfish darting through the green plants. Her heart was heavy.

"It's all rather stupid, I suppose. I'm sorry, Rob."

"Don't keep apologising."

"But I am sorry—honestly."

"So am I, but it isn't the end of the world. Perhaps you'll fix another holiday one day and let me come with you."

Now she turned her earnest eyes—eyes that he always found so honest and beautiful—towards him.

"Of course. *Of course.* I'll look forward to it. There'll be another time."

He did not ask what had actually happened with the Hallings. He didn't really want to know. But he had a shrewd idea it was something to do with that fellow, Boyce. He also felt there was some mystery here, too. What about that accident to Des? He had looked pretty ghastly. And he had been all but rude—not as usual, charming, hail-fellow-well-met. When Rob looked at Nira again he felt dismayed. Her eyes were full of tears.

"What is it, my dear? Is it anything very wrong? Can I help?"

She would have given anything to unburden herself—to tell him the whole story of Boyce and Cricket, and all about Des's extraordinary behaviour, to say nothing of her own ugly suspicions. She couldn't get the words out. Loyalty to Des would not allow it. The worst of it was that she wasn't sure about *anything*. It was just all so unpleasant and depressing and it *might* be muddled thinking.

Her own tears horrified her. Hurriedly she got up and moved away from Rob under pretence of pulling some leaves out of the pond with the shrimping net which the children used to keep the water clear.

Rob also rose. He threw away a half-smoked cigarette and with hands in his pockets looked through his glasses at Nira's tall graceful figure. He had never thought her quite as vulnerable as this. Her tear-filled eyes upset him. Never a man of great conceit, he thought it better he should make an exit from the scene. If anything was wrong between Nira and Des they wouldn't want him hanging around. Des had, in fact, made that plain.

"I ought really to get home, Nira," he said, "and the sooner I make the hotel cancellation the better."

She didn't want him to go. More than ever before she needed the warmth and support of his friendship, but she said nothing. Only when they reached the front door she tried to be flippant. "Fine thing—inviting a friend to spend a holiday with you—then when he comes for the details about the place to be told we aren't going away."

Rob fully realised that the flippancy was a façade—she was nearer tears than smiles. He took his cue from her.

"It's the end of our friendship, madam," he announced.

Now she put both hands on his shoulders and looked up at him with an expression of tenderness which he found unbelievably thrilling.

"Don't you ever dare end it. I would hate to lose it. Goodbye, dear Rob, for the moment. See you!"

She walked slowly back into the house. She thought, *He never tried to get anything out of me. He just accepted what I said about cancelling the holiday and not a reproach. He really is a sweet man. Oh, damn, damn, why did Des have to muck it all up.*

But in a flash she realised that it wasn't only Des who had mucked up the holiday. It was she herself who had told him she wouldn't go away with the Hallings.

Had she made a mistake? Was it all a storm in a teacup?

As she stood in the hall, ruminating, the bell rang.

She opened the front door. The last person in the world she wanted to see stood there—*Cricket*. Cricket looking a little less attractive than usual. Her pretty face, despite the make-up, was pale and puffy. She hadn't taken much trouble with her clothes. As a rule she was so carefully dressed and made-up. The blue trouser-suit today was crumpled. The silver-blonde hair untidy in need of setting. And she gave Nira a sullen look after the first "hello", and there was an ugly twist to her lips.

Nira froze.

"Come in," she said and stepped back, holding the door wide open.

Cricket walked in and followed Nira into the lounge.

8

"HAVE I COME at an inconvenient time?" asked Cricket.

Nira avoided answering that question. Out of politeness she offered Cricket a cigarette, which was accepted. Both girls lit up and then Nira asked her uninvited guest to sit down. Cricket looked round rather nervously, Nira thought. She said, in her high, flute-like voice, "I was away for the night last night, you know."

"I do know. Boyce told me on the phone."

"Yes, he said he had phoned you and wanted to come round for a chat last night but you had someone else here. Was Des away?"

Nira thought, *She's been too clever. She knows perfectly well that Des was away. Boyce must have told her by now.*

"I came round to talk about our holiday." Cricket added the words somewhat lamely. She was wondering why Nira was being so stiff and unfriendly.

Nira said, "Des is upstairs in bed. He spent the night in a hospital. He had an accident."

Now Cricket, who wasn't really being clever about the whole affair, gave herself away before she could exercise restraint.

"An *accident*? But how? He was perfectly all right when he left me —" She broke off, her face suddenly scarlet and her long lashes fluttering. She took one or two deep breaths. Nira felt her heart go right down.

"When I last saw him, I mean," Cricket added, stuttering.

"You were together last night, weren't you?"

"No, of course not. I mean — what an idea —" Cricket laughed hysterically.

"Then tell me just *when* you thought him perfectly all right," Nira said, feeling merciless because she was now convinced she had been deceived by her husband and this woman. "When you said good night to him, I suppose. You'd both had too much champagne, of course."

Cricket sprang to her feet. She was white and there was a sick look in her large blue eyes, but she made a desperate struggle to right her mistake.

"I really don't know what you're talking about, Nira. I mean I thought he looked all right when I *last* saw him down here."

"That was some time ago, surely. Anyhow, what bearing does it have on the accident last night? Do let's be honest with each other. Des was drunk and fell down. He hurt his face and leg and cut an eyebrow and had to be taken to hospital, on his way back from a party — *a party with you.* Maybe Boyce isn't interested in what you do, but I am frightfully interested in what my husband does."

Cricket began to shake. The ash fell from her cigarette on to the carpet.

Nira, the tidy housewife, stooped automatically to brush it away.

"You were with him at Morris's flat, weren't you?" was her next question and she looked at Cricket with hard eyes. All the softness, the friendly sweetness, had gone right out of them.

Cricket suddenly began to realise that she had a formidable enemy in Des's wife. She hadn't expected to be found out — certainly never imagined Nira would hit on the truth like this. She could see it was her own fault. She really had made a frightful gaffe just now. She wished she hadn't come to see Nira. She wished she hadn't spent those hectic passionate hours with Des last night. She didn't want trouble. She didn't want to be so involved. She liked to be gay and happy — not worried. In this moment she felt horribly nervous. She didn't know how even Boyce, who was so permissive, would react to this.

She made a last desperate effort to allay Nira's suspicions.

"Of course I wasn't at Morris's flat — whoever Morris is. I stayed with my aunt."

"But I happen to know, because Boyce told me, that you'd been out at a party. Des was at a champagne party too."

"What are you trying to say — make out that Des and I are having a secret sordid sort of love affair?" asked Cricket and burst into tears. She covered her face with her hands and sobbed childishly. "I didn't know you could be so beastly — so suspicious. I think you're awful! I shall tell Boyce that I don't want to go away with you and Des if that's the sort of thing you're going to cook up about us."

Nira felt sick. She knew perfectly well now that Cricket and

Des had been together last night. If Cricket wasn't guilty, why should she be crying and seem so scared. Besides, that half-finished sentence—"*An accident? But how? He was perfectly all right when he left me*—" And she had broken off. She couldn't go on, of course. She had been shocked to hear that Des had spent the night in a hospital—shocked into betraying herself—and him.

At this crucial point the door-bell rang. Nira was half tempted to leave it unanswered but now somebody tapped on the window and to her dismay she saw her mother-in-law standing outside. Gandy—neat, smart as ever, pale-blue dress and jacket, with a blue chiffon scarf tied over her waved white hair. Gandy never did have a hair out of place and always looked as though she had come straight from the beauty parlour; so well made up—and so young-looking for her age.

She was the last person on earth Nira wanted here now. But there was nothing for her to do but open the door. Gandy had waved a gay white glove at her. Nira gave a swift glance at Cricket whose face was still hidden in her hands.

"I've got to let my mother-in-law in. Perhaps you'd like to escape into the dining-room or go up to the children's bedroom. Susan isn't in. She's meeting them at school. You can be alone and put on some make-up and so forth—then slip out of the house."

Cricket sprang to her feet. She raised a very smudged, tear-wet face to Nira who felt not the slightest compassion for her. If Cricket was miserable she had no one but herself to blame.

"I'll hide in the dining-room, and dash off home without your guest knowing," Cricket said in a thick whisper.

"I don't suppose my mother-in-law will stay long if there's anything more you want to say to me."

"No, I don't, but I shall tell Boyce as soon as he gets back and he'll deal with your awful accusation—" Cricket gulped out the words then vanished.

Nira felt herself trembling as she opened the door to her mother-in-law. Mrs Curtis came in, bringing with her as usual a delicious odour of the fresh lemon-scented toilet water she used.

"Can I come in?" (She was already in the drawing-room by now.) "I thought I'd drive over and see you as it's such a nice afternoon. Can I have tea with you and the children? Ought I to have let you know?"

Nira dutifully kissed the pale powdered cheek presented to her and assured her mother-in-law that she was delighted to see her.

She wanted to tell her to go away and of course she couldn't. She mustn't risk her finding out that her son was upstairs, because she would insist on rushing up to see him. His bruised puffy face would both shock and alarm her. Besides, Gandy, of all people mustn't guess that anything was wrong between 'her young' as she called her son and his wife.

Nira made a desperate mental note that Susan should be back with Jonathan and Renira quite soon. She must act swiftly and suggest they all went out in the car. There was a pleasant little café not far from here where they could have tea. They would have a better one at home but the children would enjoy the change. The main thing was to get everyone out of this house. She would rush upstairs now to warn Des to keep out of the way.

Perforce she talked to Gandy for a moment. She only half heard all that the older woman had to say about the marvellous bridge she had been playing lately and how she had won a tournament with her friend, Lady Ansty, who had a flat near hers; yes, she, Gandy had won six no-trumps doubled and vulnerable, and on *two* occasions; fabulous bridge! Never stopping, she chattered on; then out from the brocade bag she carried, came a little box of sweets for each of the children, and one of bitter chocolate mints for Nira and Des who liked them.

She was a good, generous-hearted woman really, and never failed to bring little presents, but oh, thought Nira, what a moment to choose and how desperately boring it was to have to sit and listen to Gandy while her thoughts kept wandering first to Cricket (whom she hoped by now had made her exit), then to the room above where Des, she *hoped*, was still sound asleep.

After a moment she could no longer contain her impatience and with the excuse that Susan would be in any moment and she wanted to slip upstairs, Nira left Gandy to smoke her cigarette and wander around the room. She was an inquisitive woman and adored to quiz as she called it.

"*Where did you buy this?*" she'd ask, or "*Did I give you that?*" or "*Oh, I wish I'd found a bargain like that!*" . . .

To Nira's relief, Cricket had left the house—as suggested. Nira found her husband sitting up in bed, wide awake. The face he turned to her was woeful; one eye almost closed. She would have been sorry for him but for the fact that she knew beyond doubt that he was guilty.

She spoke to him in a cold voice, her long lashes fluttering with

86

nervousness. "Your mother's come unexpectedly. She mustn't see you."

"Why not?" began Des gruffly, "I could do with a little motherly love and attention. I'm not getting much from you."

She flashed a look of contempt at him.

"You know perfectly well you don't deserve it and I'm not going to stand by and hear you tell Gandy a lot of lies about your accident and how it happened because *you* know the truth and so do I now."

"What the hell do you mean — ?" began Des more heatedly. He got out of bed and tried to look dignified, but failed. He was rather a sorry spectacle.

"I mean that just before Gandy turned up, Cricket — your dear little Cricket — paid me a visit. It's been quite a party. I only just managed to get *her* away in time, before Gandy saw her weeping."

Des felt suddenly very uncomfortable — in mind as well as body. He ruffled his thick chestnut hair and looked at Nira with alarm in his bloodshot eyes.

"What in the name of God was Cricket doing here?"

"She'd come back from town to take Simon to the dentist and thought she'd pop in here to have a nice chat with me about our holiday."

"So what?"

"She said just one or two things too many and confirmed my belief that the champagne party you had last night was with *her*. You were both at Morris's flat, weren't you, Des? And I won't believe you if you start telling me all you were doing was to make plans to join the Salvation Army."

Des looked at his wife aghast. He had never heard her speak to him with such bitter sarcasm. God, he thought, what a mess he had made of things. Yet how could Nira be sure of her facts? *What had Cricket said?* When he started to bluster and assure Nira of his innocence, she cut him short.

"I've no time to talk now. All I ask is that you keep upstairs in this room. Lock your door — just in case Gandy comes up for any reason at all. Don't make a sound. You'll hear us drive off in the car. We're going to the Ponders Café for tea. I'm going to make an excuse not to offer your mother tea here, at home."

Before he could answer Nira was gone.

Susan's arrival with the two children made things a bit easier.

In a high bright voice Nira informed all of them that she was about to treat Renira and Jonny to tea with Gandy at their favourite teashop.

Gandy seemed a little put out. She'd wanted to stay in the house but the children were unconsciously helpful to Nira. They seized their grandmother by the hand and began to scream their delight.

"I want one of those scrummy chocolate biscuits."

"I want the orange cake we had last time."

Nira bustled them out into the car and almost sobbed with relief once the front door closed behind them. Before leaving the house she had rushed into the kitchen to tell Susan to take some tea up to Mr. Curtis. She made up some story about his having been in an accident and didn't want his mother to know.

Susan, a placid, capable sort of girl, asked no questions but did as she was told.

Driving to the teashop, Nira asked herself bitterly why she had bothered about Des's tea — after all the misery he had caused her. Her head throbbed and her heart ached. She was nearer to tears than to smiles. She felt positively crushed. One thing she was thankful for during the tea party — she didn't have to exert herself to talk too much to Gandy because the children monopolised the conversation and soon afterwards Gandy said she must go back to Brighton. She never liked to stay out long.

As she kissed Nira goodbye, Mrs. Curtis suddenly forgot her egotistical little self and noted that the tall, slim, beautiful girl who was her son's wife, looked unusually white and — now she came to think of it — Nira had been very silent — even odd — during tea.

"Aren't you well, dear?" she asked.

"Fine, thanks, Gandy."

"Nothing wrong?"

"Why should there be?" Nira gave a high-pitched laugh.

"You just don't look yourself, dear."

After Gandy had gone, Nira remembered those words and thought, *And I'm not myself. I'm a stranger and Des is a stranger. We aren't the same two people who loved each other so much and were so close. It's as though we'd both died and now we're in another awful world — a sort of hell — hating each other.*

Somehow Nira managed to get through the next hour, dutifully entertaining the children who always expected her to play with them before bedtime. Then she pleaded a headache and told them to let Susan give them their baths. She'd kiss them good night later on.

Heavy-hearted, with lagging footsteps, Nira then walked to her bedroom door and called out to Des.

He unlocked the door and returned to the little Victorian brocaded seat which stood under the window, where he had been sitting, smoking. Nira noted that he had finished the tea but left the cake Susan had brought up to him.

He stubbed his cigarette end in an ashtray, spread his legs out, put his hands in his pockets and glared at her. It was that glare that made her feel quite sick.

"Well, I hope you're pleased with yourself," he said. "You've mucked up everything properly, haven't you, with your idiotic suspicions."

Nira leaned her back against the door. Her eyes were as hard as his.

"Don't speak to me like that, Des. *I'm* not the one who's mucked things up."

"You made up that nonsense that Cricket said something to make you believe we'd been together last night."

"No—I caught her out. When I told her about your accident she said you were perfectly well when you left her. She was so shocked to learn that you'd had this accident, she just gave herself away. Then she tried to put it right and couldn't."

Now Des's bruised face flamed with anger—anger which was a part of guilt—of resentment because he had been found out. He spoke violently. "Since you want the truth you'd better hear it. I wouldn't have lied only I knew you'd be so bloody jealous. That's why I kept denying the truth, for your sake—to save *you*, my dear!"

Nira broke out into a cold sweat. She sat down on the edge of the bed. She thought she really was going to be sick, any moment. Her knees shook.

"My God, what a hero you are! What a noble motive for telling all those lies. Am I supposed to put a laurel wreath around your handsome head?"

"Oh, shut up."

"I want the truth and nothing but," she said, breathing noisily. "And as for my jealousy—I don't think it's altogether a question of that. A woman surely has a right to expect her husband to be faithful to her, hasn't she?"

"Aren't you exaggerating? Who said I'd been unfaithful? Cricket and I had dinner together."

"*And* went back to Morris's flat," Nira added.

"Okay. Okay. And we cracked a bottle of champagne."

"You cracked more than that. You've cracked up our marriage and done something absolutely awful to me!" she said hotly and began to cry.

He stared at her—his anger fading. He was right up to the neck now and he knew it. He didn't want this thing to go any further. He never had meant Nira to know about Cricket and he had certainly never had the slightest intention of cracking up their marriage. Never! But somehow her indignation and anger had infuriated him—made him beastly to her.

"You really are behind the times, my dear girl," he blustered. "Whatever you think happened in that flat—even if we indulged in a bit of necking—where's the crime?"

"Were you just necking?" Nira repeated the word with an hysterical laugh. "I've never heard it called that before."

"Oh, for God's sake, let up. You seem to *want* to make the most of it."

She looked at him without understanding. "And you, I suppose, have done nothing wrong in your own opinion. You are *entitled* to lie and deceive me and make love to Cricket."

He scowled. "I'm sorry, Nira. I didn't want it to happen, honestly. It was just one of those things."

Nira was trembling from head to foot now. She dug her long fingers into the side of the bed.

"Are you going to try and make me believe it wasn't pre-arranged, that you and Cricket only met in town by accident? All the old stuff about staying late at the office, too."

He shifted from one foot to the other, uneasily. "What's the good of all these recriminations? You're my wife. You are supposed to love me and where there's love surely there's forgiveness," he said grandly.

Nira almost bit through her lip. She didn't know whether to laugh or to cry. When she had said that he had cracked up their marriage she had meant it. There was a great big fissure through the mountain of content and happiness—the joy she had known before last night. The memory of Cricket's pretty, vicious face and that kitten-quality that made her so treacherous and unattractive in Nira's sight, damped her spirits.

Des said, "You don't *want* to forgive me. Is that it? Perhaps you're not so fond of me after all? I always imagined you were full of high principles. You used to talk so much about fidelity and romantic love. Have *you* always been faithful to me? I'm beginning to wonder. What about that evening you spent with Rob — alone in this house except for the kids. Or are you going to go on telling me you're just good friends?"

Nira gasped. Her breath quickened. She looked at him with positive loathing.

"You dare say a thing like that; about Rob and *me*? You know perfectly well there's nothing like that between us and never has been. Nor have I had an affair with any other man. *You know it*. It's the most awful thing for you to suggest. You're absolutely contemptible."

Des cooled down. He realised he was playing a dangerous game. He didn't want to lose Nira. He seated himself on the bed beside her, picked up one of her hands and held on to it tightly, despite her efforts to drag it away. When he tried to kiss her she drew back. But he was all penitence now.

He said, "Oh, God, we mustn't go on like this, Nirry. It's crazy. Nira darling, darling Nira, I'm so terribly sorry. I was mad — drunk. I don't love Cricket. I swear I don't. She excites me but I don't love her. I love only you and our children."

At that moment there was no comfort for her in these words. She wrenched her fingers from his and covered her face with both hands.

"So you want to love me, and make love to her too. Well — you can't, and that's that," she said and the tears streamed down her face.

He was suddenly genuinely ashamed of himself. To see his beautiful Nira like this and because of him, stabbed his heart — Des had a heart although it was of the spongy kind. You could depress it but it bounced up again. Nothing much made a lasting impression. He had in fact been quite proud of the fact that for at least ten years of their marriage he had been more or less faithful to his wife. But there were times — such as now, when he really didn't think she should be quite so conventional. Of course he realised that he was more tolerant about his own sexual behaviour than he would be of *hers*. He wouldn't want her to be like Cricket, or even like Maggie Wilson who was pretty responsive — as well he knew. Perhaps he himself was being old-fashioned in thinking that there should be one law for the man, and another for the woman, and that a good wife should be good (so long as she was sexually appealing and sensually attractive to him) which Nira had always been when it came to their intimate life. But hell! he didn't want her to become too smug, either. He felt worried and uncertain of his own feelings.

He took her hand and pressed it against his closed eyes, flinching as he did so because the cut over his eyebrow hurt.

"Oh, darling, my darling, you're wrong. I certainly don't want you *and* Cricket—only you. Last night was a moment's folly. I swear it. For God's sake be your generous self and forget it. Wipe it right out of your memory."

For a moment she said nothing but sat motionless, her face drawn with the pain of her thoughts. But for the first time that day she began to feel a little better—a little less anguished. She had despised Des for what he had done to her glorious faith and love. Now the focus was on herself. Perhaps she was being ungenerous—and as far as Des's affair was concerned she was ready to believe it *was* the first time. She was sure of that. She must try to remember that if you loved a person you didn't just wipe them out of existence because of one lapse.

Soon she turned to him, melting, utterly feminine, tender, jealous, reproachful yet still his woman, in love with him. All the passionate moments they had known together couldn't possibly be forgotten. Supposing this thing had happened to her? Supposing *she* had had an irresistible desire to make love to another man— she, too, might have given way then regretted it bitterly and hoped to be forgiven. She couldn't really imagine herself wanting any man but Des, but she felt that she would be pompous, vain— even stupid—to suppose that she never could surrender to the same sort of folly that had led Des into such a situation. And, truly feminine again, all her hatred and contempt became centred upon the woman who had tempted him.

"You didn't mean to hurt me—I know you didn't!" she broke out and sobbed the words, "You love me. You don't love her. It's her fault. That's true. It *is* true, isn't it, Des?"

"Absolutely true!" he said with an intensity that reassured her still further. "And it will never happen again, my darling."

"I blame Cricket," she said with passion, and drew a long slender hand across her nostrils, then got up to find a tissue and blow her nose. Soon she calmed down again and tried to be natural and laugh—crazily anxious to put things right. She belonged to Des and he to her—she must wipe Cricket out of the picture. She couldn't live with her husband in such a state of hostility. And she couldn't live without him. So she broke out in denunciation of the other woman. "Cricket's a little bitch. I hate her. I'll never, *never* willingly speak to her again."

God, thought Des, *how do we get out of this? What'll Boyce think? An open row between Nira and Cricket will bring him round here in the role of injured husband, unless we're careful. But was that true?* Boyce seemed not to mind what Cricket did or how she behaved. She had told him. It was only because of Nira they had been so careful. They hadn't succeeded very well. Damn Cricket for her stupidity!

He didn't think this was the time to talk too much about Cricket. The position was much too delicate. Above all he mustn't let Nira think he was in the least anxious to continue seeing his girl-friend. He wasn't. He'd had such a shock these last few hours that quite frankly he had lost all desire for fun and games. Nira was right. Cricket wasn't worth the loss of Nira and the kids.

He took Nira into his arms and went through all the old familiar motions of caressing her. He smoothed her hair back from that lovely brow that was ordinarily so serene; kissed her eyelids, drinking in her tears, repeating again and again that he was hellishly sorry he had hurt her—he hadn't meant to do it. And then he tried to lessen the blow he had given her by telling her that although he and Cricket *had* spent a few hours together in that flat—it hadn't really gone as far as Nira might imagine.

But after returning his kisses and swearing that she would forgive and forget and give him another chance, she refused to accept any more lies from Des.

"Oh, don't try and make light of it! I'm not a fool, Des. Of course you—you and that little beast—oh, *God*!" She broke off, her tear-stained face flaming, pulled herself out of his arms, and clenched and unclenched her hands. She knew she was still tormented by jealousy.

He spent the next half-hour trying to convince her that she need have no such feelings and that this was only a nightmare—she would soon wake up and could feel that she was the only person in the world he really loved. *And* he was going to be a good boy for ever more—he swore it.

She listened and accepted the protests and promises and said little. But the one thing she didn't want to be was bitter. Having forgiven him she mustn't hold the affair against him. She mentioned the children.

"For their sake you wouldn't want to break up our home, would you?"

"Good lord no, nothing further from my mind. You know what a lot I think of them."

Nira gave a long sigh, walked to her dressing-table, sat down and started to repair her face. She dabbed cooling lotion on eyes that were pink and puffy with weeping. Funny, she thought, oh so funny that a man could love his wife and children (and she knew that Des did) yet find it so easy to go to bed with another woman. And he wasn't the only one. There were others — others in this town she and Des knew about. She'd always pitied the wives. Well, she didn't intend to join those who were in need of such pity. She tried to concentrate entirely on the thought of Renira and Jonathan.

"We must neither of us ever hurt those two. One's got to set an example. The world's in a pretty rotten state at the moment, Des. If we don't want our kids to grow up thinking nothing of sleeping around and behaving all anyhow, we've got to watch what we do ourselves!"

He agreed heartily. But his mind was more on the fact that he needed a strong drink than on the moral welfare of his growing children. He made an effort to accept Nira's little lecture with a meekness which he didn't often show, and went so far as to say, "It's not that I need any woman but you. It's this bloody drink that's responsible for my stupid behaviour. I don't deny it. I'll cut out the alcohol. I'll never have another gin — you'll see."

Nira laughed, and tears stung her eyelids at the same time. She took his arm between her hands, laid her cheek against it and murmured, "Oh, Des, darling, you're so like a naughty schoolboy. Who could be cross with you for long? I bet you don't give up the gin. But do remember it's the champagne that's *your* undoing, every time."

"Then I'll never have another glass of champagne."

"Tell that to the Marines, darling."

She laughed and cried again. In a state of nerves and tension unusual for her, she had lost her normal self-control. It had been a terrible thing to her, Cricket and Des's treachery. Her deep dislike of Cricket intensified.

The next thing they had to do was to decide how best to dispense with the Hallings. Cricket, thought Nira, was not going to come into this house again if *she* could help it. She didn't care what other people thought, and as for Boyce, he had been pressing her far too hard with his attentions lately and she didn't want *him*.

However, Nira and Des avoided this issue for the moment. They went together to say good night to the children. Renira was growing very observant. Nira didn't want the little girl to see that she had been crying. She put on dark glasses and pretended that her eyes were sore and that the light hurt them. Susan went home. Renira and Jon settled down. Soon it was time for Nira to cook Des's evening meal.

He said he couldn't eat a thing but that he wanted something to drink — coffee maybe. Nira said he looked so grim, he'd better make it a stronger one. He reminded her that he'd promised to go on the wagon to please her and only meant that he wanted coffee or orange-juice. She said he needn't go as far as that if he didn't want to. Anyhow, why couldn't he be moderate about drinking? She thought it would probably do him good to have a Scotch. Also to try and eat the steak she had bought for him.

"It's a ghastly price now but I thought you would enjoy it, so I was extravagant. You can't turn it down, darling."

He was hungry and gave in. Once supper was over, the subject of the Hallings and the cancellation of the holiday had to come up again, and about this they did not altogether agree.

"We all know each other at the golf club and it'll be so damned awkward if we have an open battle," Des said, although he looked at Nira anxiously because he did not want to upset her again. But she acceded in so far as she agreed that it was all very awkward *and* that they didn't want a scandal. But she wouldn't retract what she had said about not having Cricket in the house again. There was the business of Simon Halling which worried her, of course. Simon was Jonathan's best friend. That was more than awkward.

Des, feeling better now that he was back in favour and had both eaten and drunk, suggested cautiously that the boys should be allowed to carry on with their friendship and just the parents need not go on being so friendly. They could acknowledge each other at the Club — little matters of that kind, but no more dinners and bridge. And there was still the Majorcan bookings — plus Rob's holiday — to be considered.

"I've already told Rob that we're cancelling it," said Nira.

Des looked at her gloomily. She'd been a bit quick about it, he thought, but he supposed he couldn't blame her in the circumstances. Oh, the whole thing was hellishly embarrassing and he began to wish he'd never had that abortive affair with Cricket. It had spoiled everything.

Later that evening Rob's name was mentioned again.

"If we're not going to Majorca, I suppose we could ask him to join us with the kids in Cornwall," Des said, wanting to be generous in the circumstances.

"Oh, he'd be delighted," said Nira, "but there's no necessity — he understands there's been some sort of crisis and is quite okay about it."

"Well, I'll leave it to you," Des said with more than his usual affability.

He was really anxious to get back on to the old good terms with his wife. Cricket and her luscious love-making had been all very well but the repercussions had been far too dangerous. A chap couldn't afford to make a muck of his whole married life just for the sake of a few hours in bed with a new and exciting woman. He must really take a hold on himself and not let it happen again. Nira was worth his consideration. She was a darling and it had hit him hard when she had turned on him. He'd had a ghastly fear that she might try to divorce him.

In the lounge, Nira switched on their colour television. She knew that there was a golf championship that Des particularly wanted to see, and she herself had no wish to enter into a lengthy conversation that might involve further recriminations and apologies — the wordy wreckage that a matrimonial storm so often washes up on the shore of two people's lives.

She closed her eyes to the golf match and thought about Rob and his immense kindliness. That sense of reliability he gave her. Integrity was a much-to-be admired virtue in any man, and growing more rare as time went on. Who, for instance, could depend on a man like Boyce, or several others she could name at the Club, although she tried hard to avoid putting her own husband into the category. Her feeling for Rob was strange — it almost amounted to a kind of childish hero-worship. Of him it could be said (as once indeed it had been said) of a great leader of the French Revolution: that he was *incorruptible*. She could imagine somehow that nothing could corrupt Rob. Yet there was nothing smug or sententious about him.

She knew he had been bitterly disappointed about the holiday. He had looked forward to getting away from Aunt Ida and life in The Hollies. Perhaps she would take Des up on that offer to let Rob accompany them on their holiday to Cornwall and so make up for his disappointment over Formentor.

She felt herself to be in a rather queer mood tonight. She still loved Des with all her heart, yet it was plain to her that the tie which had once been so strong and complete between them, had in some way weakened.

He wanted to make love to her that night but she rejected him—gently but firmly. She could not bear his love-making while the slightest feeling of suspicion or distrust existed. She must wait until she could get over the whole thing.

She could be friendly with Des, and even tender, but she could not measure his passion with hers. She even fancied that he was relieved when she turned from him, and was so soon asleep. After a moment she disengaged herself from the arm which he had thrown across her, and settled down on her own pillow. She found herself thinking suddenly how much she would like Rob to be with them on their Cornish holiday, even though they had to wait till the end of July.

She loved Cornwall. She thought about it drowsily before she slept. She had once discussed it with Rob. He hadn't been there, but said he felt sure the awe-inspiring splendour of the sea and the gigantic cliffs on the north coast would appeal to him, as they did to her.

For Des, it had always been purely a parental duty to swim in cold water, lie on the sands, or play cricket with the children. He preferred their more sophisticated exotic holidays abroad. But Nira loved her Cornish coast as much as the children did. It would be nice if Rob could come with them. She would try to arrange it tomorrow.

Des was asleep—breathing noisily. Nira sighed and shut her eyes. She felt very tired and most unusually lonely.

9

"I'D LOVE TO go down to Cornwall with you and the children if it can be arranged," Rob told Nira when she broached the subject of the family holiday at the Club the following day. "But I really feel I'd be gate-crashing—even more so than when I made a fivesome for Majorca. Des won't want me—just with his own family and—"

"He doesn't mind at all. *He* suggested it," interrupted Nira.

They were sitting in the sunshine on the veranda of the club house facing the first green. Des had insisted on going up to town. His eyebrow was healing and his limp less obvious, and they were short of staff at the office. Nira and Rob had arranged this game a week ago.

Rob was feeling good. What could be better than a fine morning in early summer and a game of golf with his adored Nira? But his feeling of pleasure began to evaporate as a definite change in her impressed itself upon him. He was sure something had happened to upset her—and badly. It puzzled him. She was nervy, unlike her usually tranquil self. She looked very pale, with dark smudges under the beautiful eyes.

He felt in the pocket of his suède waistcoat for a pipe.

"It's very decent of you both to offer to include me, and you know how fond I am of your young," he said.

"They are of you."

"What are your plans?"

"As a matter of fact," she said, "we aren't going to a hotel in Mawgan Porth. We've booked rooms in a farmhouse we know. It's a lovely little village."

"I've heard about it. They've got an airport there."

She nodded. "It's pretty crowded like all these holiday resorts in the West, but much less so than places like Newquay. It still retains lots of its old charm. We were only going to have ten days but I am sure we can arrange to stay longer now that we are not going to Majorca. Des will need a proper break from the City, and, of course, the children adore it. There are some lovely beaches around and the bathing can be super if we strike lucky with the weather. Trevarra Farm is an old stone-built house, owned by a retired couple—the Hoskins—both very nice and she adores Renira and Jonathan. They don't farm any more but make quite a good bit of money in the summer letting rooms. The cooking's plain but quite decent. We've known the Hoskins for years. I'm quite sure they'll fix you up. She always keeps an extra room or two for her favourites. I'll phone her after six tonight. But you must remember it'll be just a children's holiday; nothing glamorous or as exciting as it might have been in Formentor."

"If you ask me," said Rob smiling his slow lazy smile, "I reckon I shall prefer Trevarra Farm to Formentor, even if the kids don't get me into the icy water. After being so long in Kenya and the swimming out there, I'm spoilt for English sea-bathing. But I promise to play cricket with Jonathan."

Nira felt suddenly happier, less ill-at-ease. Grateful for this man's honesty and unfailing friendship. Nothing seemed to ruffle Rob. There were no awkward corners in him. *Dear* Rob! Not for the first time she thought what a fine husband he would have made. What a wonderful family man! It did seem a shame.

"Have you told the Hallings about Majorca yet?" he asked.

She bit her lip. She had not yet decided how best to deal with Boyce and Cricket. She said, "If Cricket turns up for golf I'll just tell her that the holiday's off and leave it at that. Maybe she'll understand," Nira added with a bitterness that was not lost on Rob.

"As we're such good friends, would it be impertinent of me to ask how this break has come about?" he asked gently.

The colour stained the creamy pallor of her face. She avoided his gaze. She was well aware that those kindly eyes had noticed that she was desperately worried.

She said, "Oh—it's something—rather personal. I—forgive me, Rob—I'd rather not discuss it."

Rob was sure now that the explanation for her present state of nerves lay with those two—Desmond and Cricket.

He'd bet his boots on it. He steered the conversation tactfully away from the subject and suggested that they fetched their clubs and started to play.

"I shall be awful today," Nira laughed. "Worse than usual. I've got a headache, so I'll slice every ball."

"I know what headaches are."

"Your kind must be worse than the one I've got today."

"Well, we'll play for a large sum of money so I'll win for a change."

She gave what he thought rather a hollow little laugh, but after playing for an hour in the fresh air and the sunshine, the delight of the game seemed to revive her spirits, and bring the sparkle back to her eyes.

He did beat her, but he was glad to see her relax, and whatever it was that had happened to upset her, it was obviously not troubling her too much just now. He rather hoped that Cricket Halling wouldn't come into the Club and distress her again.

A shock awaited them once they walked into the bar for a pre-lunch drink. Several of the members, drink in hand, were already there. Joyce Moffatt's voice, talking to Maggie Wilson and Colonel Moffatt could be heard above the rest.

"Isn't it *ghastly*! Poor wretched Boyce—he must be in a state."

No one could avoid hearing what Joyce said. Nira and Rob exchanged startled glances.

"What's happened?" Nira asked.

Those who were there, stopped talking and turned and looked at Nira and Rob. Joyce was once more spokesman.

"These bloody car accidents," she said. "It happened at midnight, they say. I'd been expecting to see Cricket here. She was going to play a three-ball with Maggie and me and now we know why she didn't turn up."

"But what's happened?" demanded Nira. "Has Cricket had an accident?"

"Yes. It was on the early news. I suppose you missed it. She and Boyce were coming back from a party late last night and met a lorry at the corner of Sangster Road. You know that damned crossroads—I've always said there ought to be a sort of Give Way sign there."

Nira unzipped her jacket and threw it on the sofa. Her heart beat rapidly.

"What happened?" She turned to Maggie Wilson.

Maggie, like the others, looked pale and upset.

"The poor thing—she was driving. There was a lot on the radio about it—the ghastly tangle of wreckage and so on. The lorry driver was killed and they couldn't get poor little Cricket out for nearly an hour."

"Oh God," said Nira and sat down. Rob had drawn a stool close to her and helped her on it.

"Yes, she was driving," Maggie repeated, "and they say she was on the wrong side of the road. She was — she was —"

"Let's cut the details," put in Rob tersely. He could see that Nira was shivering. He understood her feelings. She and Cricket had quarrelled. She had been about to edge Cricket out of her life. But they had once been friendly and their two boys played together. Whatever had happened in the past must be forgotten now.

The next thing Nira did was to ask about Boyce. It appeared that he had come out of it miraculously unhurt except for minor cuts and bruises and a broken ankle. They were keeping him in hospital for twenty-four hours at least. Nira felt nothing but compassion.

"Poor, *poor* Boyce, what a hideous shock for him! And poor Cricket! So young to die like that."

It wasn't until much later when Rob was taking Nira home that he heard Nira voice a personal opinion that it may well have been after a champagne party that Cricket had driven so carelessly.

In due course this was expressed at the inquest. Boyce admitted that they had both exceeded the amount of alcohol a driver should permit himself. Because he had let Cricket drive, he felt doubly guilty. He made no effort to deny it.

As soon as they reached Nylands, Nira asked Rob to come in with her. They had meant to lunch at the Club but she couldn't stand all the crowd. They *would* keep harping back to the details of the accident and Cricket's death. Maggie had always been a dramatic sort of person. Her own husband had died in a car crash, so she revived *that* story and it all became too harrowing.

Rob stayed for a sandwich lunch with Nira, glad that he was there to look after her. She went straight to the telephone and got through to the local hospital. "I must speak to Boyce and see if I can do anything about Simon," she explained to Rob.

"Yes, of course, the poor little boy—grim for him."

He didn't hear the conversation between Nira and Boyce but she told him about it while she made the sandwiches. He watched her cutting the bread. He smoked his much-needed pipe. There were tears running down her cheeks.

"He seemed glad to talk to me," she said. "He's obviously suffering from shock as well as the broken ankle. Can't you imagine it? He keeps blaming himself for letting Cricket drive him back from that party. He says they had both had one or two over the odd but had been so near their home, they had somehow never dreamed they'd meet a lorry at that time of the morning and in Sangster Road of all places."

He also told Nira that he had no idea that Cricket had drunk quite so much. Much more than he had imagined. He went on and on, blaming himself. When Nira asked if she could do something about Simon, he said yes at once. He'd already phoned through to their daily who had been spending the night at their house which she often did when Mr. and Mrs. Halling were out late, so that Simon would not be alone. She was a nice woman and had children of her own and had been deeply shocked by the news. She had seen to it that Simon had had his breakfast and gone to school without letting him know why his parents had not come home last night.

"Let me help, too, if I can," put in Rob. "If the boy wants fetching, there's my car and I'm ready to do anything."

Nira threw him a grateful look. "I might keep you to that."

Boyce had told her that neither he nor Cricket had parents. His had been killed in an air raid during the war, and hers in a car crash, when Cricket was still at school.

"All these crashes," ended Nira. "God, Rob, it's a bit unnerving!"

"Agreed, but don't think about it too much if you can help it, darling."

The darling passed unnoticed. She went on telling him about Simon. "There's no one he can go and stay with, only some distant cousins and Boyce has a step-brother in Kenya. He doesn't want Simon to go back to the house as there will be such an atmosphere there, bad for the child, with his mother dead and people ringing up, and flowers arriving and all the gruesome business — so I said he could come here. He adores Jonathan. Poor old Boyce has gone to pieces. He can't even face telling Simon about his mother — he wants me to."

Rob looked at her gravely. As she was about to lift the lunch tray from the table, he walked up to her and put an arm around her shoulders. He drew her close.

"You're all in, poor Nira. Just don't let that kind heart of yours run away with you. I know how you feel about helping Boyce out — but let me help *you*. I can fetch Simon from school. I'll even tell him about his mother, if you like. I'm rather good at talking to the young — so they tell me. I don't think I've ever mentioned it but I was a schoolteacher for a time after I left university. I didn't make a career of teaching but I did get on very well with the young ones. I think I'll know how to tackle the poor little chap."

Now Nira collapsed entirely. She put both arms around the tall man who was holding her and gave herself up to the blessed warmth and security of his embrace. Sobbing, she leaned her face against his shoulder, and between her sobs thanked him.

"You're such a dear, Rob, thank you awfully. No, I didn't know you'd ever been a schoolmaster but you're obviously just what Simon needs — a strong-minded understanding man. You'll be so much better for him than an emotional woman like myself."

Rob's pulses jerked as he felt the slim pliant body pressed against his own. He kissed her cheeks, brushing away the tears, knowing to his cost how desperately he loved her. To help her get through this crisis was vital. He was surprised to find how right she was, when she called herself an emotional woman. Of course he was an ignorant fool. She was highly-strung and vulnerable behind her cool façade. Hadn't she made it obvious what Des meant to her? He should have known.

He came dangerously close to kissing the beautiful mouth that was all too near his own, but realised that this was not the moment to swing from pity to passion. He pushed her hair back from her moist forehead, breathed in the odour of her hair, her scented skin, then gently released her from his arms. The sweat was breaking out on his own forehead now. He said, "That's settled, dear. You tell me what time to fetch Simon and exactly where his school is. I believe it's somewhere near the recreation park, isn't it? I've noticed the football-ground. Now come along and let's have that lunch and a stiff whisky and soda, too, if I might suggest it. I think we could both do with one."

At once Nira calmed down. Rob always had a soothing effect on her.

"I'm so sorry I'm behaving all anyhow. It would be wonderful if you'd collect Simon. Yes, do please tell him about his mother. Have a little talk with him, then bring him back here, by which time I'll have briefed Jonathan. They'll get together and have a game. In fact I'll go out and buy some new aircraft models. They both like doing those. Small boys are easily amused and thank God, at ten years old Simon can be managed more easily than if he were a couple of years older."

Rob agreed. Excusing herself, she went upstairs to fetch a clean handkerchief and make up her face, while he carried the tray through to the lounge.

During that meal Nira ate little. She hadn't the heart for it. She kept thinking about Cricket, broken and dying in her shattered car. What luck Boyce had had — if it could be called luck for a man to be left alive, knowing that he should never have allowed his wife to take the wheel.

Deliberately Rob avoided the subject of the crash. After lunch, he rang Simon's headmaster, who already knew the situation, and gave permission for him to fetch the boy whenever he chose.

Rob had a date with an old friend who was coming down to The Hollies for dinner, so he arranged to bring Simon back to Nira soon after five.

"You look all in — you really ought to have a rest before Simon comes, Nira," Rob said when she walked to the front door with him.

Nira was so unnerved that she burst into tears again. Unpopular though Cricket had been with Rob, he himself was upset enough. It was tragic that that pretty frivolous little creature had come to such a violent end. He could fully understand why Nira had lost her customary command of herself. Involuntarily he took her in his arms.

"Don't, darling, don't cry," he kept saying while he smoothed her hair and pressed her wet face against his shoulder.

"Oh, Rob," she sobbed, "Oh, *Rob* — poor little Simon — he adored his mother!"

"God knows why these things have to happen."

She clung to him for a moment, then remembered Des. *He* would have to be told. She wondered how it would affect him, but wondered it without bitterness or jealousy. She let Rob hold her and caress her in his tender way for a moment longer, then drew back and turned her face away.

"Do forgive me. I'm so sorry."

"You know you needn't be formal with me, my love," he said.

His love — how curious that sounded, she thought, and how strangely it comforted her. Suddenly she went back to him, put her arms around his neck and kissed him on both cheeks.

"You are a darling, Rob. Thanks a thousand times. I don't know what I'd do without you — your friendship."

"And what would I do without yours." He smiled down at her.

At half-past five he brought Simon and Jonathan back together. Nira put her son into the picture and extracted a solemn promise from him to be particularly nice to Simon. Jonathan being a kind-hearted boy, said that he would do his best and that he was "jolly pleased Simon could stay and sleep in the same room". It would be fun.

"It's tough for Simon losing his mother, isn't it, Mum?" he added.

"Very tough," said Nira who by this time was completely self-possessed again and ready for any emergency. "And don't take any notice if he cries a bit."

"Boys don't cry," said Jonathan gravely.

"I know they don't often," she agreed, "but this is a bit special, isn't it?"

He gave her a hug and said he'd hate to lose her and went off whistling. *How lucky children are*, Nira thought. The young—the ten-year-olds like Simon—were so gloriously remote from the agonies and ecstasies of the adult world. Nothing went too deep with them, fortunately. They couldn't grasp the full meaning of death. They were too far removed from it. Fortunately for them all, Simon took the news extraordinarily well. Nira never knew what Rob said to the boy or how he tackled him, but by the time he brought Simon into the lounge where Nira was waiting, the boy seemed quite calm. He had been crying, but now he was anxious to go off with his friend Jonathan and get away from the embarrassment of this terrible accident. Nira told him there was nothing for him to worry about—that his father would be out of hospital in a day or two. Then they all drove round to the Hallings' house to fetch Simon's night bag. By the time they were back in Nylands, the two little boys were giggling about something that had happened at school. Once again Nira thanked heaven for the matter-of-fact outlook of children.

Finally there was Des to cope with. Rob had by this time gone home. When Nira met Des in the hall she could see from his face that he had already heard the news. Somebody he knew on the train must have told him. He looked quite ghastly, and he immediately launched into the subject.

"My God, isn't it grim news?"

"Appalling. We've got Simon here. Boyce is in hospital."

"Gerald Robinson told me. His wife phoned him up."

"I didn't phone you. I didn't think you'd want to hear like that."

Des made no answer but went straight to the dining-room and poured himself out a strong whisky. He remembered his promise to Nira and lifted the glass to her with a wry smile.

"I still mean to cut it out, but just tonight I really need this."

Nira's eyes softened. She slipped an arm through his affectionately. "Of course you do."

He sat down heavily, spilled some of the whisky on the table, mopped it up with his handkerchief and looked around for a cigarette which Nira found and lit for him. For a moment they discussed the details of the accident. Nira could see his big body trembling. She wondered vaguely if he had really loved Cricket in his way, but there was no room for jealousy in her mind. She tried to comfort him.

"You must feel particularly awful, poor Des."

"It isn't that I was really in love with her," he said awkwardly, "but we sort of got on very well. We had the same sense of humour. She was great fun — that's all."

Nira felt her colour rise. "Okay, Des."

He gulped down half the whisky. She could see that he was badly shaken. She put a hand on his knee.

"Don't take it too hard, Des."

"She was so full of life," he went on. "She had a lot of faults but she was a gay little thing."

"And very pretty," said Nira generously.

"And now she's lying in a mortuary."

"Des, don't dwell on it."

"I'll try not to. It isn't much use, is it?"

"The people to be sorry for are Boyce and Simon."

"Oh, I don't pretend it's a great personal loss for me but it's so shocking and I — I —"

"You were fond of her," broke in Nira. "I understand."

He took her hand and hid his face — still bruised and haggard — against the palm.

"You're a wonderful person, Nirry; too good for me."

"Oh, darling, don't be absurd. Sometimes you make me feel dreadfully smug when you talk about all this *goodness*. I'm not good. I'm just rather practical and not quite so up in the air as you are at times. I daresay I'm rather dull, really."

"Rubbish — you've never been dull in your life."

She closed her eyes. She had not been able to rest and she felt very tired.

"Death's so final, Des. Nothing can bring Cricket back so we must just try and do what we can for the two who are left."

Now Des put down his empty glass and grimaced at her.

"Don't let's be hypocritical and suggest that Boyce has lost the love of his life."

She got up, walked to the standard-lamp by the desk and switched it on. The room was flooded with amber light. She needed light, she thought. The whole day had seemed to her as though she were living in a black stifling cloud.

"Let's try not to talk about poor Cricket. I don't think I can take much more. I've had it all day. But I do want you to know that I'm full of sympathy for you, darling."

"I suppose everybody at the Club is in a state. Who have you seen?"

She sighed. He was determined to go on about the disaster. Better let him get it all off his chest. She was beginning to feel confused about the whole affair — about life and death — love and hate — everything. She wondered if ever she would feel happy and carefree again.

She let Des talk and answered all his questions. When Rob's name came up, remembering how wonderful he had been with Simon, she also remembered a moment in the hall when he had held her close in his arms. This was the second occasion. She had felt so safe and comforted — both times.

She had told him she didn't know what she'd do without his friendship, and she didn't know, she thought, while Des poured out his second whisky, and continued to harp on Cricket's death. *She just didn't know.*

IO

ANY HOPE THAT Nira might have entertained that Cricket's untimely death would solve her own marriage problem, was slowly but surely dashed. There was to be little peace in her life during the four months that followed the Hallings' accident.

First came Cricket's funeral. All who had known her, including her harshest critics in the neighbourhood, and at the golf club, went to the service, if not to the cremation. She was remembered kindly and mourned because of her youth and physical attractions and the sadness of her end. Immediately after the funeral, Nira had Boyce on her hands.

Glib-tongued, amusing, self-confident Boyce, underwent something of a metamorphosis following the horror of his wife's death. He exhibited a pathetic desire to be with Nira. He haunted Nylands and because of the circumstances, she hadn't the heart to reject him altogether. She and Des agreed that Simon, anyhow, should remain with them for the present. He was happy with Jonathan and rapidly accepted Nira as an adopted mother. But his presence in the house led to problems because the two boys paired off and little Renira often found herself an unwanted third. This made her fractious and difficult—which she had never been in the past. Susan, as ever, was a tower of strength, and kept the three amused. It was a help. But Nira's most embarrassing moments were spent with Boyce who all too often came round to see her and stared at her with his mournful eyes. He talked a great deal about his poor sweet dead wife. Although Nira was full of pity, she also was far too well aware that Boyce had been on poor terms with his wife for a long time before she died. Nira could not really relate this constant show of grief to his true feelings for Cricket. Being an honest person herself, his attitude began to irritate her.

When she told Des about it, his sole comment was, "Okay—so isn't it time you asked him to take Simon back to his own home. Boyce should be getting down to the task of making a new life for himself and that boy. We can't carry on with this Good Samaritan stuff for ever. I'm surprised he's so gutless."

Nira twisted her lips.

"Charitable Des! You're harder than I am, darling. Whatever I may think about Boyce, I haven't the heart to send Simon packing. He seems so happy with us."

"Well, it's up to you. You're the one who has to have him here," said Des, and shrugged. He was no longer interested.

At the end of June things changed for Boyce. His firm offered him a job with their company in Peru where they were about to engage on a new big business project. Boyce readily accepted. He came round to Nylands to tell Nira the news. She was alone. Boyce, who since Cricket's death had been genuinely grateful to her for all she had done for him and his son, reverted suddenly to the man he had been in the past. He took both her long slim hands, pressed them against his cheek and looked at her with desirous eyes.

"Oh, Nira—lovely Nira, I shall always adore you. I'm likely to be away on this job for a couple of years. I shall only be able to see you when I come back on leave, and that won't be too often. I'm devastated, darling."

She drew her fingers away and tried to ignore this emotional approach. She said lightly, "Boyce dear, I wish you the very best of luck, and every happiness in your new life and work. Peru sounds exciting."

"Not as exciting as you are, Nira," and Boyce's gaze strayed from her face to her long graceful throat, then her waist, her long tapering legs—all the beauty he found so irresistible.

She tried to pretend she hadn't heard what he said.

"What will you do about Simon?" she asked.

Reluctantly he let the sensual moment pass.

"I've arranged for him to be a boarder at his old school. He wants that. He's used to it there and gets on well with the boys and masters. Will I be asking too much if I suggest you take him out now and then?"

"Of course, Des and I will cherish him. We love him. And it'll be nice for Jonathan to go on seeing him at school, too. He'll always be welcome here."

"I can have him out in Peru during the holidays. Another chap from my office is going out there with his wife and family. They say Simon can stay with them when he's on holiday. I shall be living with our assistant manager and he's a bachelor. We couldn't really do with a small boy in his flat."

Nira nodded. "Well, it all seems arranged and I hope your luck will change from now onwards, Boyce. You've been through a bad time."

"You're determined not to be anything more to me than a friend, aren't you?" he asked sadly.

"Boyce—*please*—you know that I—"

"That you're in love with your husband?" he broke in, "Nonsense, I'm not a fool. I don't want to refer to anything that happened in the past but I just can't believe you're as much in love with Des as you were."

Now she was angry.

"Boyce, *please*, I don't like what you infer and if we're to go on being friends you really mustn't say — or think — things like that."

"Certainly I shall go on thinking them," he said with a short laugh, and taking one of her hands again, kissed it from fingertips to wrist. "I adore you," he repeated, "Remember that."

The kissing left her cold. She did not find Boyce physically appealing. In any case it was Des she loved *that* way, and Boyce was all wrong about it.

But as he left the house she faced the fact that he had both confused and upset her. Why should he think that she didn't love Des as much as she used to? Why must he stir up the ghost of the past — especially now that Cricket was dead? And it wasn't true anyhow. She *did* love Des — just as much as ever.

But did he really love her? Could she really regain her old confidence in him, and could a woman, no matter how much in love, ever really forget a husband's infidelity, even if she forgave it?

One afternoon in July Des phoned to say he wouldn't be back for dinner that evening and might be late home.

"So sorry, darling, hope you haven't got my favourite dinner prepared."

Her spirits drooped.

"No, it's quite all right," she said. "I've got to help Susan sort out the children's clothes, anyhow. I never seem to get down to it when you're at home."

He told her that he loved her and hung up.

As Nira put down the telephone she found herself wondering . . . wondering if this late work at the office excuse was genuine, or if he was slipping again. Was he taking some girl out in town . . . *any girl?* . . .

She checked her thoughts, ashamed of them and remorseful. She had absolutely no reason to believe that Des was not to be trusted now. She was being absurd. But somehow the prospect of helping Susan sort the children's clothes bored her to death.

She rang up Rob.

His reaction was immediate and gratifying.

"Funny," he said, "I was going to ask you and Des if you'd seen that film at the local. It's an old one — *Dr. Zhivago*. Let me take you, will you?"

"I've seen it but I adored it. All that fantastic Russian scenery —

that terrible train journey, and the marvellous way Omar Sharif played his part—all *her* love and self-sacrifice—oh, it was stupendous!"

"Then come and see it with me again."

Of course she went. She always enjoyed being with Rob. There was nothing awkward or difficult about their friendship, only the warmth that she valued so highly.

Des had begun to call him her boy-friend whenever he was mentioned. She accepted the term with good humour. That was all there was in it—Rob was her friend, nothing more. Des knew it.

She was once more enthralled by the great Zhivago film and sat eating the chocolates Rob bought for her, yet she could not quite forget Boyce's unwelcome allusion to the affair that had existed between Des and Cricket, or his suggestion that she and Des were not as much in love as they used to be.

The love element in the film appealed to her deeply emotional nature. When Rob glanced down at her he saw tears glistening on her cheeks. He felt more than a little distressed. He saw far too many signs these days that Nira was unhappy. He wished he knew more about it, so that he might be of more help. But when they parted she seemed composed—smiling again—full of warm gratitude for the evening's entertainment. Rob went home, still troubled.

Once Nira was back at Nylands, she determined to give Des a warm welcome when he returned. She remembered suddenly that it was over a month since he had held her in his arms like a lover. She felt a tremendous longing for their love to be as passionate tonight and complete as it used to be. She put on one of her newest, most attractive nightgowns and sprayed perfume over her throat. She would show him how much he meant to her and he would respond and dispel the shadows and make her feel safe and content again.

But Des came home flushed and talkative, bringing a very strong smell of drink and cigar smoke with him. He had obviously been to a party. He was certainly in high spirits, talking non-stop about his work and the Common Market and nothing she wanted to hear. She asked him what sort of work had kept him in town, and he told her it was the office—just something that had happened—a fault in the computer, and they had to have a conference and go further into the accounts. There was never enough time during the day, he said. Of course he wanted to be with her, Nira, but couldn't make it, etc.

She listened, wanting to believe, but with her heart full of disappointment and disbelief.

She couldn't accuse him of not trying to make love to her. He made every effort to do so — but he failed. Then he sheepishly kissed her good night and excused himself by saying he was over-tired.

"Sorry, darling, but you know I love you," he mumbled, and went to sleep.

Nira lay awake staring into the darkness. A depression descended upon her such as she had never before experienced A lowering of her entire spirit, her morale, her fundamental belief that all was well between Des and herself.

She was too sensitive, she thought, perhaps psychic, for in the depths of her heart she *knew that Des had been with a woman tonight*. Who, God alone knew, possibly some girl in the office. *But she knew it.* She said nothing because she also knew that she could be wrong. And that next evening when he came back, he was his old gay attentive sober self, and she hoped to enjoy a pleasant evening. They were going to dinner at Maggie Wilson's. This would of course include the American mother — Mrs. Kennett — and Rob had been asked as well.

They were late in reaching Maggie's attractive ultra-modern bungalow which had huge picture-windows facing the golf course. Rob was already there. Des nudged Nira and whispered, "I'll be darned well jealous soon. Wherever you are, your boy-friend follows."

She found his humour not very funny tonight — even annoying. She kept her lips tightly shut. During dinner she was quieter than usual. Rob glanced at her now and again and wondered what had happened to make his Nira so subdued. The look of strain that had been on her face quite often lately had returned. He was very aware of this. Des was slightly more boisterous than usual and talked a lot to Maggie. Rob noticed this, too, and felt more and more uneasy. What was happening between Nira and Des, he wondered.

Maggie's mother helped her daughter with the meal and kept up a flow of chatter. She was born and bred in California, and although in her sixties, still attractive. It wasn't the first time she had met the Curtises. She admired Nira immensely — found her both beautiful and charming.

Maggie was, as always, a good hostess and a Cordon Bleu cook. She produced an excellent dinner. As a rule Nira liked Maggie. She was sympathetic and good value. Tonight she looked particularly attractive in her long, pale-yellow organza hostess-gown. It had a low-cut neck which showed the curve of her beautiful white breasts, and went well with her red-bronzed hair which was her outstanding beauty. She wore it parted in the centre, looped back on either side and coiled in the nape of her neck — an old-fashioned style that suited her admirably.

Des sat on her left. Rob, the older man was on her right, but he was for the most part caught up with the conversation between the garrulous Mrs. Kennett and Nira, while Maggie concentrated on Des.

It was during the cheese course that Nira suddenly turned her head, glanced down the table towards her hostess, and noticed the way she and Des were looking at each other. In that split second they were not laughing, but staring intently into one another's eyes. Maggie's long-shaped eyes, brown, moist, thickly fringed, held an expression that no one — let alone Nira who was so perceptive — could mistake. It was the look of a woman in love and Des was returning it to the full. Nira knew *him* well enough to be sure of *that*, too.

For Nira, time seemed to stand still, then Des and Maggie both laughed, Maggie said something frivolous for everyone to hear, and the moment of revelation passed. But so revealing had it been that Nira experienced a sensation of hopeless loss. The repeated loss of her confidence in Des and the awful suspicion that now Cricket had gone and some weeks had passed, he was having another love affair; this time with Maggie.

Would Maggie do such a thing? Maggie, who was supposed to have been devoted to her doctor-husband and so heart-broken when he died? Well, why not? Nira asked herself. She was lonely, hungry for love perhaps, after two years of widowhood. It was common talk that she wanted to marry again. And it was well known that she found Des attractive. Of course, Nira thought miserably, Des had a strong animal attraction for all women. *Didn't she know!*

Oh, God, she thought, *oh, God!*

Suddenly her gorge seemed to rise and she went ice-cold. She leaned across the table and spoke to Mrs. Kennett in a voice that could not be heard by the two at the top of the table.

"I suppose you and Maggie didn't see *Dr. Zhivago* last night at the local cinema, did you?"

"No, we didn't. We're going tomorrow night. Mag went up to town last night; to a party. Don't ask me where. I never know what my dear daughter does. She's a law unto herself, that baby. But aren't all girls the same these days."

Nira nodded. She couldn't speak. She locked her cold hands in her lap so tightly that the points of her nails grazed the palms. And she thought; *Maggie was in town last night, too. At a nameless party. So it's Maggie this time. It's Maggie.*

At once this thought was followed by self-reproach. She mustn't be stupid. She mustn't allow herself to become a jealous wife just because there had once been an affair. She had no real reason to suspect Maggie and her husband. Surely *this* wouldn't follow the Cricket pattern? It couldn't. Des wouldn't hurt her again in such a way so soon after *the other*. She, if she loved him, must trust him now.

Let Des and Maggie gaze into each other's eyes. As for Maggie being up in London (the Cricket pattern again), it was out of the question that he should have spent the evening with her and if he had, it mightn't be anything more than that they dined together, and he hadn't told her, Nira, because he knew she'd be upset. She had herself to blame. She never had been as free and easy with other men as Des was with women. He frequently teased her about her old-fashioned views.

On the way home she didn't even mention Maggie's name, but he did, and she thought he was so frank that either he was being very clever or was quite innocent.

"Mag looked terrific in that long yellow job she was wearing, don't you think, Nirry? What a dress and what a figure she's got!"

Nira sighed but she put a hand on his knee and pressed it lovingly.

"Better than your old woman's?"

He covered the hand with his. "No one's got a better figure than my old woman, if that's what you want to call yourself, my love."

Then rightly or wrongly she decided that she had just been idiotic about Maggie. So the night ended on a gay note. Des had certainly had plenty to drink but she couldn't accuse him of not being lover-like and once the new day dawned she had put the whole episode out of her mind. The only thing she did was to warn him with mock severity that she wouldn't stand for it if he kept on having late nights in town, and he could tell his boss so.

Des gave one of his hearty laughs, kissed her and assured her that there wouldn't be another late night at the office for some time to come so far as he could see, besides which they were off to Cornwall in a fortnight's time. And after that Nira was fully occupied getting everything ready for the holiday.

She saw Maggie and her mother once or twice up at the golf course and each time Maggie was warm and friendly and Nira began to feel that she had been quite on the wrong tack. She could cut out any idea that there was anything between Des and the attractive widow.

The holiday in Mawgan Porth was now arranged. There was room for Rob at Trevarra Farm. Poor little Simon had flown with his father to Peru a week ago. He was much missed by Jonathan but not at all by little Renira who openly expressed that she was glad she wouldn't have to be left out of everything by the two boys. Jon would be forced to play with *her* now.

Late in the afternoon before the Curtis family were due to set out for Mawgan Porth, Nira went to tea with Aunt Ida at The Hollies. The old lady had asked her long ago. Rob was at home. During the hour Nira spent with them, Miss Bessiford told her how pleased she was that her nephew was going away with the Curtis family tomorrow. The only thing that worried her was that he was driving his own car—they were going in convoy—setting out at seven in the morning. Aunt Ida was terrified of accidents.

"Mind you make him follow you, my dear, and don't let Mr. Curtis drive too fast. Rob will keep up with you and his eyesight isn't all that good these days."

"Nonsense, dear aunt," Rob grinned across the room at Nira. "She gets far too nervous about me, Nira. I've got to wear a scarf in case I get cold, and I've got to eat slowly because of my diges-tion and I take vitamin pills to please her every morning," he ended with a laugh.

Nira laughed. "I'll take care of him, Miss Bessiford," she said. "I never let Des drive too fast—especially when the children are in the car, I assure you. He's very good, anyhow."

"And my eyesight is perfectly all right now, otherwise I wouldn't be allowed to drive," put in Rob, patting his aunt's thin delicate hand.

She looked with great affection at him, then with pleasure at the graceful girl sitting opposite them. Nira always seemed so young to the old lady, too young to be so long married and the mother of two big children. But then they all looked like that today with their trouser-suits or mini-skirts and their long hair. Not that Aunt Ida disapproved. She wished she had been a young girl herself during this period of history. She was not narrow-minded, neither had she joined the band of elderly people who disapproved of the young moderns.

She knew, of course, that her nephew had more than a special feeling for Nira Curtis and it grieved her sometimes to think that he would probably never marry now, and she would never see a child of his. She loved him very dearly. He was like a son to her, and Nira was just the sort of young woman she would have liked him to marry.

Nira went home in better spirits. Not only did she look forward to getting down to her beloved Cornish coast, but it would be extra nice this summer to have Rob with them.

She mentally enumerated the things she still had to do before they went off. Des would lock up the house and see to all that side. She would finish the last-minute packing and get the picnic together. She intended to take their lunch so that they could stop on the way and sit in the sun in some beauty spot rather than go to a crowded restaurant. She mustn't forget canned beer for Rob and Des, she reminded herself, and a Coke each for the children. Rob was bringing the usual box of chocolates for them. It really should be fun — especially as the weather this last week of July had been exceptionally warm and bright. That reminded Nira she mustn't forget her own swimsuit and cap. She and Susan had been so busy with all that the children wanted, they had left Mum out, *and* they must put a pack of cards in the car. The children sitting at the back liked to play games when they grew bored, although on the journey this time it had been promised they should ride some of the way in Uncle Rob's Rover.

Once home, Nira had half an hour in the children's bedroom with Susan and a wildly excited pair of children — too excited. It ended with Renira chasing her brother up and down the stairs trying to beat his bucket with the end of her wooden spade and never being able quite to get it and finally, tears.

Nira sent the screaming pair to bed an hour early and was secretly glad the punishment was justified by the fact that they needed the extra hour's sleep. They would have to be up tomorrow at half-past six. Susan was going away, too; not with them, but with her own family, on a package holiday to Torremolinos. She, like the children, was excited, too. Nira suddenly felt her age. It seemed sad yet it was a fact that often when you reach thirty you began to feel already approaching middle-age.

Des seemed quieter than usual. There was nothing very hearty or boisterous about him tonight. He went out to fill the car up for the journey tomorrow. When he came back, she teased him.

"And did my dear husband fill up too?"

He rounded on her and answered irritably, "If you want to know I stopped at The Rose and Crown for one—okay, I did. Was it a crime?"

She flushed hotly. Perhaps she'd been tactless but she used to be able to pull Des's leg and joke with him without his taking offence. Things between them were really changing and not for the best. A slow corrosion was weakening the whole structure of their marriage. It terrified her.

"Sorry," she said briefly. "Perhaps I'm envying you, darling. I've had rather a hard day and I'm exhausted. Let's have a drink together now. I wouldn't mind a soft one, and perhaps you'd fancy a beer."

He brought her the lime-juice she liked but didn't bother about a beer for himself. He said he needed a bath and an early night and was going up to pack his own case.

"I've just got one or two things to see to in the kitchen, then I'll be up too," she said.

Once in the kitchen by herself for no real reason she started to cry. A crushing sense of loneliness weighed her down. She and Des seemed so far apart. Inevitably her thoughts turned to Rob. It was pretty good to know there was at least one man she could depend on.

She was still depressed that next morning when she got up soon after six, to cook the breakfast and fill the Thermos flasks with coffee. It wasn't even fine enough to cheer her up. The sky was grey. It was definitely cloudy and cooler. She faced the unwelcome prospect of poor weather down in Cornwall—of a cold wind sweeping the beaches, of cold clammy swimsuits and the children getting chills. What a bore!

She hoped once they got off that Des would be his usual friendly affectionate self, but he seemed as quiet and preoccupied as he had been last night. Inevitably she thought, *He must be sorry he is leaving Maggie behind*.

Rob drove up on time. The children elected to sit in his car for the first lap of the journey. She let them go. She wanted to be alone with Des and try to talk to him.

He grumbled at the weather, and having to wear a pullover. Once out on the main road to the Winchester By-pass (they planned to stop at Exeter for lunch), Nira wondered why she had bothered to come and sit beside him. He was unresponsive to any of her attempts to discuss themselves and how they were feeling about things in general. He was obviously in no mood for that. He continued to grumble about the other drivers, then in due course, they met the holiday traffic which brought fresh complaints from Des. It was a slow almost bumper-to-bumper drive down the motorway. Nira, resigned, lapsed into silence. She felt shut out—rejected. Finally when they began to talk again, he snapped at her undeservedly. She snapped back at him.

"Oh, really, Des! You're so unpleasant this morning."

"I didn't know I was."

"What's biting you, anyhow?"

"Nothing."

"Well, you behave as though you've got a king-size chip on your shoulder."

"You're too imaginative. You're forever thinking things that aren't—well, they don't exist."

"Since when?" she asked indignantly, "Generally when I think things—they *do* exist."

He gave a quick look which she found nothing short of surly.

"A man can't always be at his best and particularly so early."

"It isn't all that early. We've been on the road for hours. Really, Des, I don't know what's come over you."

He opened his lips to speak and shut them again. He knew perfectly well what was wrong with him and it annoyed him because he also knew that Nira was right. She rarely did use her imagination without cause. She had an uncanny way of guessing the truth. Not that he imagined she had the least idea of what had been going on between Maggie and himself. He was sure he had managed to keep that from everybody. He had acted with absolute discretion. Lately he had wondered what had possessed him to start this affair with Maggie. He'd always had a bit of a yen for her, of course, and knew from the way she looked at him that she wasn't all that cold about him. But it wasn't until after Cricket's death that he felt the necessity to get on more intimate terms with her. Then, once it all began, and she had been warm and willing to respond, he was lost. He couldn't keep away from her.

It had always been the same with him. He couldn't withstand the lure of women as seductive as poor little Cricket, and now Maggie. He had even talked himself into believing that he was doing Maggie a good turn by becoming her lover. She was lonely and wanted a man in her life. They had actually agreed that it wouldn't hurt Nira so long as she didn't *know*.

He and Maggie had stolen some splendid passionate hours together.

He still loved his wife. Of course he did. He would never stop loving her and the kids. He wished he could be a better husband — but he just wasn't cut out to be faithful. But last night Maggie had given him a shock.

They had arranged to meet in Ponders Wood (it was during that hour that he had been busy filling up the car and having a drink). He had phoned her from the office earlier in the day and told her he must just kiss her goodbye. But there had been no kissing; no passionate farewells. Right from the start she stood aloof and told him that their affair had got to end.

"I've had a chat with Nira up at the Club," she said. "I know I've had lots of them but this was a particular talk. We just happened to be discussing marriage and she asked me if I would like to be married again and I said yes but that I didn't somehow think I would ever find the right person."

"Well, you know my position — I can't do anything about that," Des had said gloomily.

"That's not what I meant. I just meant that I don't think I would even marry you if you were free, Des. What I'm getting at is, Nira said if you died, she wouldn't know what to do because you've always been so close, and I can't tell you what she made me feel — too awful! She's really such a sweet person, and I can't go on having an affair with her husband. It may be awfully silly of me but I can't and won't be responsible for hurting her."

"Why should she be hurt if she doesn't *know*," he had tried to argue.

"She just might find out. I have an idea that she already guesses we have a thing about each other."

Des protested in vain. Maggie had been adamant. When he

kissed her goodbye he had been forced to realise it was for the last time. And Maggie had a strong side to her — she wasn't as weak as Cricket — she wouldn't come back. He knew it. He knew also that she was right but he had gone home feeling gloomy and frustrated. It all had the effect of making him hostile in some funny way towards Nira. It was quite unjust, he admitted that. But he felt depressed about losing Maggie and quite frankly he was bored — for the moment anyhow — with domestic life. Possibly after a couple of weeks by the sea with the family he'd feel better. He'd try to dig in his heels and be a good boy but he couldn't even pretend this morning to act like a devoted husband.

Nira no longer tried to get nearer him or lighten the gloom between them. By the time they reached Exeter she felt as depressed as ever.

The picnic lunch was gay despite the grey coolness of the day, by virtue of the fact that the children were madly excited and talked non-stop, and at least Nira could feel glad half the long journey was over. It was more than trying for Renira and Jonathan, patient though they were, but they grew bored. On the whole they were good travellers and had never suffered from carsickness like many of their friends.

Rob said they'd been splendid during the drive with him, but after Exeter they switched over to the family car. They would drive with Daddy, and Nira would keep Uncle Rob company.

Nira was relieved to find herself in Rob's comfortable car. It was good to talk to somebody who was completely responsive to everything she said and so anxious for her comfort. Beside which, he was never a bore. He always had plenty of things to talk about. She found him an excellent companion. But she was still subdued, and unlike herself, and Rob noticed it.

"You've been doing too much lately, haven't you? All those preparations for the holiday, and looking after everyone. I'm afraid it's tired you out," he said in his gentle way.

She denied this but suddenly asked him a question that confirmed the suspicions he had had for some time that things were not as right as they used to be between Nira and Des.

"Do you think a man needs more than one woman in his life?"

The question came as a slight shock. He didn't quite know the answer. He took his pipe from his mouth, put it in the glove-box and was silent for a moment or two, keeping his eyes on the tail-end of Des's car. Des was driving at a reasonable pace anybody could follow.

"Well, my dear," at length Rob answered, "that's not a subject on which one can generalise. Everything depends on the sort of man. Some men do need more than one woman. Some don't need *any* women in their lives at all. What sort are you referring to?"

She knew quite well but she wasn't going to tell Rob. She invented a fictitious character. "Oh, a friend of mine has a husband who seems to love her all right but also needs a new love from time to time. I just wondered what *you* think. I—I'm confused about it."

"Sounds like your friend's husband would like to go back to harem days," said Rob smiling. "The age-old necessity of man to renew the force of his sex-urge from time to time by planting a new young beauty in his home."

Nira laughed, too. "Oh, I don't think in this case that the man actually needs a *harem*, but don't you think that a man on the whole wants variety—he gets tired of the same old wife? He looks for fresh excitement."

"Perhaps—in order to bolster up the feeling of youth and vigour, and so on. But there are a lot of chaps who don't want anyone but the chosen wife. I tell you, it's all a question of temperament."

Nira kept her fingers locked together in her lap. She stared at the traffic ahead, then she said, "Perhaps it's a lot to do with the temperament of the woman, too. Some wives become bored or love their husbands too much and show it too plainly. Men can get bogged down by too much adoration. Besides it's their nature to want what's hard to get. In fact I've often noticed that they seem to go for a girl who's undemonstrative and keeps them at arm's length."

Her sudden cynicism surprised him. He looked down at her uneasily. "I wouldn't exactly say that. I think what a man really needs is a warm, sweet, affectionate creature who is also a good friend to him—and a good cook," he added jokingly. "Of course she must be a good cook."

Nira was glad to laugh with him again. She decided not to continue the discussion. She was treading on dangerous ground. In another moment she'd be saying something that would leave no doubt in his mind that it was Des and herself she had been discussing.

She steered the conversation into a new channel.

Rob played along with her but he was troubled. Her attempt to philosophise over the matrimonial troubles of a 'friend' had been really rather pathetic. Of course she had been alluding to her own marriage. He was sure of it. Des had had an affair with Cricket Halling. And who else besides? *He* was the sort to need a harem. Rob thought he knew Des pretty well these days. Nira had become sad and disillusioned. Rob felt desperately upset, because he loved her with his whole heart and soul, and he knew he couldn't do a damned thing about it.

II

THE ARRIVAL AT Mawgan Porth was nothing short of dramatic and quite different from anything Nira had expected. The weather was perfect. Hot sun and cloudless skies, quite different from when they left home. They made good time despite the slowish crawl, traffic jams, and frequent stops for the children. On the whole the journey was uneventful until they came to within four miles of Mawgan Porth. By this time the children were growing fretful and heartily sick of the long drive and Nira had a headache which was unusual for her. She presumed it was nerves as much as heat and dust, for it had been a close day as well as a fatiguing one. She cheered up at the first sight of the magnificent coast she knew so well — the dark purple-blue of the Atlantic — the creaming foam fringing the great breakers — the jutting rocks with their crusts of violet mussels — the gold of the wind-swept sand. Not even the march of time which had brought far too many little houses and kiosks and small shops to spoil the beauty of this place could destroy its intrinsic magic. Still sitting beside Rob, Nira enjoyed the sight doubly because he, too, was so enthusiastic. He had revived some of his youthful eagerness to take photographs and there were going to be some splendid opportunities down here. It couldn't be the sort of photography that had made him so successful in Nairobi, but there were wonderful colours along this coast. He was glad he had brought a special wide-angled lens.

"It makes one glad to be alive and very glad to be here," he said. He took off his glasses, shut his eyes and drew in a breath of the salty air. "Makes you feel better, doesn't it, Nira?"

She nodded. Now she had an idea. "Let's just hoot Des and the children to stop and tell them to take the road that leads to Sandy Beach."

"Is that very special?"

"It's the one with the least people on it because it's such a steep climb down and difficult for charabancs. I'd like to make sure it's still there," she smiled.

Des pulled his car up and waited for them to stop alongside. He had nothing against Nira's idea except that he thought perhaps it might have been best to get straight to Trevarra Farm.

"I don't know," said Nira, "it's just a feeling I have that I want first to catch a glimpse of Sandy Beach."

"So do I!" put in little Renira, jumping up and down in the car.

"So do I," echoed Jonathan. "It's where I first swam without my arm bands, isn't it, Mum? I want to see it."

So they all drove to Sandy Beach. And there the shock awaited them. A year ago it had been a lovely secluded spot—one of the few left. This afternoon it was unbelievably changed. Not only were there a mass of cars and caravans ranged along the top of the cliff, but a crowd of people were milling up and down the narrow zigzag path that led to the beach. In the hollow itself, encircled by a crowd of onlookers and obvious enthusiasts, were a party of cameramen with full equipment for shooting a movie. Nira, Rob, Des and the children got out of the two cars and stood staring. Now they could see a man standing on a promontory just below them shouting through a megaphone, "Cut! Cut—for God's sake! I don't want any more of this. It's bloody awful. Start again, please, all of you—from the beginning—*all of you!*"

Dismayed yet fascinated, Nira shielded her eyes against the sun and went on staring at the crowded beach trying to make out what was happening. Des seemed to come alive. He had been moody and apathetic all during the journey. Now he was alert.

"Look at them. A film company on location—they're making a film down here. D'you see, Nira? Great fun!"

"It may be fun but bang goes our sleepy Sandy Beach," said Nira sadly.

"I'll trot down and see what they're shooting," said Des.

"Well, don't be long—we ought to get on," Nira reminded him.

He in turn reminded her that it had been *her* idea coming here, and started to make his way down the steep path. As he did so, a man and a girl climbing up to the top stopped just short of a collision with him. They seemed to be having an altercation. The man—young, bearded, burnt red by the sun, and looking decidedly harassed—was pleading with the girl.

"Now, Frankie, don't be awkward. You've got to let me shoot it again. It was all wrong. You know it was, darling."

The girl addressed as Frankie turned around to face him. She was sensationally beautiful, thought Nira. In a yellow bikini showing most of an exquisite slim brown body she had a huge peasant straw floppy hat on her head, and wore large round dark glasses. These she suddenly whipped off and pointed them accusingly at the man beside her, tossing back a mane of rich red hair.

"If you're trying to say that I'm the one who spoilt the scene, why not just say it? You can go to hell, Vince. I'm hot and I'm tired and I've had enough down on that god-damn beach. I want to rest and I want a drink, and I'm not staying below one moment longer. No more shooting today for little me."

"But Frankie, we haven't time to spare. You know we've got to get on with this sequence. We've only just started and we've a bare fortnight to finish the sequence. Be reasonable."

She screamed at him, "Go to hell!"

Nira exchanged glances with Rob. He smiled at her. He had been less interested in the row than in the camera equipment on the beach. That was more his line.

"Is this part of the act or what?" he asked Nira.

"I reckon it's a row between the director and the leading lady," she said.

Then something clicked in her brain. Frankie—of course—this was Frankie Motte, the famous new star who had made such a success in that big film last year—*Night of the Fifth*—(that's what it had been called), and there had been more than ordinary Guy Fawkes fireworks in it, too, she remembered. One of those fast-moving films with brittle witty dialogue and fantastic drama—and sex which suited Frankie, who was then only twenty. Nira remembered, too, how Des had tried to make her go up to

London with him to the cinema, and how fascinated he had been by Frankie's photographs. He had been to see the film and come back raving about her. After that he used to talk about her fabulous red hair and figure and gorgeous long legs and jokingly call her his 'dolly-bird'.

Nira had taken it all lightly as a kind of joke. She was amused today to see the way he sprang to life when he actually saw his 'dolly-bird'. She seemed oblivious of him and the rest of the crowd on the cliff top who were watching and listening to the unrehearsed row. It was clear to Nira that she was exercising her right to be difficult and greatly embarrassing her harassed director.

Now Des suddenly became a participant in the scene because the fabulous Frankie wrenched off her dark glasses and threw them at her director. He ducked. The glasses landed on the turf at Des's feet.

He picked them up and handed them to her. He knew of course exactly who she was. He had so often made a study of that splendid body in pictures and now that he saw her in the flesh, he thought Frankie Motte attractive enough to stir any man's passions. She was heavily made-up. Her false lashes were incredibly long, but there was nothing unreal about the blue of the blazing eyes. They were magical. Des grinned at her, and when Des grinned like that, few women were ever unmoved by his charm. Even Frankie succumbed. She calmed down, and examined the tall handsome stranger through the glasses that were miraculously unbroken.

Her whipped-up rage evaporated. She drew nearer Des.

"Thanks awfully. I hope I didn't hit you."

"The glasses fell at my feet. All wrong — I ought to be falling at yours. Frankie Motte, I presume? You're my favourite film-star, d'you know that?"

She put a hand on her hip and gave him her most fascinating smile. A little studied, he decided, but most enticing, and he was enjoying the fact that the film director stood sullenly mopping his forehead, looking daggers at him.

Frankie asked Des for his name, then said, "You're sweet. Did you see *Night of the Fifth?*"

"Of course," he said, and made the two words sound like hot honey.

She cast a rather ugly look at the unfortunate Vince.

"I don't suppose you'll have a chance to see this new one we're supposed to be shooting in Cornwall because if Vince doesn't stop making me repeat and repeat and repeat, I'm quitting."

"Don't do that," said Des. "You'd rob the world of some worthwhile entertainment."

Vince looked at Des more kindly.

"You've said it, chum," he muttered.

"What I need is a drink and a rest," said Frankie, and stretched her arms above her head and stood there on the edge of the cliff like a nymph poised for flight, giving Des the works as she called it. She knew exactly how fabulous she looked.

Des was fascinated. He was well aware that she was the incarnation of artificial charm and that her looks were aided by every possible gadget. But nature had given her that superlative shape, and the blatant invitation in her marvellous eyes was more than enough to storm through Des's façade of the dutiful husband and father. He glanced toward his wife, and at the man standing with her, then at the children who were still in the car. If ever he'd wished he were a bachelor again he wished it now. Quickly he said, "My family and I are going to be down here for a couple of weeks, Miss Motte. Perhaps we shall see you again."

She smiled. It was a warm inviting smile, and Frankie had a big amusing mouth and exquisite teeth. She said, "Why not? We'll be on location here for another fortnight, I don't doubt—do you, Vince?" And she turned to her director, still smiling, for which he was devoutly thankful. Frankie in one of her tempers was unmanageable and he wanted to finish the Cornish scenes in his new film before the end of the month. They had plenty more stuff to shoot when they got back to the studio and one particular act due for a Rome setting.

"I'm sure we'll still be here," he said and ran a critical eye over Des—a fine-looking man. Photogenic, he'd wager. He added a few words to Des. "We want people who look good in the background for a couple of scenes. Come on down one morning and join the crowd."

Des's spirits, which had been rising ever since he saw his favourite film-star, rose a bit higher.

"I'd be amused," he said.

"Then we'll see you," said Frankie. "We're all staying at the Headland Hotel in Newquay. Come along one evening and have a drink with us." And with a friendly glance at Nira whom she thought a nice-looking but rather dull girl, she added, "And bring your wife."

Nira heard this. "I must say I'd adore to see Des — my husband — in a film — so thanks awfully." She smiled at Frankie.

Vince, watching, thought Nira rather lovely; very English, cool but attractive. He was experienced with women. In his job as a film director he met hundreds of seductive girls. There had been a time in his life when he had thought he would like to settle down with a woman like this one, and have two nice kids, like hers. He might make use of them, as well as Nira — put them all in the next scene. The public liked kids and animals. When he looked at Frankie, he grimaced. She was enticing, amusing, all the things that could get a man — that was if he didn't need peace and quiet, but for the moment, Vince was thoroughly involved with his leading lady. He turned and put an arm around her shoulders. They were tanned and glistening with little drops of perspiration.

"Back to the job, sweetheart," he coaxed.

"Like you say," was her reply. She was not particularly concerned with grammar. She was in a better humour now. Her marvellous eyes still responded to the admiring glances Des was throwing in her direction.

She put an arm through Vince's and started to walk down the path — then she turned to wave at Des.

Vince growled, "Now, now, honey-girl, leave that nice guy alone. He's got a wife and kids and I know that look in your eyes."

She gave a low laugh. He knew that laughter, too. It was rather like the purring sound from a panther about to spring.

"I'm not so sure he's all that nice," she said lazily, "but he's got something for me, baby. Ring him up and ask him over to The Headland for drinks."

"Ask her, too, then. She's got something for me."

"Oh, she won't want to come. I know her type. I don't know who that older man is — her brother or something. Maybe he'll take care of her."

Vince looked down at the beach, crowded with the members of the cast plus the extras and all the paraphernalia of his film-making. "I don't think you've got one single moral, Frankie Motte," he said and stuck a cigar between his teeth.

She giggled. "Who wants morals? They're too deadly. Don't start preaching, baby. It doesn't suit you, and if I want a kiss

127

from a stranger I'll have it. You still want *me* as your leading lady, don't you?"

He gave a sardonic grin. "You've got your contract."

"Okay, lover-boy, let's finish our scene and get back to the hotel. I'm fed up with the sand and the sea and the sweet pure air of Cornwall. Let's shoot the sequence where I've got to be carried into one of the caves by Chris."

Christopher Baker who was playing lead opposite Frankie was an actor of some note and a big draw with the slinky figure teenagers—long hair, side-burns, groovy outfit—all of it. He was as dark as if he had Mexican blood in him—a good foil for Frankie with that hair that held the burnished red-gold of satin in the light. But they fought like cat and dog. The trouble with Frankie was that she fought with everyone unless she happened to be going through a phase of what she called being 'loving and giving'. She seemed to be falling into one of these states at the moment. She said to Vince very softly, "Why can't you arrange for that gorgeous-looking man up on the cliff to carry me into the cave instead of Chris. Then I could play the giving part with genu-yne—feelings."

Up on the cliff the gorgeous-looking man stood watching the film-star walk on her sandalled feet with feline grace, slowly down the zigzag path until she reached the shore. He was quite sure he had not mistaken the message in her eyes. He had seen it so many times before in the eyes of other women. The memory of Maggie and the frustration he had felt at losing her before he left home vanished completely. He barely recalled the fact that she, too, had had a touch of red in her hair, and sweet invitation in her eyes.

He felt as excited about Frankie as a schoolboy. What luck, being able to muscle in on her and her film company, like this. Who would have dreamed they'd be on location so near Mawgan Porth. As for Frankie, he knew perfectly well he'd see her again because she wanted it that way. There was absolutely no room in his mind for compunction when he turned to his wife and children again. He only thought what a good thing it was that old Rob had come with them. No reason why he, Des, couldn't slip away discreetly whenever the occasion arose. He could leave Nira quite happily with her family and the boy-friend.

The two cars headed for Trevarra Farm. The children drove with Uncle Rob again. Nira sat with Des.

She said, "It looks as though it'll be quite an amusing holiday. It would be super if we could all be filmed together. Renira and Jonny are thrilled. Frankie Motte is quite a girl, isn't she? Terribly attractive — Miss World standard."

"She sure is," said Des, feeling in the best of humour.

And that was how it all started.

12

THE FIRST WEEK of the holiday was hardly a success for anyone in the Curtis party — except Des. The weather changed again as so often happens on the Cornish coast even in the middle of summer. The wind blew from the south-west bringing heavy cloud and sharp storms of rain. The temperature dropped. The sands were deserted. The seagulls wheeled in towards land, crying desolately.

Trevarra Farm was not the big success it had seemed in former years. The Hoskins were as hospitable and amiable as ever but Nira noticed a decline in the general amenities of the place. The bathwater was never really hot — the food was uninspired, less lavish than it used to be, although there were plenty of eggs and milk for the children, and Mrs. Hoskins' saffron buns which they all enjoyed plus those little dishes of dark yellow Cornish cream with a thick crust on it which were so good to spread with jam or honey. But because of the cooler weather they all felt cheated.

Renira fretted because she wasn't allowed to wear her bikini. Jonathan was incensed because there was no swimming, no real fun on the beach. Not only was it cold but the wind whipped the sea into great breakers and Des warned them all that it wasn't safe to swim. Only twice during that first week were Renira and Jonathan able to find a pool in which they could paddle, and take advantage of a sudden break in the sky when the sun came through and it was warm enough.

Then Nira developed severe toothache and had to go to a dentist who diagnosed an abscess. After unsuccessful treatment the tooth had to come out. A penicillin injection did nothing to add to her comfort. She was, as she admitted, a bit of a wreck at the end of it all—disappointed not only for the children's sake—but for Rob. She had praised life in Mawgan Porth so warmly and knew he had looked forward to the sort of lazy life in the sun one could lead down here in fine weather.

As usual, Nira was more than thankful for his presence and support. It was he who drove her into Newquay to have the tooth out, because Des had been called by Vince and asked to take part in the film. Nira didn't want him to miss it. So it was Rob who took his place—and amused the children when she felt too miserably in pain to organise them and wanted only to be allowed to lie down in a darkened room. Antibiotics did not suit Nira.

As the days went by, Des became the one really cheerful person in the party. He went around the place whistling, saying that he didn't mind the rain or the wind and he was always out walking or driving into Newquay where the film crowd spent a lot of time in their hotel, drinking away boredom, waiting for the sun to come out again. They could only shoot the film spasmodically.

Two days after Nira had had her tooth extracted, she and Rob walked into the little village shop where one could buy anything and everything. She needed more Anadin. Her face hurt and her head ached. She felt wretched, although she appreciated the fact that Renira and Jonathan had gone out for the afternoon.

Rob looked at her anxiously. She looked white and ill. Her eyes seemed to have sunk into her face.

"That damned tooth still hurting?" he asked.

"Yes—where the damned tooth *was*, it still hurts," she said with a faint laugh.

"Poor girl, it's a frightful bore for you and the last thing you needed on your holiday."

"Well, at least we've got rid of my darling children," she laughed again. "I love them to death but they've been so difficult because of this awful weather and having to stick indoors and amuse themselves—poor angels. And me being so off-colour, hasn't helped them. I'm glad we met those other people—the Wilsons. It's a godsend."

Wilson was a major in the Army. The family were on leave from Singapore and had met the Curtis family in the local. They had two children of their own, much the same age as Jonathan and Renira. They had all gone to see a Disney film in Newquay.

It wasn't that Rob found the children trying, but he hated to see Nira looking and feeling so ill and being constantly nagged at by the boisterous pair. At their age kids could be exacting and remorseless.

It was raining again. Where the devil was Des, Rob wondered, although he could guess. At The Headland again no doubt, with that film bunch, including Frankie. It was obvious to Rob that Des had gone off his head about the red-headed star. He had been behaving disgracefully—neglecting Nira shamefully. She never complained. She wouldn't, Rob thought, but he knew well how she must be feeling. Des spent far too much time with Frankie and her set. Nira went to one supper party with him, but never again, neither did she tell Rob much about it. Two nights ago, Des came back from one of his Newquay jaunts the worse for drink.

Whether there'd been a row between husband and wife, Rob did not know, but he imagined so because they were not on speaking terms when they all breakfasted in the big kitchen that next morning.

Rob was deeply disturbed. He didn't like the look of things for Nira. He could only guess what was going on in her mind, but he had little doubt that Des was no longer the faithful devoted husband Nira had always believed him to be. He made a great show of being devoted when he was with her. Rob was certain he was putting on an act for the family. He did a lot of laughing and joking. He bought the children toys, and gave Nira a large bottle of perfume, but the whole situation stank in Rob's nostrils. Des wanted both to eat his cake and have it. He was perhaps still fond of his charming wife but one woman wasn't enough for him. In the past there had been Cricket (perhaps even others). Now there was Frankie. A domestic storm was brewing. Rob felt that he would be involved. But he had no wish to go away and leave Nira, even if it meant unpleasantness for him. If she needed him, he was going to stay.

It was raining hard by the time they finished shopping and got back to the farm.

"I'd better change, I'm drenched," said Nira.

"Me, too," said Rob, "I'll meet you in ten minutes. Don't catch a chill now—you've had enough this last few days."

She left him standing in the Hoskins' parlour which had been given to them for their private use while they were here. There was only one small electric fire with a single bar—another sign of the Hoskins' new economy. It threw out little heat. The room was cold and dismal. Nira looked around and sighed. What a a difference the weather could make. The last time they had been at Trevarra they had been out all day and it had seemed such fun.

As she put on dry jersey and slacks, she turned her thoughts to Des.

She had to face up to the fact that she'd hardly seen him this past week except when he had played the part of loving husband and father and joined them for an hour or two. And at night when they shared the big old-fashioned bed in the low-ceilinged room above the parlour, she had felt she might as well lie alone. A quick kiss and a 'Good night, sweetie' from Des—and he was fast asleep. They seemed no longer able to communicate.

While her tooth had been so bad she had felt too ill to protest much but now that she was beginning to feel better, she could see clearly what was happening. Her resentment was growing. The jealousy she used to feel over Cricket—her suspicions about Maggie—her fears for Des when he started to drink too much— all these things had accumulated and formed a black ugly picture in her mind.

They had quarrelled openly one night when he returned from Newquay in the early hours of the morning, so drunk that she wondered how he had driven back in the car without having an accident. It had set the seal on her unhappiness.

She had turned on him the next day. "It's that girl—your precious film-star who's been keeping you out—you call it a party with all the actors, etcetera, but it's a party with *her!*"

He made one or two feeble protests, then snarled at her, "Oh, shut up, Nira . . . I'm fed up with your nagging and possessiveness. You've got your dear Rob—let me alone—why don't you have a party with *him?*"

In her pain and bewilderment she had told him what she thought of him. "Don't dare try and bring Rob into this. You know perfectly well there's nothing between us."

"Don't tell me he isn't crazy about you!" he had retorted.

"If he is, it's in the nicest possible way. And if he was mad about me he'd keep it to himself. He isn't as unscrupulous as you are. Oh, Des, how you've changed!"

"We both have."

She had stared at him wild-eyed, her world falling apart.

"How have *I* changed?"

"Oh, I don't know—why don't you quit arguing. It's all this arguing that's driving me away from you."

"That's cowardly of you—you're just trying to put the blame on me. You're trying to say that it's because I've become a possessive sort of wife that you're fed up with me."

"I don't say anything of the sort, but I do say I'm a gay sort of chap and no saint and you knew it when you married me."

"I was gay too. We had wonderful times together, but always *together*."

"We're still together. What are you moaning about?"

With the back of her hand against her trembling lips, she looked up at his sullen, handsome face and shook her head, completely incredulous. He bore so little resemblance to the husband she had once adored. Her voice was broken as she said, "We were in love with each other for ages. Terribly happy—at least I thought so. It wasn't until I found out about Cricket I began to lose my faith in you and ever since then you've seemed to want to be what you call gay all the time."

"Why don't *you* try to be a bit more amusing for a change?"

Her head throbbed. The cavity in her mouth where the wretched wisdom tooth used to be, throbbed too, and she felt sick.

Suddenly Des noticed the way she put her hand against her cheek and how tired she looked. Weak character though he was, he had his kindly and gentle side. He took Nira in his arms, and tried to be nice to her.

"I'm a monster. I don't know what's come over me. Sorry, darling. You're the best girl in the world, and the only one I really love—honestly."

She pushed him away, her eyes blind with tears of sheer despair. "But I'm one of so many. I know it now. You can't leave the girls alone. And you'd like me to have an affair with Rob so that it would make *you* feel better. I can't accept that. Neither can I keep forgiving you for what you do. I *can't*."

"Hell! Who said there was anything to forgive at this moment?"

"You know there is. We came down here to have a lovely holiday and you've been out most of the time with Frankie Motte. You're absolutely fascinated by her, aren't you? *Aren't you?*"

"It doesn't say we're having an affair."

133

"But you are, aren't you? *Aren't you?*" she cried again, the tears pouring down her face.

He was fed up with having to lie and dissemble. The flame that had sprung up between him and the famous Frankie had burned a little too swiftly and fiercely for him to resist. He never really wanted to resist. She was the most exciting and powerful magnet that had ever drawn him away from hearth and home, and she had told him that out of all the men she had made love to since she was sixteen, he was the greatest. She admitted she had a thing about him. His gaiety matched hers. She was bored by the film actors in her own profession and fed up with producers, managers and agents who followed her around, hoping to pick up money or bask in the reflection of her glory. Des was new and smart and he amused her. He was splendid to look at, wonderful to be with, and she had every intention of enjoying a swift affair with him. For the time being she wanted him, and what Frankie wanted, she got. The wife and children were a background nuisance and that was how she treated them.

While he was brooding about this, Nira shot another bitter unexpected question at him, taking him off his guard, giving him little time to think up any more lies.

"What about Maggie? It isn't just Frankie Motte. We've only just left Ponders Heath and I realised it was you and Maggie at home. You were after her. She was Cricket's successor. You take so many mistresses, don't you? And you tell me you don't love any of them, so you don't even betray my love for something real or big. I might try to understand and forgive if it was a real thing. But you have just little petty affairs. That's how you seem to like it. You don't deny it, do you?"

He made one feeble protest.

"I don't know why you're bringing up Maggie. We were attracted to each other, yes, but in actual fact she didn't think it fair to you and we ended it before we came away."

Nira gave a hard laugh. She sneered, "Charming! I'm glad she has that much conscience. Were her kisses better than mine and are Frankie's better than Maggie's? And when dear Frankie goes back to town, having enjoyed a little summer madness with a handsome stranger, will you find someone else and—"

He broke in, furious, on the defence; startled by the fury of her outburst. He had never seen her like this before. It confused him.

"Look, Nira, I deny nothing. You have every right to be hurt

134

and angry but it was only because I didn't *want* to hurt you. That's why I kept it all from you. If you had been a different sort of person, I'd have been much more honest."

Nira turned her eyes heavenwards.

"My God! So you wanted a halo of honesty to make things easier. It never entered your head that you not only dishonoured us — our love — our belief in each other — but our children. I can see from your face that you think that stuff old hat. You think I'm a prude — like your mother — or Aunt Ida. But you're wrong. I just won't admit I'd have been a better wife if I'd let you do what you want and turned a blind eye until you got tired of your various girl-friends or they got tired of you."

Des kicked the toe of his shoe against the floor, hands in his pockets, eyes sullen. He didn't like what was happening between them. He hadn't meant it to turn out this way. But he was in the mood to feel himself aggrieved. She had become an over-possessive wife who, to use her own words, was as old-fashioned as his mother or Rob's aunt. Of course he was grateful to her for her fidelity and respected her for it in the depth of his heart, but with Cricket dead and Maggie backing out, Frankie remained a new powerful magnet — beautiful, famous, glittering. He was both dazzled and enslaved. Eventually he tried a new line with Nira.

"Don't let's split up over this. You know you're still number one with me. If I behave like a so-and-so, do try to turn a blind eye. You know I'll always come back."

She stormed at him, "No, I don't intend to sit back and wait for you to get tired of making love to other women. You can follow your fascinating Frankie back to London or New York or anywhere you like. You can ruin yourself for her, but first of all you'll get out of my life. I won't have you, and I won't let the children have you. I'll finish with you *absolutely*."

For a moment Des looked startled and apprehensive, then he laughed.

"You don't mean it, ducky, you're just being hysterical."

But after a few moments when she had proved to him that she did mean it, he climbed down. He hoped he could go on seeing Frankie in London anyhow. But divorce, no — he didn't want one.

"You know I'm devoted to you and the kids and I don't want to break up our home," he muttered.

"You've said that before. I don't believe one word and you're not going to have it both ways. I refuse to face that sort of life. I may be dull compared with your film-stars and I'm sure *she's* a big attraction, but I'm *me*. I want a decent husband and a decent life and if you can't give it to me any more you can go. I will divorce you."

The bitter fight continued for hours, leaving them both exhausted. It all began again the next day. Nira had been perfectly well aware that he was down on Sandy Beach watching them film Frankie, because the sun had come out again. That was yesterday and he had walked out of the farm this morning without even saying goodbye to her. They'd hardly spoken a word to each other last night. She had lain awake, her nerves jumping — feeling that the bottom had dropped out of her world. The clock merely ticked around, and she did the best she could to amuse the children and ignore the nagging pain in her face, and — with much more difficulty — the pain in her mind.

She had lost Des. He had lost her. It came to the same thing. Now this afternoon, sitting alone with Rob in the oak-beamed chintzy parlour at Trevarra Farm, she suddenly collapsed. She looked, Rob thought, terribly pale. He kept a close eye on her. After lunch he made some pretence of talking about a letter he had had from Aunt Ida this morning. "She doesn't seem too well at the moment. She's been in bed for a couple of days. What's the matter with my two best girls?" And he stretched out a hand to Nira, adding, "My ancient aunt and my young sweet friend."

"Oh, Rob," she said, "Oh, Rob, I'm a mess! I'm in an awful state. I feel so old it isn't true. If you're too nice to me I'll begin to cry. That would embarrass you terribly."

"I'd be upset but not embarrassed. And you needn't imagine I don't understand what's wrong. Of course I do. It's all too obvious."

She flushed, crouching there in front of the little electric fire, her cold hands spread to the inadequate warmth. She felt chilled right through her whole body, and inexpressibly sad.

"About Des, I mean. Have you — guessed about Des and me?"

He looked at the back of the dark silky head. She seemed so unsophisticated this afternoon. Her hair tied in a pony-tail and the slenderness of her neck made her somehow look so young. She had a fawn-like quality — a grace which he found both innocent and touching.

"I think I know. Do you want to tell me about it?" he asked gently.

She no longer felt she could put up even a small fight. Des mocked at Rob and tried to turn him into an image that made *him* feel less guilty. Rob seemed all that she had left of strength and security. The love she felt for Rob in this moment was sexless yet absolute. She knelt at his feet, folded her arms on his knees and cried until she could cry no more.

He took off his glasses and bent over her, embracing her shuddering body, stroking her head and the nape of her neck. He pressed his lips against her hair and did what he could to comfort her. To hear her uncontrolled sobs and to know the depth of the pain she was suffering went through his heart like a knife. He had seen it all coming and not been able to do a thing to help her, and while she had hidden behind pretence to save her pride—he had respected her wishes—but not now. Now that she was broken and turning to him for help. He said, "Oh, my darling, my poor darling, my poor love, don't cry like that. I can't bear it."

"I wish I were dead."

"No, you don't. You've got the children. Whatever has happened between you and Desmond, you've always got Renira and Jonathan."

"I know and I oughtn't to want to die, but I do. We've been so close—Des and I and the children. We were such a happy family. I suppose I was just living in a world of romance. I was quite sure of him right up to the time that he and Cricket—"

"I know," Rob broke in, "I know."

She lifted a pitiful face, disfigured by grief yet still lovely to him. "I expect everybody knew but me." And down went her head again, hiding from Rob's compassionate gaze.

He pressed the fine bones of her skull between his warm hands. His own face was deeply grooved. His emotions ran high. He had not imagined that loving a woman as he loved this one, could be so agonising. He said, "Don't think I haven't noticed the change in you two and worried about it for a long time. But, my darling, even if Desmond has toppled off his pedestal, it needn't be the end of the world."

Up went her head, blue-grey eyes blazing through the tears. "How can you say that?"

He had to force the words now. "I mean that I haven't the slightest use for the way Desmond is behaving. In view of the fact that I love you very, very much; it doesn't make sense. I can't understand him, I'm sorry, but I'm close to hating him. It's murderous for me to know he's had the chance he's had with you and thrown it over. At the same time men don't love the way women do, of that I'm certain. Women like you give completely. There are men like Desmond who want love both in their own homes and out of it. But if you could accept the fact that he's no saint—and—"

"Rob," she broke in, speaking more calmly, "Are you trying to advise me to shut my eyes to Des's behaviour even though he'll keep on betraying me? If you are, I don't understand it. I should have thought that you of all people would realise I couldn't accept what Des is offering me in the future. Just one affair after another. No security—no trust—the sort of love-game some of the couples we know are playing—switching from one to another. It makes me sick—I couldn't do it. But he wants me to accept what he's done and carry on as though it hadn't happened."

Rob's face turned a dusky red.

"It makes me sick too, darling, but—"

"But you're trying to defend him because you are a man and men ought to stick together," she said with a cynicism he had never expected of her.

"Oh, Nira," he said, "forgive me, my dear, if I'm a bit off-beat but I really am shaken by all this."

"You're trying to be charitable to Des because you're fond of me and you want to do what you think best for me and my family."

A bit startled he acquiesced. "Very well, perhaps that's it."

Then she reached up her arms to him. "Rob, I think you're the most marvellous man in the world, and in my way I love you, Rob, very very much."

He felt a lurch of his heart—a throb of his pulses that threatened to break his control. He drew her up and held her against him. For the first time, with passion, he covered her face and throat with kisses. Then at last, her lips. Now it was her turn to be startled by the depth and significance of that long, long kiss. But almost immediately he pushed her away and stood up.

"I'm not being at all helpful to you, Nira," he said tensely, "The whole damn thing is getting too much for me. I love you and not only with affection and friendship. I'm heart and soul in love with you. All I can say is, please forgive me. We both seem to be letting down the defences. It's hopeless for me to pretend any more. I'm a man—a one-woman man if you like. It's *you*. It's been you for a long time and there'll never be another."

Her tears dried and her eyes shone suddenly with a joy she made no effort to conceal.

"Oh, Rob—darling Rob. I do thank you! I feel so proud— you're such a wonderful person. Rob—dear, *dear* Rob—"

She hid her face from him but clung tightly to him with both hands. He held her, in silence. In that complete silence and understanding they stayed close and warm, drawing comfort from each other.

He thought, *To her I am like an elder brother. She feels platonic affection for me, but I cannot feel only this for her. To me she is not a sister. She is the woman I love. I've never felt hatred for any human being before, but I hate Desmond Curtis. I loathe him for what he has done to her. And I hate myself because I want Nira— and I shouldn't. God, it's wrong!*

He was a man of principle. Whatever way the world was going at the moment, he had no use for married men who fooled around with other men's wives or indulged in promiscuous sordid little affairs just because they needed a new excitement to stimulate their appetites. Especially not men with wives like Nira. But while Rob held Nira close—Nira who was so unhappy, spiritually wounded, lost in her woe—he was all too conscious of the physical, as well as the spiritual side of things. He had never in his life before loved a woman seriously. There had been one or two brief affairs during those early days in Kenya, short-lived, half-hearted, almost forgotten.

One in particular with a girl older than himself. She worked in a big photographic centre in Nairobi which he visited regularly. When he had been shooting movies of big game he had seen her quite often and taken her out from time to time.

There had come a night when she had asked him back to the bungalow which she shared with her sister who was away. She was attractive, warm and enticing and had wanted him for her lover. He had learnt quite a lot about women during that brief hectic affair. He had not been the first with her and had no need for compunction, but he had felt remorseful because she had seemed to care a lot more than he did. It ended in them agreeing not to see each other again. He had been frank from the start that he didn't intend to marry but for a long time afterwards she had written him sad little letters. Not for a year had she found another man.

Then, happy and relieved, he sent her a wedding present, and for her generosity and sweetness he had always been grateful. But it had made him careful not to become involved in the future. So the years for Rob had gone by, during which he made sure there were no more such episodes. He didn't like hurting anyone and he didn't want to be drawn into marriage before he was sure he could settle down to the domestic scene. By nature he was really a lone hand, until now. Nira was different. Now, especially when Desmond looked like breaking up their marriage, he was doubly conscious of the tremendous pull she had at his heart-strings. He wanted to swing from the brother-image to the lover. He felt the crazy beat of his pulses and with passion sweeping him up to heights he had never meant to climb, he began to kiss her madly. The slender vulnerable neck he had always admired so much, the soft pale face wet with tears, and then her lips again. But he put an end to it. He stood up, and taking her by the hand lifted her to her feet.

"I can hardly judge other men. You can see how I feel about you," he said huskily.

For a moment she stared at him with wide startled eyes. Her own blood was leaping *and she knew it*. It confused her and more still was she bewildered by the sudden change in Rob. Old Rob — great favourite at the Club — famous for his integrity, and his quiet authority and his interest in everything. Suddenly today Nira had felt the strength of passion in him. There was a definite vibration between them. Because she was so unhappy she wanted his kisses. But she steadied herself, taking it for granted that this storm had blown up only because he was sorry for her, full of the pity that is so near to love, and that she was in the emotional state to respond.

She thought it best to ignore what had happened, and it was in the old friendly voice that she said, "Thank you, darling, that was sweet of you. Sorry I've been such a drip. I ought to have more sense — and more courage. I'm not the first wife whose husband has gone astray —" she punctuated the last word with a laugh, "and I won't be the last. Here am I a woman of thirty with two children behaving like a teenager!"

Rob put on his glasses He was alarmed by his own reactions. They were so conclusive. It had been proved to him that he was as vulnerable as any other man in the circumstances and that he was wide awake—in mind, body and spirit. In every way, as he had never been in his life before. It was quite obvious that he was capable of loving this girl— this married woman with her two children—with all the strength of his being. He was like a boy again—intoxicated by the rich promise of her lips. But he was not to allow himself to be led away by what he thought of as *promise*. She had only kissed him back in a sad very human moment of weakness. It promised nothing for the future. It mustn't. The one horrifying thought that followed was his fear that he might lose her altogether now that she *knew* he was in love with her.

But when she spoke again, she said, "I'll never forget all your goodness to me. You'll always be my dearest friend on earth," and she reached up and brushed his lips with the lightest kiss. It filled him with relief and gratitude. He had to exercise all his control as he lightly returned that caress, then gave her a brotherly hug.

"We understand each other completely, my dear. Forget my idiocy and remember only that anything I can do for you in this world I'll do. But what, *what?*"

She smoothed back her hair and put a handkerchief against her lips.

"I don't know." Looking at her reflection in the little mirror over the parlour fireplace she touched her lips with rouge, turned back to Rob and gave a long sigh. "We'll have to see how things work out. I suppose I've got to be sensible and not panic. As you and I once agreed, heaps of couples today have affairs on the side and think nothing of it. I could never lead my life that way, but perhaps Des will settle down in time. So the poignant question is, am I prepared to accept his present behaviour and wait for him to change—or part from him?"

Rob pulled his pipe from his pocket and stuck it between his teeth. He had never felt more inadequate—more reluctant to advise her in the right way. He would liked to have told her to leave Desmond and go away with *him*—just anywhere—yes—so that he could hold her loveliness in his arms for ever and for ever safeguard her from the sort of misery Desmond was causing her.

He forced himself to speak, "I think you should wait awhile as you suggest and perhaps Desmond will see what a fool he is and stop this nonsense. You don't want to break up your home— it wouldn't be good for the children. It never is."

"I agree. If it wasn't for Renira and Jonny perhaps I'd do it."

"I understand."

Not long after all this the children came back from Newquay full of the film they had seen, noisy and excited.

Nira felt a pang of conscience as she looked at her two. Whatever happened, she mustn't break up this marriage — the old charmed circle. It must return. She must think of Des as a boy who was sowing his wild oats and would get tired of the frolic and want to be his old self; the much more reliable and devoted Des she had married and who was father of the family.

Rob left them to go for a long walk by himself across the cliffs. At least the weather seemed more promising. The late afternoon was golden, beautiful; the sky, above a sea that was gradually settling down, blue, shot with green, looked like wrinkled silk with a long frill of cream as the breakers moved in to shore at ebb-tide.

After Rob had gone, Nira read to the children, gave them their milk and biscuits and put them to bed. Whatever the outcome of this holiday they, at least, looked radiant. The wind and the rain and the salt air beating against their little faces had made them as tanned as though they had basked in perpetual sunlight.

As Renira kissed her mother good night she nuzzled her cheek and giggled. "Mr Wilson said I was a pwitty girl. Am I pwitty, Mummy?"

"Very, my darling."

"There!" said Renira defiantly to her brother, "I told you I was."

"Oh, but you mustn't be vain," Nira smiled, her arms around the small adorable figure in the short floral nightie.

"What's *vain* mean?"

"Too fond of yourself. You mustn't *ever* call yourself pretty. People won't think it nice. Let *them* always say it — never you."

"Why not?"

"Don't ask so many questions," Nira laughed again and pulled the blind down against the last red-gold rays from the setting sun.

Jonathan flung himself on his back, tossed his legs in the air, laughing loudly.

"I don't think she's pretty. She's hideous."

The corners of Renira's lips turned down. Nira hastened to

kiss and console her and to tell them both to keep quiet. Then she left them before there could be any more trouble.

Once in her own bedroom she sat down on the edge of the bed and for a moment stared rather miserably around the room. She was so tired. The emotional scene with Rob had disturbed her even while it consoled. She had just told her small daughter not to be vain. Here was she, Nira, against her better judgment, proud and pleased because Rob had called her beautiful. "*You can see how I feel about you,*" he had said, and she had certainly felt the quick tell-tale throb of his heart against her breast. It hadn't left her cold nor had it irritated her, as Boyce's attentions had done. Yet while she analysed the whole situation she knew that she was still Des's wife—Des's girl—and the jealousy was still there, too, stabbing her while she imagined what he might be doing with Frankie Motte. How badly he behaved! Shamefully, *shamelessly* with Rob to see it, too. He had broken every promise he had made to her.

"Oh, what a muddle," she said the words aloud, and the tears pricked her eyelids, but she was determined not to cry again, and when Des came home she wouldn't say a reproachful word. She would pretend that it was quite in order that he should have walked out on his family all day and 'been on a party' as he called it, with that film crowd. Of course if it had been with the crowd it wouldn't have mattered. But Nira knew that Frankie and Frankie, alone, was the draw.

13

WHILE THE RAIN continued to fall during the early part of that afternoon, the actors in Vince Lord's film, and the camera crew, had been forced to idle away the time in their hotel. Vince held a conference and informed them that the forecast was good so they would probably be able to shoot the rest of the beach scene tomorrow and get it finished. Then he went off to his own room to sulk. He hated bad weather interfering with his plans and he was more than a little annoyed that Frankie was showing such a marked interest in Desmond Curtis. When he had tackled her about it she had only laughed and said, "Don't be so stupid, darling. You know I hate my boy-friends to go all possessive and that's what you're trying to be. Besides, it's dull down here and Des is terribly good to look at, rather groovy altogether, don't you think? If I want fun and games with him, please shut your blood-shot eyes to it and stop nagging."

"Thanks very much," Vince had answered tartly and disappeared.

Des at her request drove Frankie away from Newquay and down the coast road towards Portreath. Just before they came in to Perranporth, they found an attractive roadhouse where they could have sandwiches and drinks. There was a small sitting-room at the back of the bar which they had to themselves. The landlord was only too pleased to accommodate them. He recognised the famous exciting-looking red-haired film star, and the gentleman was lavish with his money. Good enough! He ordered champagne instead of beer.

Inevitably there followed a session when Frankie, in the best of humours and fortified by the champagne and Des's companionship, ended up in his arms. He amused her. She adored his looks and his sense of humour. He was such a change from Vince. Vince was the clever one all right but she was sick of him *and* that crowd she worked with. They were all the same; weak-sycophantic. There was no such sick-worship in Des's handsome eyes. He asked for nothing. He just *took*—and she was in the mood to be taken—wooed out of her utter boredom.

Later while she dressed again, ran a comb through her glorious hair and put on the white anorak which she wore with white hipsters and long black shiny boots, she smiled at Des's reflection in the mirror.

"Well, lover-boy, are you going to follow me to Rome? You know we're shooting the end of this film there at the end of the week. I want you there with me, baby. What about it?"

Des, sitting on the sofa, a cigarette between his lips, looked at her provocative figure with narrowed eyes. He had had a lot of women in his life but never one quite like Frankie Motte. She was terrific.

He knew that he was behaving shockingly to Nira. Without doubt she *knew*—and old Rob guessed what was up and must think him pretty ghastly. But he couldn't help it. There had

144

never been an opportunity such as this for him to have an affair with a girl like Frankie—an international star. She flattered his ego and made it almost impossible for him to say no to her. When all was said and done he couldn't really understand why she wanted him. She had her pick of so many men, some of them millionaires. But he took what the gods offered and enjoyed it.

Yet in his way, unstable—inconsistent—the image of his wife and children and the home they had built up together, prevailed. What conscience he had was uneasy.

Frankie smiled at him, moved close and rested her hands with their long silvered nails, on his shoulders.

"It was great just now, wasn't it, lover?" she whispered.

He seized one of the hands and kissed it. "You can say that again."

"We just—click—don't we?"

"As far as I'm concerned, you're a riot—a riot, my darling."

And now he pulled her down on the sofa beside him. But she didn't let him hold her for long. She moved away, shaking back her hair, her eyes mocking him under the long false lashes.

"Steady. I've just tidied up. What about Rome?"

He stubbed his cigarette end in an ashtray.

"Darling, I can't possibly. How can I? I'm a married man and I've got a job."

Frankie shrugged.

"You shouldn't have married. It's a stupid institution anyhow."

"I suppose so. You certainly make me feel it is. Like hell I'd like to be free to follow you to Italy."

"And you will, won't you?" she asked softly.

"It's tricky, darling. It's all very well for me to play truant and come over here like this, but to take a week off in Italy—that's not quite the same thing. I'd have frightful trouble with Nira."

Frankie yawned. "She's a nice girl, I'm sure, much nicer than me, but we've only got one life to live and I can't waste mine worrying about other men's wives. She's got her kids and she's got this fellow you call Rob, hasn't she?"

"Not in the way you think. It isn't as simple as all that. She still happens to be in love with me."

"Too bad for her. *I* want you in Rome, lover, and I'm used to getting what I want."

He glanced at his wristwatch, frowning. His brain was still a bit bemused with all the champagne and the events of the afternoon. But he realised that the kissing had got to stop. He must get back to Mawgan Porth, or he'd start a major row between Nira and himself which might have unfortunate results. He was not used to having to face serious decisions of the kind Frankie was trying to impose on him. He liked his affairs to be easy. Nipping in and out of somebody's bedroom was altogether different from throwing up wife and work in order to follow your girl-friend to Italy, even if she was Frankie Motte. *God*, he thought, *what a jungle I'm getting myself into. What's the answer?*

Now suddenly Frankie showed her other side. She went for him as she had gone for Vince when the Curtis family first saw her. She sprang to her feet in a rage and her huge eyes glared down in anger at the man who a few moments ago she had been smothering with kisses.

"Well, listen, baby, I'm not prepared to sit back and wait while you have fits of conscience about your wife and family. If that's the way it is you'd better go back to them right now. We could have had a marvellous time together in Italy—and after that. But your attitude bores me. Please drive me back to New-quay."

Des stood up, his pulses jerking and his face very red.

"Look, Frankie, you don't have to shout at me. Surely we can just talk things over."

"No, we can't. You're a drip. That's what you are. One of these creeps tied to a wife's apron-strings. No use to me—or anyone else who wants fun. Okay! I made a mistake ever thinking you different. But don't start trying to get what you can from both your wife *and* me. Frankie never takes second place to anyone. Just drive me home."

He looked at her. The fever that had crept into his blood for this girl began to simmer down. She was marvellous to look at and to make love to, but she'd be hell to live with, he thought, or to be with for long in any part of the world. Suddenly he remembered Nira—her cool sweetness—her tenderness—her trust in him. A trust that he had betrayed so often.

He felt sick and dispirited. He picked up his jacket and scarf.

"Okay," he said briefly. "Come on."

"No, I've changed my mind. I don't want to drive back with you. You bore me to sobs," she said with a venom that amazed him.

Her vanity, her greed and her belief that the world was her

oyster and that she could do exactly what she wanted, was frightening, he decided.

While he struggled into his jacket, she dashed out of the room, crashing the door behind him. A few moments later she came back.

"I've phoned Vince. He's driving over to fetch me. *Goodbye.*"

This was a bit much even for Des. The sudden metamorphosis left him more than a little confused.

"Oh, hell, don't be like this. Can't we part friends? We've had such a wonderful few days together —" he began.

She broke in, "I'm off to the bar to buy myself a drink. I've *had* you, and you needn't bring your precious family down to join the crowd while we're shooting tomorrow. Stay at home and cherish them. That's what you really want to do, isn't it? *Goodbye.*"

She was out of the room again in a flash before he could answer.

He stood a moment lighting another cigarette with shaking fingers. He felt as though he had been swept off his feet in a tornado and he couldn't pick himself up again. Oh, well, let Vincent Lord comfort Frankie and keep her. It would obviously never have worked with him, Des. Unspeakable gloom encircled him as he left Frankie in the bar surrounded by admiring fans. He heard a champagne cork popping as he went out to his car.

God! he thought, and put a hand to his forehead. He was in a wave of perspiration. He had drunk far too much this afternoon. As for Frankie, she could drink him under the table.

He'd have to think of something on the way home that he could say in order to put things right with Nira. This time he really would try to play straight. Frankie had been a new experience and she had had him hypnotised. But there was a sort of corruption under her glamour and today it made him feel lower than he had ever felt in his life before.

Disgusted and remorseful, he climbed into his car and set out for Mawgan Porth. He felt a sharp reaction as the cool evening breeze blew against his hot face. A bit dazed. He must drive slowly, he told himself. He'd had a lot more than any test for alcohol content would permit. His eyes weren't focusing all that well, and these damn Cornish roads were narrow and winding. They could be tricky. He drove carefully for the first few miles then speeded up, anxious suddenly to get back to the wife he had treated so badly. He wanted to be in time to say good night to the kids. Poor old Jonathan — he hadn't played much cricket with the boy this holiday, but he'd make up for it tomorrow. It looked like being a fine day.

Just before he came into Newquay, Des was doing a steady sixty miles an hour in the Marina. His brain had not cleared. He felt suddenly sick and dizzy and afraid that he might pass out. He jammed his foot down on the brake and swerved across the road. It was at this point that an articulated lorry came round the corner on the wrong side. It hit the bonnet of the Marina with a sickening impact, buckling metal, shattering glass, and hurling Des from an instant of pain and panic into darkness and silence. For him it was the end not only of marriage but of life itself.

It took over an hour before a police car arrived on the scene followed by an ambulance. It took another half an hour before Des's body could be taken from the wreckage of the car. Then, with the lorry driver who was suffering from shock and cuts, they were taken to Newquay Hospital. There, a letter in the dead man's wallet, revealed his name and gave the police the information that he had booked rooms at Trevarra Farm in Mawgan Porth.

At seven o'clock a telephone call to the farm broke the news to Mrs Curtis.

Nira's Story

I

WHEN YOU GET hit really hard, if it doesn't kill you it affects your mind. On the day that the police told me that Des had been killed on his way back from Newquay, I felt absolutely stunned and numb. I didn't feel any pain. I couldn't cry. I remember calling for Rob who came running down from his bedroom. He told me afterwards that when he saw me he was positively scared because I looked so ghastly. He took off his glasses and came up to me quickly.

"Nira, what is it? What's happened?"

"Des has been killed," I answered his question, and told him all that the police had told me. Rob looked quite blank at first then, as the truth broke over him, he was as shocked as I was. He took my hands, drew me to the sofa and told me to sit down while he fetched me a brandy. There wouldn't have been any in the farmhouse but dear Aunt Ida had packed a flask in Rob's case. She believed in using brandy medicinally in times of stress. "I can't believe it," I kept saying to Rob, my teeth chattering, "I can't."

"My God, how awful!" Rob said, staring down at me.

"History repeating itself," I said. "When are the horrors going to end? It isn't so long ago that Cricket died in almost the same way, crushed in the wreckage of her car."

The ever-resourceful Rob refused to let me talk about that.

"I'd better go to the police station at Newquay at once," he said. "Yes," I nodded.

He went off to fetch his car-keys. I found Mrs Hoskin and told her what had happened.

"Oh my *gracious!*" exclaimed Mrs. Hoskin and put a hand up

to her mouth. "*Never* such a thing! It can't be true. Oh, you poor dear, you do look bad!"

"I'm all right," I said. "But I've got to go and identify the body." It sounded crude, even callous, saying that, but there it was.

It was such a peaceful fine evening—never had the sea looked calmer or the sky more wonderful, full of amber and crimson light. The air was soft and gentle as it could so often be during a Cornish summer. One could never dream there were such things as storms or the havoc of gales—or the horror of sudden violent death.

Rob drove very quietly—out of consideration for me of course. I sat with one hand in his. He released it only now and again when he had to turn a corner.

I was haunted for ages by the memory of that grim session at Newquay police station. First the mortuary. A Des I just didn't recognise lay there on a slab, white and still, and quite remote from life. His face was extraordinarily untouched and handsome. It was his body that had received the full impact in the crash. I remember looking at my poor dead husband in a dazed sort of way, thinking how young he looked in death. He had recently been growing rather fleshy about the jowl, and was all too often flushed and rakish. But this was the Des I had married—or, at least a white marble image of him. I couldn't believe that he'd never laugh again—never again be the boisterous racy Des of former times—the good raconteur, the splendid lover I had loved so well.

Without Rob I couldn't have got through those dark hours. In the mortuary I held very tightly on to his hand. Before I left Des I leaned down and kissed his forehead, then turned away shuddering because it had so soon grown icy-cold. A kind policewoman took me away to have a cup of tea while Rob made all the necessary arrangements on my behalf.

I had told him that Gandy would never forgive me if Des was buried down here. She wouldn't travel so far to the funeral. She would expect me to take Des back to Sussex, and possibly want him buried or cremated in Brighton, because it was her present home. I didn't care—it didn't seem to matter. Neither did I count the cost of it all. I was quite sure that when I came out of this stupor, this being what the Americans call 'in shock', I would start to cry and feel desperately sad—even though Des had betrayed me, and I was no longer his lover. But I was still his wife and he was the father of my children. Poor Renira and Jonathan—they had lost their father. That wasn't a good thing. It was only fortunate they were so young and wouldn't feel so upset as they might have been if they were older.

Gandy was the one I was sorry for. Des was the apple of her eye and her only child. I dreaded what it might do to her.

We went back to the farm. I eventually told the children that Daddy had gone away. I didn't want to tell them the truth just then, I couldn't, personally, stand any more emotional scenes. I just wanted them to go up to bed and to leave me alone. I didn't even want Rob at that time. I longed to be left quite by myself to think everything out, and to try to see the situation more clearly.

Des had left me for ever. I was his widow. I would never see him again. I stood in the same shoes that Boyce had worn when Cricket died. Funny that I kept thinking about Cricket. I even wondered crazily if they were now meeting each other in heaven— and what they would be saying. Or wouldn't they get to heaven? Hadn't they been good enough Christians?

In my nervous rather hysterical state I started to laugh. Rob was in the room and he immediately came and treated me quite roughly. He shook me and said, "Now stop it, Nira. *Stop it.* You've been marvellous up to now. Don't lose your grip."

I did stop laughing, I must say. I just felt desperately tired.

"Sorry," I said, "I think I had better go upstairs to bed. Tell Mrs. Hoskin that I don't want any supper. You have yours, please. And thank you, dear, *dear* Rob for all you've done."

"I've done nothing," he said. "But I don't want you to go without supper. You can't afford to be ill. You'll need all your strength during these next few days."

Darling Rob, I am sure he was quoting Aunt Ida; as if going without my supper would make me ill! But I made no further protest when he said he would ask Mrs. Hoskin to take me up a tray, even if it was only a cup of tea and an egg.

"Oh, Rob," I said, "it's a sort of nightmare. Can you believe that Des is dead and never coming back—and that we'll never see him or speak to him again?"

"It must be terribly hard for you to accept," he said gently, then in his practical way, reminded me that I hadn't yet contacted Des's mother.

So before I could go to my room and shut myself in and give way to the tears that were beginning to burn against my eyelids, I had another miserable task to perform. Perhaps the hardest of them all. I had to break the awful news to Gandy. I didn't dare leave it, in case it was put in the newspapers and she'd see it like that. So many bad accidents are reported and Des worked for a very well-known firm, which reminded me that I had also to contact Mr. Steadman, Des's chief.

Oh, there were going to be so many things I must do — gruesome, ugly things. I was quite capable of carrying them out, but on that night I didn't feel I could face too much without cracking.

Rob offered to ring Gandy for me, but I wouldn't let him. I had to speak to her myself. How I managed to get the words out I don't know. She had answered my call so brightly, saying that she had been thinking of us all enjoying ourselves now that the weather was improving, and was Des brown and how were the darling babes? She even began to tell me what a big success she had had at bridge the night before and how she'd won a little slam, doubled, redoubled and vulnerable. Wasn't it thrilling?

Feeling sick, I then interrupted her chatter and told her about Des.

I must say she took it fairly well. She was quite a good person in her way, my mother-in-law, and of course, she knew absolutely nothing about the rift between Des and myself. She was for once decent enough to think of me before herself.

After she had groaned a little, she said, "Oh, my God, my God," and then, "Oh, my poor Nira and those poor children! What a terrible thing. Oh, *why* did it have to happen? I was afraid of it."

"Why?" I echoed her words.

I could hear her crying. I felt dreadfully sorry for her.

"Try not to be too sad, Gandy," I said. "At least we can be sure that he'll never grow old or have to bear a protracted illness or anything. He's at peace. They say he couldn't have known anything — just died instantly. He didn't suffer and he was having such a lovely time down here. He said it was the best holiday he'd ever had, with all that film crowd."

The words almost stuck in my throat. The telephone was in the parlour and Rob was there because I'd told him not to go. He had his back to me. I knew he was smoking his pipe and I wondered what he must have been thinking when he heard all the lies I had to tell. I had to make things as good as possible for poor Gandy. When she stopped crying and spoke to me again, I told her we would be coming home as soon as we could bring Des.

Then Gandy made the really big gesture. "That would be an awful business," she said. "Why not let our poor boy be buried in some nice little Cornish churchyard. I'll come down for the funeral. You arrange it and I'll get a hired car. I'll take the children back with me and I'll look after them while you are sorting things out. I know Susan's away," she went on, "so I'll be as helpful as I can, my dear," then she burst into tears again.

I comforted her and thanked her and told her we'd always stick together and all that sort of thing, then she thanked me and said she'd let me know when she'd arrive. I hung up. It was then the tears began to roll down my cheeks. I think I was so touched by the way Gandy had taken the news. I was sure she didn't really want to come all the way down to Cornwall. As a rule she was such a selfish, self-centred woman, but she had loved Des and she loved the children, and I made a vow that I'd always make it easy for her to see plenty of them.

When I put down the phone and turned to Rob, he took me gently in his arms and smoothed my hair as he had done so often. Once again he was the big brother I needed.

"There, there," he kept saying, "I know what you must be feeling."

So ended that tragic day.

Then came the funeral, Des was buried, as his mother wished, in a lovely little cemetery between Mawgan Porth and St Columb, and the children and I were back in Nylands before I felt the full impact of what had happened. This time I wasn't stunned. I was cool, self-possessed and capable, even though fully alive to all the pain and trouble that followed Des's death.

Gandy kept her promise and took the children off my hands. Susan was due back in three days' time—we had all about reached the end of our holiday fortnight, but Gandy said she'd keep the children as long as I liked if Susan would take the train into Brighton every day to help her. The high-spirited pair were a bit much for a woman of Gandy's age and temperament, but she continued to be very unselfish about the whole thing.

The first week back in Ponders Heath was ghastly for me of course. The local paper was full of the accident. Pictures of Des and of me and the full story of the accident in Cornwall. There followed the usual spate of letters from friends and relations all of which had to be answered by me. A personal visit from Mr. Steadman who said the firm had lost an excellent man, much to be regretted. Flowers from dozens of my friends. Unexpected bouquets from people I hardly knew in Ponders Heath. It was amazing how much kindness one could be shown at such a time. Of course all the members of the Club were stunned by the news and although I didn't go up there at all, Rob, who came daily to see if he could do anything for me, said they all told him how sadly they would miss Des's cheerful attractive presence. Like me, they also looked back to poor Cricket's accident and the superstitious among them wondered gloomily if there would be a third accident among the members.

I told Rob that I'd received a huge bunch of roses—long-stemmed pink ones, with asparagus fern—from Maggie and her mother. A letter with it. Rob read it.

"My dear Nira,

You've no idea how grieved my mother and I were when we heard your dreadful news. It must have been a terrible shock for you and we send all our sympathies to you and your children. Des will never be forgotten by any of us. He was a great person. Please do let me come and see you one day.

Maggie."

Rob took off his glasses and met my gaze—a sort of under-standing look passed between us. I gave what he must have thought a wintry smile.

"Nice letter," he said.

"Very nice," I said. "Poor Maggie."

"Why poor Maggie?"

"Never mind," I said, "death wipes out everything, doesn't it?"

And after those cryptic words I put on a coat and went out with him. I'd promised to have dinner at The Hollies. I was eating so little, Rob was worried about me. He said I looked like a ghost. Perhaps I did. I'm sure I'd lost weight, and that was only ten days after Des was laid to his last long rest.

Then came the business of sorting out all his things, most of which were his clothes which I gave away to the W.V.S. His personal valuables like his gold watch and his nice cuff links, of course I kept for Jonathan. It was a bleak job emptying his cupboards and drawers and still I couldn't quite believe he would never come back into his room, and this house. There would be no more love between us, and no more hate—which was the other side of love. I must let him remain in my memory not as the man who had made me so unhappy towards the end, but as the Des who had given me years of happiness when we first married.

Then there was all the legal business. Des had made a will. He left everything to me. Gandy came over to be present when the solicitor, Mr. Parsons, lunched with us and told us all about it.

Now came a fresh blow—a financial one for the children anyhow, although I didn't seem to mind much what it did to me. But Des, having left me everything, seemed to have borrowed so much in recent years without me knowing it, that most of his assets had already been swallowed up. The house was mortgaged, though not for much. I would at least have that to sell. All the shares his father had left him and which I thought were safely tucked away to bring in dividends and profits, had been sold. Bills came pouring in. I thought I used to know everything Des did, but I was wrong. He had his suits made by the most expensive tailors. He had ordered so much drink, and so many boxes of cigars and spent so much more in town than he ever did at home or on his family—it was little wonder he had accumulated big debts. Mr. Parsons said after they were paid there would be practically nothing left for me except Des's office pension and I'd have my widow's allowance, and something for the children. Obviously I should not be able to go on living at Nylands.

I didn't want Gandy to know all the things that Des had done but couldn't stop Mr. Parsons letting the cat out of the bag. He told her that Des had even borrowed on his life-insurance. I wouldn't get much of that.

Gandy's delicate powdered face turned quite red with anger and disbelief.

"But Des wasn't like that. He was a good family man. I can't believe he has left his wife in such poor circumstances," she declared.

Mr. Parsons coughed and cleared his throat, and said he was sorry but those were the facts.

Gandy turned to me, utterly woebegone.

"Is it true, Nira? Had you any idea Des was being so extravagant?"

"No," I said, as steadily as I could.

"He was such a wonderful husband to you always."

"Yes," I said.

Gandy put a handkerchief to her eyes and her lips.

"Oh, *dear!*" she wailed.

I looked at Mr. Parsons.

"I don't really understand what he spent all this money on, because we weren't so terribly free with it when Des was alive," I said. "How can he have spent it?"

"Gambling on the Stock Exchange, much of the time—that's how a lot of men lose their money," answered Mr. Parsons.

I nodded. It was possible. Des had always been unpredictable, and at times he used to rush into all kinds of projects without due thought.

So, to the list of his other follies—the ones I knew about—I must add gambling.

"Oh, well," I said, "I can always get a job. Anybody of my age with any intelligence can get a job these days. But it'll be hard on the children."

Gandy sniffed into her handkerchief.

"I shall still continue to make you a small allowance," she said, "but I haven't got so much money myself after paying tax and my own bills. I'll go on supplying the money for the children's education, but I couldn't begin to keep this home going for you. After all, I'm only in my sixties. I might live for a long time yet. I mustn't touch my capital."

"Very wise, Mrs. Curtis," said Mr. Parsons, whom I thought a rather smug stupid man. I wondered why Des had dealt with him, then remembered his father had dealt with Mr. Parsons' father—he was Gandy's solicitor as well. I said no more. I felt so tired. A feeling of absolute exhaustion weighed me down.

After Mr. Parsons had gone, Gandy went back to Brighton. She had left the children at the flat with Susan for the afternoon.

The *children*, I thought—I must have them home this weekend. Gandy was looking weary and no doubt she would like some peace and quiet just now. I personally didn't think I would ever know peace or quiet again. I was living in a sort of cyclone that continued to whirl around me. On top of the horror of Des's death I now had to face the fact that I was going to be very badly off in future. Probably I'd make a profit on the sale of the house. But I would have to live on my investments. I began to see myself and Renira and Jonathan caged in a little place somewhere, counting every penny. I would certainly have to resign from the golf club. There would be no more golf parties or expensive holidays abroad.

It should all have been so different.

Oh, Des, I thought, *Oh, Des, what have you done to us?*

Yet I knew that what I was suffering today was as nothing—compared with the pain I had felt when I first learned that he had been unfaithful to me.

Without undue flattery to myself I think I had been a good wife to Des but I was never much of a hand with the accounts. That was something he always saw to. He used to pay the bills (so he said) and keep the receipts. I left the financial side to him. But I'd made a mistake. For here I was—each morning receiving another little bill—or a big one—for Mr. Desmond Curtis, and it all had to be sent to Mr. Parsons to be paid for out of Des's pitifully small estate.

I don't know what I'd have done without Gandy. Tiresome she used to be but now she was kind and sympathetic. Of course I bolstered up her image of her wonderful son. "He was a faithful devoted boy and we shall never see his like," she once said to me, weeping into her handkerchief. All I could do was to agree and try to remember the Des I had married.

Most of our old friends and acquaintances either called on me or phoned to say they wanted to come and see me. Lady Conniston stooped from her self-made pedestal and sent a gracious little note sympathising with my dreadful loss and begging me to take the children up to the Manor House any time I wanted. So once or twice I sent Jonathan up to play with the Conniston boy but I refused all invitations to meals with his parents. The Moffats were very kind—Joyce having lost her twins in an accident, was swift to try and be a help and comfort, but I didn't feel close to her. Nor did I to any of my golfing friends. Strange and sad to say, it was Maggie I had liked best but she most of all I did not want to see. So I was very much alone and once the children were in bed I found myself wandering desolately from room to room and ending in my solitary bed, crying from fatigue, grief, all the emotions that could weigh a widow down. I didn't want to talk to anyone about Des and I didn't want to be the object of pity. Crushed though I was by this avalanche that had suddenly descended upon me, I had, as they say, my pride. I couldn't parade my sorrows. I devoted myself entirely to the children. Needless to say I had to send Susan packing. I couldn't possibly afford her now. She was very upset and even offered to take a lower salary in order to stay with us but of course I wouldn't let her. I could deal with driving the kids to and from school, and here, at home.

I could also afford to keep Mrs Tulk, my daily, once a week, while I was selling up. I know I should have felt that losing my lovely home was a real tragedy but somehow I couldn't wait to get out. Everything reminded me of Des. Unfortunately I remembered all too vividly the rows we had had in recent months, and the tears I had shed, lying in that double bed of ours when he left me alone. The sooner I could make a new life for myself and the children elsewhere the better.

This sentiment was intensified after I received an express letter from Boyce from Peru (Jonathan would love all those huge exotic stamps) but the contents of the letter were slightly alarming. Boyce had heard about Des from Colonel Moffat who corresponded with him. He said how shocked and distressed he was and sent his deepest sympathies, then added that he more than anyone could feel for me after what had happened to Cricket. The important line was to say he was coming back to England.

The job in Peru hadn't worked out. To begin with, Simon had had perpetual sinus trouble since he arrived. He had also grown very thin and nervy and didn't seem to want to leave his father and fly back to England. Boyce disliked the set-up in Peru and had asked Head Office to send him home. It wasn't a good thing to do but Boyce didn't think the firm would sack him. He might just have to accept a lesser position. However, as a good research engineer he had no fears of not finding another job, even if he quit the firm. He ended by saying that he had booked a flight back to London on the 1st October. He would bring Simon to Ponders Heath to his old school and he, himself, would look for a flat there. He had missed his old friends at the golf club and life in the Heath generally. He ended:

It seems years instead of months since I left England. It's you I miss most of all, dear lovely Nira. Maybe we shall be able to comfort each other a little. At least I can bring you my friendship.

He signed himself *Forever, Boyce.*

I could feel his presence as I read that letter and see those rather bold hazel eyes fixing me with a look that gave no room for doubt as to how he was feeling. *Comfort each other!* For heaven's sake! The last thing I wanted was to be comforted by Boyce or to renew that particular friendship. I had hoped I'd cut right away from him, or the memory of Cricket.

I took the letter up to The Hollies and showed it to Rob.

"I don't think I could take another session of Boyce. I think I'll sell Nylands at once. You know I've been putting it off because I just didn't feel I could tackle all that had to be done. But now I'm better. I *must* start sorting and packing. I did phone two agents who both said they were sure they could get me a handsome profit. Some of it of course will go toward settling overdrafts and bills, but Mr. Parsons thinks I'll have enough left to buy a nice flat somewhere for the children and myself."

We were sitting out in the small walled garden at the back of The Hollies, drinking our before-lunch sherries. Aunt Ida had been in bed for several days with one of her bronchial-asthma attacks.

I saw Rob's expression alter. He looked alarmed.

"But you're not going to leave Ponders Heath?"

"Everything's very expensive here," I sighed. "It's the commuters' paradise and Des's mother is terribly anxious for me to get a little place in Brighton so that we'd be near her."

Rob didn't answer for a moment, but he took off the tinted glasses and blinked his eyes at me.

"Shan't take kindly to that idea. I'd feel it an awful loss if you leave this vicinity."

As ever, my heart warmed to him but I was still uncertain as to whether I wanted to go on living in this town. It was so full of memories of Des — and Cricket — *and* Maggie. I'd be certain to meet *her*. Or would I soon stop letting anything upset me? Would I grow indifferent — even callous — reach a pitch where the name of Des would neither hurt nor distress?

Rob, his brows raised, handed me back Boyce's letter.

"Has this got you down? Because if you don't want to see Boyce we'll just make it plain to him. I can't say I'm all that pleased that he means to come back to the neighbourhood. Sorry about the little boy, of course, but I never did think Peru a good idea for Simon, even in the holidays."

"Oh, I could tackle Boyce—it isn't that—oh, Rob, I don't know *what* it is. I just want to get away."

"I understand," he said gently, "but would you be any happier in Brighton?"

"I don't know," I said, "I don't seem to know anything any more."

He picked up my right hand and touched it with his lips.

"Poor darling, it's all such a grim shake-up of your life. Everything seems to have happened within such a short time. I can't say I blame you for wanting to get away but I do feel while you are in the Heath I can keep an eye on you and the children and be of some help to you."

Now I took his hand and pressed it between my own. I felt the tears well into my eyes.

"Oh, you are marvellous to me. You've done everything so far. But I just honestly *don't* know what to do."

"Sell Nylands, and get what money you can," he said quietly. "Then why not store your things and take a little furnished flat or go into a small hotel until you've made up your mind where you do want to live permanently."

"You mean near my mother-in-law?"

I could see before he answered, that it wasn't at all what he meant or what he wanted. It was always a comfort to feel the warmth of Rob's tender affection for me. He was in love with me. I learned that from the passion of his kisses, his touch, down in Cornwall, on the day Des died. But he hadn't shown me that side since. He had been strictly controlled. He had given me just what I wanted—friendship and advice, and great kindness.

"I'll have a talk with my mother-in-law and see what evolves," I said.

The woman who came in to cook the hot midday meal for Rob and his aunt announced that lunch was ready. Rob pulled me up from my chair, tucked my arm through his and walked me into the dining-room.

"Now stop worrying and puzzling and planning. Just enjoy your meal. I've opened a half-bottle of claret. It's rather good, and it'll do *you* good!"

Later, after seeing the old lady, I went back to my home to prepare supper for the kids and then fetch them back from school. I looked with slightly worried eyes at the car. How much longer was I going to be able to run *that?* Despite Gandy's help I really had to cut down drastically. A car was a luxury even in this day and age when everybody seemed to have one. But, my goodness! I'd miss it, I'd be absolutely pinned wherever I was if I hadn't got a car. It wasn't all that old. No doubt I could sell it quite well, but I determined to keep it as long as I could.

I was glad there was no need for me to answer Boyce's letter. He would be home almost as soon as a note would reach Peru. The irritation I had felt when I first learned that he intended to come back to the Heath—and pursue me again—soon faded. I had so much else to think of and do.

There were many more miserable moments ahead. So far, I hadn't begun to go through letters and papers except those Mr. Parsons had asked for and which were kept in Des's bureau. But suddenly I found a cigar-box in one of the drawers. I lifted up some of the cigars to see how many there were, wondering if I could give them to Rob. Underneath the bottom row lay a letter. Obviously he had put it there, in order to hide it.

My better self told me to tear it in half without reading it but I wasn't strong-minded enough to do this. I pulled the letter out of its envelope. It was written in a curly sort of feminine hand— vaguely familiar. I looked first at the signature. *Maggie*. I thought I'd recognised her writing! She had sent me a letter of sympathy after Des died. As I scanned it I began to feel sick and thoroughly resentful of this pretty dewy-eyed woman who had so ruthlessly taken Des's love from me. There it was for me to see in black and white and to make me all the more convinced that Des had been slightly sex-mad and ready to give way to his passions.

Maggie wrote like a lovesick schoolgirl. She mentioned that it was the first time she had dared write to him. He must have kept the letter out of sheer vanity because it was so full of praise for his looks, his strength, his wit, all the things that attracted her.

One paragraph stood out:

It was that first long kiss between us that decided me I couldn't say no to you any more. You were the lover I've always wanted. I've been so lonely since Bill died. I know you belong to Nira and I feel guilty but I must have you. Last night was marvellous. Oh, Lover, let us somehow preserve our feeling for each other. No one need ever know. I don't want to take you away from Nira but I do want your love. Oh, my darling—

I didn't read any more. I felt a sudden blind rage and tore that letter into shreds. How dared she? *How dared she* take what she called his love behind my back, even for a single night? She should have known better, seeing how she had loved Bill. How would she have liked it if I had tried to take him from *her?* Of course, she was lonely. So was I *right now* but I'm damned if I'd go and steal some other woman's man.

When had they spent this night together? I racked my brains and supposed it was any one of the nights when my dear hardworking husband said that he had to work at the office.

So when it was no longer Cricket, it was Maggie. Maggie was supposed to have given him up because of her conscience. But he had been her lover; and from her arms, he had come back to mine then to Frankie Motte's

Suddenly hate surged over me. I literally sobbed in sheer anger and disgust. Then I rang up Gandy. I said, "I'm selling up Nylands as soon as I possibly can now. I don't want to do anything permanent in a hurry, but the children must go on with their schooling here, it suits them. So if you'll forgive me, Gandy, I'll just take a little furnished place or go into a small hotel like The Swan, outside Ponders Heath. They let rooms. No, I don't want to come to Brighton at the moment, Gandy. Forgive me and try to understand that there is so much for me to do here."

Gandy, kind and generous though she had been, did not quite understand and seemed upset. But that was her selfish side. She wanted the children to be near her no matter how awkward it made things for me. I managed to smooth her down and rang off. Her final words echoed in my ears:

"The tone of your voice tells me that you are changing, Nira dear. You mustn't let grief harden you."

I didn't know whether to laugh or cry about that. Hard! Yes, I had had to harden up. I wanted to. But my grief, if she but knew, was not so much because I had lost my husband as because I had lost my faith — my intrinsic belief in goodness, in fidelity. Of course I had learnt what he was like before I ever came across that letter in the cigar box, but I admit that it upset me. It made me feel so utterly humiliated, I'd had to *share* Des. How horrible!

That night, when I was putting the children to bed I looked at Jonathan. How like his father he was growing, with that mop of chestnut hair, his fresh complexion and tall lanky body, and the cleft in his chin! Would he turn out to be a good stable kind of man or would he be another Des? Heaven forbid! I wouldn't want him to hurt any woman as Des had hurt me.

Jonny was putting on his pyjamas. He turned and gave me a roguish look.

"Renira and I have got a secret, Mum. We're not going to tell you."

I said nothing. That look was so like Desmond's and I'd had enough of secrets and things being kept from me. I suppose I was silly, but I just turned and ran out of the room, shut myself into my own bedroom and cried as I hadn't cried since Des's death.

2

IT WAS JOYCE Moffat who gave me the not unattractive idea for making a little money, and keeping Nylands a bit longer, which I now decided that I wanted—mainly because the children were so attached to it. They loved the garden in the summer. They had a fishpool and they each had a little plot of their own. They would be sad if they had to leave it at once. Then Joyce, who I met at the greengrocer's—it always seemed to be the meeting place for the shoppers in my circle—said, "Why don't you put an advertisement in the paper and take in two or three students? There's that new college that's opened in Reigate and everyone says that they can't get rooms for love or money. It isn't too far from Ponders Heath. Would you hate the thought?"

For the space of a minute I did hate it and said that I had made up my mind to leave Nylands, then Joyce embroidered on her theme. Some nice youngsters would undoubtedly help me in the evenings and I wouldn't feel so lonely, and they might baby-sit in Susan's place if I wanted to go out to a meal or a theatre or something. I'd get an income out of it even if only during the winter. I could sell the house next summer.

"I know how you feel—all at sixes and sevens," Joyce went on sympathetically, "but nice houses are so expensive — or even flats — and a friend of mine who has wanted to come to Ponders Heath for ages, hasn't been offered a thing worth having. You'd have a job getting fixed up."

I went home and brooded over this idea.

By this time — October — I'd told the children the truth about their Daddy. Jonathan, the older of the two and most sensitive, cried a bit. Renira looked puzzled, and pouted, but ended by saying with a cheerful smile, "I expect he's gone to heaven, don't you, Mummy, so he'll be able to make it all nice for us."

Whatever Des had done to me I couldn't feel hard or cynical in the face of that sort of remark. I just hugged Renira and hid her pretty face against my shoulder so that she shouldn't see that Mummy was crying. Lucky children! The thought of death held no sinister meaning for them. Almost as soon as they broke away from me they were giggling over some shared joke.

I wandered around my lonely house and felt it would be ghastly every night once the children had gone to bed. I wouldn't go out much in the winter, no matter where I lived, and if I got a smaller house or a flat, I wouldn't be able to have anyone to stay. If I let rooms here I'd have to cook a bit extra for the girls but no more than I used to cook for Des and myself.

Some gay teenagers! — the idea grew on me. Joyce had got something.

When I next saw Rob, I asked what he thought and he gave me that little enigmatic smile that grooved lines on either side his mouth, and said, "A very good idea if it's going to keep you in Ponders Heath, my dear. I agree with Joyce. Don't be in too much hurry to sell till after Christmas, particularly if you can make a bit of money out of your lodgers."

I gave him a rather wintry smile in return. I knew of course that he wanted me to stay so the idea appealed to him. Strange to say, when I asked Gandy, *she* too agreed with Joyce. "I'd been thinking it over," she said, "and I actually talked to my lawyer about you yesterday. What with the mortgage you'd have to pay off, you wouldn't get all that much capital out of the sale and there'd be agent's fees and the expense of moving and getting a new place together. When you move, windows are always different and you can rarely use your old curtains — or carpets. You'd only have to give the students breakfast and an evening meal. Try it — see how it goes."

She added that she'd been concerned about the children moving so soon from their old home — especially as I didn't want to come to Brighton. I might as well stay at Nylands, she said.

"Are you very lonely, my poor Nira?" she then asked.

"Yes," I said flatly.

But I couldn't explain to her that it wasn't so much the loneliness that hurt me as the awful misery and resentment that kept sweeping over me at the thought that Des had never really belonged to me. *Never* in the way I had imagined. He had also blotted his copybook so badly during our last year together that he had destroyed the romantic love I had found so lovely. There was nothing left for me but bitterness and I didn't find it easy to get over it, despite the fact that I knew that sort of feeling gets you nowhere and only makes things worse.

I was very close to Rob during this crisis in my life. He was my backbone. I often felt I'd have fallen right over, mentally, without his steady devotion. But I was also unable to forget that he was in love with me. It didn't worry me particularly except that I didn't want him to be hurt, and it was a dangerous situation because I was only human and the passion I had shared with my late husband was a passion not to be easily annihilated. Just because I was widowed and Des had behaved badly, it couldn't quite kill my longing for the warmth of a man's embrace and the touch of his lips on my mouth and all the shared ecstasy of the union between male and female which can be the most marvellous thing in the world. Bitter I might be, but I could not suddenly turn myself into a frigid cynical creature who found sex ugly and mistrusted all men.

I wasn't particularly ashamed of my natural inclinations, but I *was* rather ashamed because I didn't find my children enough. They were a tremendous comfort and a reason for living, but I was only just thirty. How was I going to live for so many more years being only a mother and housewife? *How?*

The real danger lay in Rob's tremendous love for me. He said nothing, did nothing, but I always knew it was there. I was sure that I had only to hold out my arms and he'd take me in his. It wouldn't be fair, because I didn't want him as I had wanted Des — with *all* of me, and Rob was too good a person to be given short measure.

I was growing thin and nervy. The sooner I filled my house

with people and tired myself out with work, the better. So I set out to get my students.

I had room for four and finally I took in four, despite Rob's fear that I might find it all too much with only Mrs. Tulk to help, and my two obstreperous children, plus the cooking and shopping.

"Let me get on with it, Rob," I told him. "I *need* to go to bed worn out. Just try and understand."

I think he did. He seemed to understand everything. He just patted my shoulder and said, "Okay, but try to take it a bit easier, darling."

I had learnt to be a careful shopper and I quite enjoyed giving the girls nice little meals when they came back from Reigate. Two of them were English—nineteen-year-old sisters named Moira and Jennifer Williams—from the Lake District. Nice quiet girls. One of them, obviously brilliant, was reading pure mathematics, the other history. They shared my spare room. Des's room I changed completely, steeling my heart against memories. The girls I put in there were both over twenty and foreigners—a fair-haired Danish beauty, Ingrid, and a petite dark little French girl from Boulogne. They were both reading English.

Ingrid was the star-turn.

She played a guitar and quite often entertained us in the evening, and of course the boy-friends began to arrive. I was determined not to be a difficult landlady. I gave the girls a key and told them to come in when they wanted and just not to make too much noise and wake the children.

I must admit some of the boy-friends were hardly my type— long hair, hairy faces, strange garments. One had a bushy beard and looked like a disciple. But they were all so nice, so interested in culture, in books or art or music—or in politics and events of the day. They treated me so sweetly—just as though I was their age. We had tremendous fun over our debates.

Renira attached herself fervently to the beautiful Ingrid and begged to be allowed to learn the guitar. Jonathan had a crush on Moira, because she was reading history and that was his subject at school. She couldn't have been nicer to him—treated him as though he were a fellow student, which thrilled him. So it worked out quite well and I suddenly found my life growing fuller. It had more purpose and it was almost as though the voices, the laughter, the music, the comings and goings of all these youngsters drove away the ghost of Des. My house was not now so full of painful memories.

I tried not to be extravagant and only at times gave the kids expensive food and had the odd bottle of wine. I made enough profit to satisfy me. My health and spirits improved. Rob was pleased about that.

"You're beginning to look your old self," he said. "You might be one of the young students instead of the lady of the house."

He came in to see us several evenings. He admired Ingrid. Everybody did. She had long beautiful legs, long silky wheaten-coloured hair and eyes as blue as forget-me-nots; plus a dimple in one cheek. She laughed a lot and had an engaging broken accent. She talked enthusiastically to Rob because he had been to Norway in his youth and loved salmon fishing, so they found a lot in common. In fact Rob was very popular with all the girls who ended up by calling him Uncle Rob, as the children did.

"It makes me feel older than Abraham," Rob laughed on one occasion when we were talking.

"I don't think Ingrid looks on you as Abraham," I said a trifle drily. "She told me the other day that you were *too* charming — so English — so dignified."

"Dear, *dear!*" murmured Rob.

"Don't you think she's marvellous to look at and enchanting when she sings?" I asked.

"As a matter of fact I do," he nodded.

It was at that precise moment that I became conscious of jealousy. If Rob fell in love with some beautiful girl and tumbled into the marriage he had avoided for so long, I would definitely be upset. My heart-beats quickened. I felt my cheeks grow red. But I grinned at Rob.

"You ought to take her out one evening," I said deliberately.

"I'm sure she has plenty of boy-friends to do that."

"Her particular boy-friend has gone back to Norway," I persisted, "and she hasn't got another."

Looking up at him I saw him smiling — rather a mysterious little smile. I didn't know what it meant but I just went on attacking him. "Well, why *don't* you take her out? She doesn't think you old at all and she'd be thrilled."

He caught me suddenly by both my hands. "What's all this about? Are you match-making? Are you suggesting that I should start an affair of sorts with the beautiful Dane?"

I felt quite childishly annoyed with him. I pulled my hands away, and shrugged my shoulders.

"Well—why not?"

Then he grabbed hold of me and held me very tightly.

"There are moments," he said, "when I could beat you." And he kissed me on the mouth. It wasn't a light kiss. It was long, passionate and demanding—even more so than the ones he had given me down in Cornwall when I first realised how he felt about me.

When he lifted his head he was breathing very fast. He said, "Don't you dare try to pair me off with any of your students, and that goes for Ingrid or anyone else. You know perfectly well who attracts *me*, and now if you don't mind I've got to get home. Sorry if I lost my head. I'll be seeing you."

Just like that! And he went off before I could call him back or say another word to him.

He left me really confused. I didn't know what I felt about Rob, or what I wanted, or anything else. I just sat down and put my face in my hands and cried. But I couldn't even give way to the luxury of that for long because it was time to fetch the kids from school.

As I washed my face and hands, made up again and brushed my hair, I looked in the mirror. There were shadows under my eyes—lines, too. I needed more colour. I wanted a hair-do. Surely I wasn't beginning to let myself go just because I was running a guest-house for students and scarcely ever sat down. How could this woman in the mirror possibly line up in any man's eyes with a glowing exquisite young girl like Ingrid? She was all curves, and seduction, and I wasn't at all sure she wasn't in love with Uncle Rob. But he had just said I ought to know who really attracted him. His long deep kiss had left little room for doubt that he meant *me*. I had always known it. What I couldn't be sure of was how *I* felt about *him*. The need for kissing—the need for being held as he held me—was not enough. If there was ever to be another man in my life it would have to be because I loved him as wholly as I had loved Des. Besides, I'd only been a widow since August and this was mid-December. Four months; it would have seemed disgraceful to the Victorians who considered there should always be a year's mourning for widows, if not two.

I really felt harassed and worried when that day ended. At times I was tempted to ring up Rob and tell him to come and see me. But *that* I didn't do. Whatever happened I wasn't going to be unfair to him.

All the same when I sat with my students that night I looked into the Danish girl's brilliant blue eyes, listened to her husky voice crooning folk-songs from her own land, and I was surprised that Rob didn't find her far more attractive than poor old haggard me!

That next morning I made a point of having my hair set. I even treated myself to a facial. The beautician found my skin much too dry and I surrendered to the luxury of being creamed and patted and soothed. Then I had a make-up and I had to admit I looked quite good.

Des used to think me beautiful. Apart from Rob, a lot of men in the past had admired me. As I came out of the shop, I began to feel much better. I decided that I must never let myself go down again or start imagining that at my age I was through with life. Also it was wrong to think that the extreme youth of girls like Ingrid was the only draw. Some men preferred older women. Age has its compensations. Besides, I wasn't even middle-aged yet.

Then Boyce came back into my life.

He had meant to return to Ponders Heath in time to bring Simon to school. But his plans had gone awry. First of all because he had contracted some strange virus which kept him in hospital in Peru. Simon had to travel to England with friends. We had already had the little boy out from school several times, which pleased Jonathan, and I was glad to see Simon, only there had been something about his face nowadays which reminded me painfully of his mother. Cricket was a person I'd sooner forget.

I heard from Boyce several times during the next few weeks. He was determined to keep in close touch with me but as soon as he recovered from his virus, he was persuaded by the firm to stay out in Peru till after the New Year. His replacement had not done too well. The affairs of the firm seemed to be in a bit of a muddle. Anyhow, Boyce's return was postponed until mid-January.

We all got through Christmas. Naturally I found myself looking back to a year ago when Des was with me and I hadn't known about his infidelities and we had seemed such a close-knit family. We always had such fun. Des and I used to hang up our stockings, like the children, then opened them with Renira and Jonathan who woke us at crack of dawn.

This year it was so different; so quiet. I didn't even have my students here to make the house gay because they all went back to their respective homes for the holiday.

The inimitable Miss Bessiford insisted on me and my family spending Christmas Day with her and Rob at The Hollies. I helped Rob decorate the house. There was someone to cook the turkey and wash up. Little Simon Halling was with us, too, because it wasn't expedient for him to go back to Peru. So there was a party — tree, crackers, and the spirit of Christmas prevailed.

Despite her great age, Aunt Ida enjoyed it all hugely. The children and I stayed to tea, then Rob drove us home. He said good night to me while the children were sorting their presents out in their own room. Dear Rob! He had been so good to us all — given such generous presents, including a beautiful scarlet leather shoulder bag for me — his own choice. Rob had good taste. And I'd given him a Dunhill pipe because I knew he always smoked that kind.

When we were alone in my drawing-room, he said, "I hope it hasn't been too bad a Christmas for you, my dear. I expect you've suffered from a few unhappy flashbacks, but that was inevitable."

"I'm okay,' I said. "I've enjoyed my day with you and Aunt Ida."

"I'd have taken you out this evening only you said you couldn't get anyone to look after the children."

"I couldn't. Why don't you spend the evening with me?"

Abruptly, suddenly, he said, No, — he had to get back home because when I'd turned down his original invitation, he'd asked some old Kenya friends of his who were staying in Brighton to drive over and spend the evening with him.

The good humour I'd felt all day seeped away from me. I felt suddenly dreary — disappointed Rob wouldn't stay. Since that moment when he'd lost his head and kissed me again, he'd been his old friendly self and not shown one sign of wanting to touch me or kiss me again. I even wondered if he'd decided not to repeat it. So tonight we exchanged the usual sort of sister-brother peck on the cheek. Then he was gone.

Perhaps I was silly and over-sensitive, but when I lay in bed that night I began to wonder if I had shocked Rob by the intensity of my former response to his kisses. Would he think that I was insensitive, turning my back on the memory of Des so soon, even if he *had* killed my love for him? I didn't know. I was only aware that above all things I wanted to keep Rob's respect, affection and friendship. Those three things mattered vitally. All this going-to-bed-together which Des had thought nothing of, could only lead to disaster—or at least remorse. What was that poignant quotation I had read the other day? Something about '*No more passionate midnights and famishing tomorrows*'. Famishing means hungry—yes, one could give way to a bodily urge and after it was satisfied, feel hungrier and lonelier than ever unless the love was the kind to last for ever. But it wasn't always that sort of love.

I put my face against a pillow. I felt a sudden sense of despair and apprehension. And the worst thing of all was the hatred that would keep sweeping back into my mind and heart—hatred for Des who had destroyed even the memory of our former happiness.

When my children woke me up the next morning and, as usual, climbed into my bed, I put my arms around them and tried to make up my mind to think of nothing *but* them. I wouldn't make myself cheap with Rob again and kiss him wildly like an excited girl. Hadn't I sworn not to encourage him? I'd see less of him—that was it.

Being a Saturday, I drove the children out into Brighton to spend the day with Gandy who was never happier than when we were all with her. I steeled myself to listen to her repeated praise of her darling son. At least I could keep up that myth of the good faithful husband—allow *one* of us to retain her illusions.

3

NEW YEAR APPROACHED. As was to be expected, Rob invited us all to The Hollies for lunch on New Year's Day, and suggested that I should go to a New Year's party with him at the hotel. However, having made up my mind not to live in his pocket, I thanked him gratefully, sent old Aunt Ida flowers, and accepted an invitation which came at the psychological moment from a married cousin who had just arrived in England from California.

I hadn't seen Penelope since I was a teenager. She had married an American and lived in Hollywood. Her husband was something to do with the film industry. I used to be rather fond of Penny as we called her. I remembered her as a petite fair-haired girl with a merry smile — a plump, cuddly little soul, always ready to be friendly. We had let our correspondence slide after my marriage to Des. I had not heard from her for years, until she received my notification of Des's death. Now her husband, Jack, had been called over to London suddenly on business. They rang me from their hotel in London. Money was no object. Jack was a success. Penny hired a car and came straight down to Nylands to see me, and issued an invitation to me to go up to town on New Year's Eve to a party at the Savoy with her and Jack and some of her American friends, and stay the night. I asked my Mrs. Tulk if she would look after the children and sleep at Nylands with her husband (who was a retired gardener). They loved to watch colour television, so that was arranged. Why not go up to the party and stay with my cousin? I was so tired of work and worry and of trying to reshape my life. As Penny said, one shouldn't spend too much time repining, and what was to be, was to be.

I shouldn't think Penny ever repined about anything. At thirty she was as gay and amusing as she used to be at seventeen. As I anticipated she had run to fat, which made her look like a dumpling, she was so short, but she was sweet and easy and as well-groomed and made-up as most American women.

"You poor honey," she kept saying. "What a *thing* for you to lose your nice husband so tragically. Jack and I'll just cherish you while we're over here and I only wish it was for longer than a week, but we've got to fly back because Jack's doing the script for a new film. Things aren't too good in Hollywood in the studios, but we hope to collaborate with an English producer."

Then she said how cute and pretty little Renira was, and what a *darling* boy, Jonathan; but after a critical look at me, shook her head, "Honey, you're as beautiful now as you were as a girl, but you're much too thin and your eyes are sad. Why don't you all pack up and come out to California to live?"

"I couldn't," I said, "there's my mother-in-law. She dotes on the children and she has nothing now Des has gone. I couldn't take them so far away from her."

Penny rolled her eyes upwards.

"Mothers-in-law!"

"Mine's not so bad," I said with a smile. "She's been very good to me really."

Penny pushed a lock of fair hair (I swear it was a wig) into place, and walked over to the bureau where a portrait of Des has always stood and which I kept there for the children. He had looked very young and so very handsome when it was taken. Penny raved about him, turned back to me and said, "Why I just break my heart for you, honey, you've lost a wonderful looking guy."

I said nothing, only nodded with a tight smile.

She was right. Only I'd lost him long before he died.

It all ended in me going up to the Savoy and staying the night as my generous cousin's guest. I felt rather guilty because I enjoyed myself—especially the dancing. I always did like that. I knew that I looked good in that dark violet dress with the long sleeves and high Russian collar which I'd worn at Rob's party at the Club. (Not so long ago, though it seemed a positive age.) I threw off all my cares and laughed and sparkled which I used to do in the good old days. Jack's English producer who was in our party—by name Roland Martin—seemed to take a special interest in me. He kept whisking me on to the floor before the others. We certainly danced well together. He was the exact antithesis of Des—not tall, with very dark hair, grey clever eyes and a lot of charm. He was gay and witty and Jack had told me he was a brilliant film producer.

Before the evening ended, Roland asked me when I could get up to town again as he'd like to take me out to dinner. He wasn't married. He was about my age, I should think, and Penny had whispered that he was very well-off and had a lovely little mews cottage in one of those streets leading off Park Lane.

I wasn't particularly thrilled by the thought that Roland was well-off and successful, but I liked his personality and it was good to be admired and wanted. What woman didn't like that? I didn't promise to meet him again but said I'd phone him. He gave me his office address and phone number. Our Savoy party ended hilariously with me putting an absolute blanket over creeping memories of last New Year's Eve at the golf club. Des had kissed me and whispered, "Happy New Year, my one and only sweetheart."

One and only — dear God! that hadn't been true, but I refused to let the thought do more than rear its head for a second, then I flung myself into the fun. At midnight I linked hands with Penny's nice husband, and Roland, and we kissed each other, wearing silly paper hats on our heads, and behaving like a lot of children.

It was great. When I left the Savoy, Penny remarked that I had made a terrific impression on Roland Martin.

"Don't you sit fretting, you follow your star, honey," she advised. "Roland's fallen for you. He says you're *so* distinguished, and he's just fine and I can't tell you how glad I am we asked him along."

Of course when I got back to Nylands, reaction set in. I'd lived for a few hours in a different world — the gay carefree world Jack and Penny always lived in and Roland Martin did, too. His hand had pressed mine very tightly when he had said good night and he had repeated his New Year's kiss in a way that left no doubt as to his sentiments. Yet I couldn't get up any real enthusiasm. In a funny way I was glad to be back in my home. The children were so ecstatically pleased to see me. Then I followed the old routine.

Mrs. Tulk and I had to get the house ready for my four students who were coming back in mid-January, so there was a lot to do. Gandy was coming for the weekend — just to make a change for her from her Brighton flat, *and* there was Rob.

My first thought after kissing the children had been to ring up The Hollies and tell Rob I was back. I wonder what made me resist that inclination. Just that feeling I'd had for a few days now, that I'd been seeing too much of him.

But *he* didn't feel the same way. Within twenty-four hours of me being home — on 2nd January in fact — he came round to Nylands bringing with him a huge pink and white cyclamen with lovely pale green variegated leaves.

"Just to say Happy New Year — a bit late, perhaps," he said.

He took off the tinted glasses for a second to smile at me. I looked up into those very blue eyes and felt all the old warmth and affection envelop me. Oh, I loved Rob in my way (not that I knew what sort of way it was) but I *did* love him. He was so sweet to me. He couldn't dance. He wasn't brilliant. He was just *Rob* and the dearest thing on earth.

I took the cyclamen, put it on the table, lifted his right hand and held it against my cheek.

"You are an angel. Thanks awfully, Rob."

"Can I come in a moment?"

"You know you can."

In the sitting-room he sat and smoked with me. I made him a cup of coffee and he asked what sort of a party I'd had in town. So I told him all about it and rather wickedly added that a very fascinating film producer had fallen for me and invited me to dine with him in town any time I liked.

Rob didn't speak for a moment. He had put his glasses on again so I couldn't see his expression. But his lips smiled.

"Goings-on at the Savoy, eh? So that's what you do when you're let loose, and I'm not around to control you."

"Rob darling, I had a *wonderful* time — honestly, even if I did let myself go a bit. It was such a change. My cousin's a sweetie and it was all very expensive and lush and I had a super bedroom looking over the river, and one of those old-fashioned sunken marble baths of all things, can you believe it?"

"It sounds fine," said Rob, "and I'm very glad you enjoyed yourself."

"Have some more coffee," I said.

"Tell me more about this fascinating fellow. Is he married?"

"No."

"H'm," said Rob.

I could guess then exactly what he was feeling — thoroughly put out because I'd met an attractive bachelor. Jealous — darling old Rob! But he didn't say another word about it. He changed the conversation and asked me when I would be free to go and have lunch with him and bring the children. Aunt Ida, it appeared, was not quite as fit as usual. The doctor had warned him that it was on the cards she wouldn't leave her bedroom again. She was a great age and might become bedridden.

"I hope the poor old darling won't just fade away," Rob said with a sigh. "But I looked at her this morning and thought how frail she looks. Her little hand when you take it is quite brittle. I can't help wondering, will 1972 be her last year?"

"Oh, Rob!" I exclaimed. "Don't let's have any more dying. We've had enough."

"I'm feeling a bit depressed," he said. "Take no notice. The doctor hasn't given her a death-sentence, nothing like that. As he told me—these old ladies of around ninety sometimes go on and on, they have such strong hearts. God bless her, I wouldn't like to see her go. But you will come and eat with me, won't you?"

"Of course I will," I said.

At that moment I heard a car out in the drive. Then the front door bell rang. I opened the door and had quite a shock. There stood Boyce Halling. Rather a changed Boyce. He had lost some of his dashing looks; even though he had been away such a short time I could see there was some grey in his hair and his face had a yellowish hue. Obviously he'd suffered from that virus quite considerably. He was a lot less bombastic, too.

"It's wonderful to see you, Nira," he said, and bent and touched my cheek with his lips. I felt suddenly sorry for him and kissed his cheek in return.

"Poor old Boyce, you've had a foul time."

'Yes, and whatever it was that hit me in Peru, hasn't altogether left me, either. They think now it was some sort of tropical bug. It's playing havoc with me. I haven't left the firm but I'm not going to take up my new post with them for another fortnight. I'm in town now. A friend of mine lent me a flat and I'm going to take Simon up there for the rest of the holidays. Then I don't know what I'll do, although I do want to come back to Ponders Heath and join the old commuters."

I took his coat and scarf and led the way into the sitting-room. "Rob's here," I said, "having a coffee. Can I get you one?"

"I can't drink coffee," he said. "Not allowed it."

"Tea?" I asked.

"Yes, I'd like a cup of weak tea very much. It's damned cold after Peru. I only landed yesterday. But your house is warm."

He didn't seem pleased to find Rob here with me and I don't think Rob was very pleased to see him. However, the two men were polite to each other. While I made the tea, they talked. When I took in the tray Boyce looked at me in the old familiar way and remarked that I'd lost a lot of weight.

"So have you," I said.

"I'm right off drink and cigarettes and rich food," he told me gloomily. "I saw a specialist yesterday afternoon as soon as I got back. A friend of mine arranged the interview for me. He said

I'd got to go to The School of Tropical Medicine and have various tests."

"I'm sorry for you," said Rob. "Being well means such a lot in life. I've been through a bit of trouble myself in my time."

I, too, felt sorry for Boyce, but I didn't really want to be left alone with him. Rob, however, must have imagined that he was an unwanted third because soon after Boyce arrived, he departed. I asked him to stay but he said he had a prescription to pick up for Aunt Ida and had promised to get home.

Once Boyce and I were alone, he became a little more intimate. He moved to the sofa beside me and took my hand. "You look more beautiful than ever, Nira. Your gorgeous eyes are sad, but sorrow becomes you."

"Well, I wouldn't exactly *want* it as a beautifier," I said rather tartly and drew my hand away.

He said that he knew how I must have been feeling as he'd gone through it when Cricket was killed and how we ought to understand and comfort each other, both having lost the other half in a fatal accident and so on and so on. I listened to it all patiently but of course the moment came when he went too far.

He took my hand again and kissed it with passion.

"You know I've been in love with you for a long time, Nira. This may not be the right time to say it—I don't really know whether you've got over losing Des or not but—"

I broke in, "I haven't been a widow more than five months."

"Time enough," he said. "I'm quite sure you feel as I do—that it isn't good to live alone."

"I've got the children," I said hurriedly.

"*And* Rob," said Boyce with a sarcasm that wasn't lost on me.

I felt my cheeks grow hot. The old irritation Boyce used to cause me returned.

"I don't know what you mean by that," I snapped. "Rob has always been my greatest friend."

"Isn't he seizing his chance to step into Des's shoes?"

That was too crude for me. I got up. I felt my heart beat fast with anger.

"Now look here, Boyce—" I began, but he interrupted.

"Don't be cross with me. Ever since I left England I've had you in my thoughts. You've always driven me mad, Nira. I'm sorry if I said the wrong thing about old Rob. I don't suppose for a moment you'd marry him even if he asked you."

That had the effect of making me indiscreet and rash.

"How do you know I wouldn't?" I demanded.

"He's just not your type."

"And pray what is my type?"

"Des was, I suppose," said Boyce, then walked over to me and put his hand on my shoulders. "Oh, Nira, please give me a chance! We've both suffered. We're both alone. I know you've got the children and I've got Simon, but surely man needs woman and vice-versa. No, don't move away from me. Tell me that you'll give me a chance. Let me see a lot more of you. Perhaps by the end of the summer you'll be thinking of remarrying. You'll give me that chance, won't you? There's nothing on earth I wouldn't do for you and I swear I'll work hard to get a bit more money behind me so that I can offer you and the kids a really nice home."

Whatever I tried to say, he interrupted. Simon needed a mother. I would make the perfect one. Simon adored me. Our two boys got on so well. Wouldn't it be an ideal marriage? I'd never really given him the opportunity to show me the love he was sure I needed, and so on.

Love, I thought, *a man like Boyce doesn't know anything about real love. It means something quite different to him.* It was odd but all through this emotional assault and battery from Boyce, the image of Rob kept appearing in front of me. I could feel again as I had felt a short time ago, that once again I was clasped in his answering his kisses with mine. And each time I thought of it, I resented Boyce taking it for granted that I wouldn't *want* to marry Rob, if he asked me—and that he wasn't my type.

Of course Boyce eventually tried to kiss and embrace me—to make me feel warmer, more yielding through the force of sheer physical passion. But I'm afraid I disappointed him. I pushed him firmly away.

I said, "It's no use, Boyce. It never has been between us. Thanks awfully for asking me to marry you, but I just can't. I never could. We're not right for each other. I'd love to do anything I could for young Simon and he's always welcome to come here and stay with Jonathan—but that's all."

Boyce looked sick. When he left Nylands, I felt sorry for him. He really had changed, and whereas he used to inspire contempt in me, I now felt only pity—but that was as far as it went.

Standing in the doorway, putting on his gloves, he said, "I won't give up hope. I won't bother you—you obviously don't want to see me, but I have contacts at the golf club and I'll find out how you are and perhaps in a few months' time you might think differently."

"Sorry—I won't," I said firmly, but added, "Let us have Simon to stay sometimes if he'd like to come, and it suits you. I don't want to end the friendship between our boys."

"Thanks for so much," Boyce said rather bitterly and got into his car and drove away.

I hadn't asked whether he still intended to come and live down here but I rather thought that he wouldn't, after I had made it so plain that I had no intention of taking Cricket's place or letting him take Des's.

Once he had driven away and I was alone—Renira and Jonathan had gone in to the house next door to play with the children there—I began to prepare their lunch. But in the middle of it I had the most extraordinary wish to see the man who Boyce had said was not my type. Rob—I wanted to see *Rob*—my one great security—my one firm friend—*the one I loved*. Yes, I loved Rob. To hell with what Boyce had said. I loved Rob with all my heart. I couldn't bear my life unless I knew that he was somehow—somewhere—in it. But this new love must remain my secret. I would cherish the thought and say nothing. Life must go on just as it was. When I saw Rob again he must not know how I felt. So I didn't ring him. And he didn't ring me.

And that is the way my life continued—for quite a while.

4

FEBRUARY CAME IN with snow, and with the first snowdrops blanching our walled garden in diamond brightness. Things suddenly changed disastrously for me, at first. The children were back at school, which was a help, and the students were back, too, and their presence in the evening gave me more freedom to go out. I had decided that I mustn't continue to refuse invitations or nobody would bother even to ask Jonathan and Renira to their houses. So I went out to dinner with the Moffats, and even accepted an invitation to a women's lunch-party at the Manor House, where I rather reluctantly received the gracious patronage and pity that Lady Conniston bestowed on me in her subtle way. The Parkinsons also asked me to a meal, and play bridge, and invited Rob, too, tactfully, thinking, I suppose, that I would like him as the fourth.

That party took place towards the end of the month.

The snow had begun to melt. Grey, stained-looking slush bedevilled the streets of Ponders Heath. The ice-cold winds gave way to a milder sou'-wester. It rained furiously, while the first bulbs of the year tried bravely to thrust their delicate yet fantastically strong green spears through the sodden earth.

It was during that evening at the Parkinsons' — Rob was my partner, husband and wife liked to play together — that I began to realise even more intensely how much I loved him. I was frightfully careful not to show it because I was still ashamed of loving any man quite so soon. I think I behaved in the normal friendly manner and Rob was his usual charming self — until he drove me home. Then when he stopped outside my house and I asked him to come in for a night-cap, he refused.

"No thank you, my dear. I meant to have an early night really, and it's elevenish now. I've got some packing to finish."

I couldn't see his face clearly in the dim light inside the car, but I sat very still. I felt a horrible sinking feeling.

"Packing?" I repeated. "Are you going away somewhere?"

"Yes," he said, "As a matter of fact things have rather altered since you last came to The Hollies."

"What things?" I asked stupidly.

He explained that the doctor thought it best for Aunt Ida to have a resident nurse-companion and although it was about as much as they could afford, he had agreed and managed to get hold of one. He needed a break, Rob said — he was beginning to feel out of sorts. Fortunately he had been told by Aunt Ida's doctor about this very nice elderly woman who had been a nurse in her time. She took up residence at The Hollies yesterday. She was a bit slapdash and untidy, Rob ended with a laugh, but Aunt Ida quite liked her. They had the same sense of humour and got on well. She was good at taking care of the old lady and cooking for her which was all that mattered.

"It makes me feel I needn't worry about going away," Rob said.

I began to shiver—cold through and through. "I think it's a great idea for you," I said with false brightness. "Where are you going, Rob?"

"Well, you know that I told you about those Kenya friends of mine who arrived from Nairobi just before the New Year, well, they're staying on for a few weeks and they have asked me to go down for a bit to their place in Kent. They've got a lovely old farmhouse in Cowden which isn't very far from here, really. You go through East Grinstead."

"I see," I said in a small voice, "and maybe you'll fly back to Nairobi with these people."

"I think I'd like to," he said (to my dismay) "I'm so much better and my eyes are almost normal. I feel I could very well stand a few weeks in the old climate and enjoy seeing a lot of old friends who used to go on safari with me."

I didn't answer. He vouchsafed the further remark that he wouldn't have thought of going so far away if Aunt Ida's doctor hadn't assured him her heart was strong and her blood pressure not too bad and it was only that she was a bit frail. Age had sapped her natural vitality. But in these days, why worry, Rob ended, when one could fly home at a moment's notice. One needn't today have the same fears of leaving someone you loved for a short time.

Those last words somehow found a dismal echo in my mind. *Leaving someone you loved.* I had thought he loved *me*, but he was leaving me. I'd never doubted his love. Why had he suddenly changed his mind? *What had I done?* Was it because of me that he was going? I felt so desperate that I resorted to flippancy in order to cover up.

"Now don't tell me you're about to contract a secret wedding with beautiful Ingrid and take her out to Nairobi for your honeymoon."

That actually brought a chuckle from Rob.

"How ridiculous can you be?"

"Oh, well, I hope you'll have a wonderful time, and it'll be a splendid change for you," I exclaimed in a loud cheerful voice.

I really was so surprised by what he had just told me and so anguished by the thought that he was going to put thousands of miles between us—as from tomorrow, perhaps—that I couldn't think of another thing to say. A dozen burning questions were on the edge of my tongue and not one could I ask.

Were you shocked by the way I kissed you back the other night?

Has that driven you away?

Have you suddenly decided that you don't love me that way any more and you just want to go on being friends?

Have I done something or said something so that I've fallen short of your idea of me?

And a dozen more queries. I was hopelessly puzzled. I only knew that life had played a pretty scurvy trick. It was all very cynical now that I had made up my mind that I was in love with Rob, but it was too late. He didn't want me any more.

I was wretched but managed to pull myself together sufficiently to put on a nice brisk manner and thank him for all he had done for me and the children since Des died, also say that I would go and see Aunt Ida regularly and write to him, and all that. Then I felt his hand take mine. He lifted it to his lips and kissed it in the old delightful way, but let it drop again. He made no attempt to kiss me on the mouth. He just said in a gentle voice, "I've more need to thank *you*, Nira, believe me. I look on you and always will as the most wonderful friend in the world."

"And that's how I look on you," I said, trying not to sound absolutely desperate.

"I'm sure we'll always be close. I'll be back home very soon. The end of March at the latest — that is if nothing brings me back sooner. Write to me, won't you, dear?"

"You know I will," I whispered, but suddenly the enormity of the pain and the grief I was going to suffer once he had gone, struck me so forcibly that I couldn't stand sitting in that car with him a moment longer. I tried to lift the door handle of the car but it stuck and as I shook it Rob suddenly grabbed hold of me and pulled me against him. His long sensitive fingers passed over my face. The tears were pouring down my cheeks and he began to kiss me quite wildly. This was no grave, self-possessed man, no reluctant lover. This was a man who loved with passion and plenty and he kept saying, "Oh, God, I love you, Nira — *Nira*, my love! I don't know how I'm going to leave you but I know I've got to. Why are you crying? Oh, don't cry like that, it breaks my heart. You're everything in the world to me."

I drew away from him with a great gasping sigh. "Rob, I

thought maybe you'd grown tired of me or didn't like me any more, or something. I thought you were running away from me."

"I was running away from myself," he said. "I've loved you a long time but I couldn't trust myself to go on being platonic, and anyhow I thought you were still in love with the memory of Des. Besides, I didn't imagine for a moment that you minded about me. And there's this Roland fellow."

"Idiot!" I laughed and cried together. "You must have known what *I* was feeling about you last time you took me in your arms. I was quite shameless. It's because of that I thought you were sort of put off."

"You're the idiotic one, my beloved *darling* Nira. Nothing on earth could put me off you. But I took it for granted you were only het-up after all the emotional storms you'd been through. Honestly, I know you kissed me with passion but I thought you were just momentarily stirred."

"Now you know the truth," I broke in, and put my face in my hands, not knowing whether I was the happiest girl on earth or the most miserable.

Very soon I knew that I was the happiest. Rob, my dear, dear Rob, gathered me in his embrace again. Later he said, "I'm still going to Nairobi. Not because I really need the holiday but just because I must give you more time to think things over."

"I don't want it," I said. "I know how I feel."

"All the same I think it would be right and proper for me to go away and come back as I've planned, towards the end of March, or beginning of April."

I found myself giggling like a schoolgirl with my face hidden against his shoulder—that strong wonderful shoulder that I seemed to have been leaning on for ages.

"You always do the right and proper thing."

"You make me sound a prig."

"You're not a prig," I said indignantly, "but you're different from so many men I've known. You have some splendid old-fashioned principles. We're neither of us very permissive. Des often used to call me a prude."

Rob laid his lips against mine and murmured, "The way you kiss doesn't suggest that."

"I hate you," I laughed, and we clung madly and stupidly like two young lovers, in the darkness of the car. I became more and more convinced with every passing moment that I was in love again for the second time in my life — really and truly in love with Rob. I had loved Des, but with a sort of idolatrous passion because he was so handsome, so dashing and amusing. I was grateful to him, too. He had given me two lovely children and, up to a little while ago, a very happy life. I couldn't deny that, even though the happiness had at last been so badly tarnished.

Then in the midst of kissing Rob a distressing thought hit me. *What on earth would Gandy think?* But I must leave that problem for the moment. I couldn't cope with it. Anyhow it was my life and not hers.

"You're going down to these people in Kent tomorrow — *tomorrow*. Oh, Rob!" I sighed.

"Dearest," he said, "I don't want to leave you but I think I must. You're altogether too much of a temptation. Your so-called right and proper Rob would like to pick you up this moment and carry you into the house and —" he broke off.

The significance of this was plain. I clung to him in silence for a moment, then, "All right," I said, "I understand. It might spoil things — I agree."

"You know of course that I'd rather marry you as soon as it could be arranged," he said, "but in my opinion, and providing you do still want to marry me — we should make it the late Spring. We could even go all conventional and announce our engagement in the papers just before I arrive back from East Africa. Then everyone in the Heath will know, and we can face the music together. Not that they don't all guess already I'm in love with you. I'm sure they do."

"But they don't know that *I'm* in love with you," I whispered, "and remember they don't know about Des and our marriage — the disastrous end. Only Maggie knows, and she no longer counts. They might think me beastly if I marry again *too* soon. Oh, I want you right now, darling, but I admit we ought to wait, so shall we?"

Rob answered my question with the wonderful words that I was convinced were the absolute truth.

"I shall always want you to do exactly what *you* want, my dearest dear. The choice is yours."

Nira and Rob

I

DURING THE TIME Rob spent in Kenya he wrote to Nira every day. She answered. She loved to write. She had never found Des good at letters. His used to be rather immature scrawls — sometimes full of little intimacies which *could* be coarse, but Nira hadn't minded because she had loved him. She had smiled over them. But Rob was different. He was a great reader and thinker and his letters were quite literary. He said the most beautiful things in a beautiful way and never let Nira doubt that he was going to make her a wonderful husband as well as a tender lover.

By the middle of March, she and Rob had come to a full understanding. They agreed that she should give her students notice before Easter. She was to do no more slaving in order to augment her income. Rob didn't want it and they wouldn't need the money, he said. He had a small but adequate income and when dear old Aunt Ida passed on, he would have a little more. Aunt Ida was the only one in the Heath who already knew that he was going to marry Nira. It had been his wish that she should tell the old lady at once. She received the news with joy.

"It's nice that you've decided to wait a while, but I fully approve. My dear boy has always loved you and so have I, my dear."

Although Nira could not discuss the glowing future with anyone else in the Heath she could talk about it with Aunt Ida. The old lady's health improved while Rob was away, and Nira had an idea Miss Bessiford would reach her ninetieth birthday, even though she might spend it in bed.

Nira and Rob weren't going to rush into things, but for the time being, because of the children, Nira stayed at Nylands. She and Rob would marry at the end of April. They planned to spend their honeymoon in Corfu. Then she would sell Nylands and move to The Hollies. They'd pool resources. Aunt Ida wished them to redecorate the best bedroom and a small sitting-room for themselves.

The companion-nurse would stay on to look after the old lady as there was plenty of room, and the faithful Mrs. Tulk would help Nira by working full time at The Hollies. Despite protests from Rob, Nira volunteered to take on the cooking. She quite liked it.

There were so many plans and readjustments to make. Susan wasn't happy in her present job. She agreed to return to Nylands to look after Jonathan and Renira at least until Jonathan went to his public school.

So once more, Susan would take on the washing and ironing and help with the children and leave Nira free to be with her husband.

The week before Rob was due to fly home, Nira broke the news about her forthcoming marriage to the children. It would be nice, she said, if they would go on calling him Uncle Rob — not Daddy. They were delighted.

"Super!" said Jonathan. "Uncle Rob'll be able to play lots of cricket with me and help me with my prep."

"Super!" echoed little Renira. "'Cos I love Uncle Rob."

"So do I!" Nira whispered and kissed them both on top of their heads.

Renira was growing more enchanting every day. She was going to be a real beauty. Jonny did look like his father at times but Nira adored him and he would have a wonderful example before him of what a man should be — once Uncle Rob started to live with them.

The hardest thing Nira had to do was to tell Gandy of her intended remarriage. To her it would surely seem too quick — an insult to her son's memory — all that sort of thing.

At first Gandy received Nira's confession (given when she went over to Brighton to lunch) with dismay and even disapproval.

"It's so *soon* — barely nine months! I didn't expect it of you, dear. Of course I know you must have been lonely but I thought as you had the children," she broke off, in tears.

Nira's cheeks felt hot. She experienced a slight feeling of guilt but she tried to make Gandy see that a woman needed a man in her life and Rob after all was an old friend. She and Des had both known him for some time and grown very fond of him. He'd been the greatest help to Nira since Des died. The children loved him, too. She wouldn't need any financial help from Gandy in future because she and Rob had their own incomes. And so on. Nira talked rather quickly — trying to make the older woman understand.

It took a little time to thaw Gandy. Once she had softened up, she admitted she was glad to see Nira looking so happy again, and hoped she would put on weight now as she was far too skinny. She also generously announced that she would not back out of paying for the education of her grandchildren, and that she relied on Nira to let her see a lot of them.

Impulsively Nira hugged her mother-in-law — kissed the pale powdered cheek and told her she would always be just as welcome at The Hollies in the future as she had been at Nylands.

The sudden change in her life was so unexpected and exciting, that Nira often wondered if she would wake up and find either that it was a dream, or that something awful would happen to bring her fresh disaster. But nothing bad happened, and the day came when the announcement of her engagement to Rob was put in *The Telegraph*. After that, Nira's telephone never stopped ringing. Most of the members of the golf club who had known her when Des was alive seemed glad that she was marrying again, and especially that it was to Rob Bessiford. It was a genuine romance. The locals loved it. Maggie was the one person Nira heard nothing from, but that didn't surprise her. Anyhow, she'd been told by Joyce Moffat that Maggie and her mother were selling up and leaving the district. Nira was glad. She didn't want to see Des's girl-friend again.

She started to go through her house and put away small personal things such as souvenirs and photographs relating to her first marriage. She had placed Des's nicest photograph in the children's bedroom. She would never disillusion them. They must always remember their father with love and respect.

It was rather a misty sunless April morning when Nira finally drove to Heathrow to meet the aircraft bringing Rob from Nairobi. All kinds of thoughts crowded through her mind while she sat in the Arrivals Lounge, waiting. Waiting for the man who had once been her dearest friend and was now her dearest love as well.

She recalled the many times during the past when she and Des used to drive down here, either when they were going abroad or in order to meet friends. Des used to like Heathrow—all the noise, the people, and the drama of the great airport attracted him.

Poor Des!—lying down there in his quiet grave in Cornwall. Nira no longer felt resentment or bitterness against him. She was grateful for the happiness she had once known with him, and had forgiven him for his betrayal. She hoped if he was anywhere around he would be glad about Rob and herself. She could almost see his mocking smile and hear his gay voice, "So after all you're hitching up with your boy-friend, your dear old Rob, eh?" Yet in spite of the mockery, he had admitted many times that he admired Rob—thought as many other people did in Ponders Heath, that he was one of the nicest of men. Perhaps Des would be pleased that Rob was to take his place in the family.

How different life would have been for her if Des had not been killed in that accident, Nira's thoughts continued. She had suffered so much before he died—she might have been forced to go on suffering. Now she wanted so desperately to be happy and to regain her joy in living and her faith in man.

The big graceful aircraft bringing Rob from Nairobi, touched down. Nira watched it, her heart beating madly fast and her cheeks pink. She was a little frightened yet absolutely happy. She couldn't wait to see him—to feel his arms around her.

She walked quickly out of the Arrivals Lounge and took up her position outside the door through which he would emerge from the Customs. She was glad that she had put on a little weight and looked better and younger than when he had left. She had bought a new suit for the occasion—a shortish skirt and jacket in fine cream jersey. A silk scarf, scarlet and blue, was knotted around her neck. Her dark silky hair—which Rob had personally forbidden her ever to cut short—fell to her shoulders. She really did look quite young and pretty today, she decided.

Rob thought so too, as he walked through the exit and saw her again. She appeared to him the most beautiful woman in the world. No woman of thirty this, but a young glowing girl—*his* girl—soon to be his wife. All the time he had been away in Kenya he had thought about her and their future. It had seemed miraculous that he, the confirmed bachelor was going to be married at last and to this glorious creature whom he had once thought utterly out of reach.

Nira moved toward him. He dropped the overnight bag he was

carrying, and without inhibition, took her in his arms in front of the crowd at the barrier and kissed her on the lips.

"Nira — *Nira* — my love!"

"Oh, Rob." She could think of nothing more to say but just that. "*Oh, Rob.*" The cry coming from the depths of her heart.

Then without speaking, their hands linked, they walked out to the front entrance . . .

The mists had cleared. The sun had come through, and suddenly it was Spring.

To Love Is To Live
Denise Robins

Paris and Edinburgh, the most romantic of cities, provide the background for this poignant drama of a young woman striving to remain loyal to her handsome and ambitious soldier-husband when the ghost of her first love reappears in the guise of a laird in his ancestral castle.

Laurence My Love
Denise Robins

Vere Rowland still thought of herself as a schoolgirl when she left the convent, but when she saw Laurence Bracknell she knew she had become a woman.

At first it seemed highly fortunate that Laurence lived near the great house where Vere's mother was housekeeper; but this coincidence led Vere and her lover to the brink of tragedy.

CORONET BOOKS

Best Selling Romantic Fiction from Denise Robins

☐	15809 3	Swing Of Youth	30p
☐	16082 9	All That Matters	30p
☐	16080 2	Put Back The Clock	30p
☐	16081 0	Reputation	30p
☐	15810 7	The Wild Bird	30p
☐	17311 4	And All Because	30p
☐	17318 1	To Love Is To Live	30p
☐	10522 4	The Cyprus Love Affair	30p
☐	17408 0	Forbidden	30p
☐	17842 6	The Boundary Line	30p
☐	17850 7	Desire Is Blind	30p
☐	17855 8	Love Was A Jest	30p
☐	16716 5	The Enduring Flame	30p
☐	01459 8	The Noble One	30p
☐	12963 8	Laurence, My Love	30p
☐	18291 1	The Snow Must Return	30p
☐	02919 6	Gay Defeat	30p
☐	18300 4	Do Not Go My Love	30p
☐	18605 4	All For You	30p
☐	01065 7	I Should Have Known	30p
☐	15084 X	The Unlit Fire	30p
☐	15110 2	Shatter The Sky	30p

All these books are available at your bookshop or newsagent, or can be ordered direct from the publisher. Just tick the titles you want and fill in the form below.

CORONET BOOKS, P.O. Box 11, Falmouth, Cornwall.
Please send cheque or postal order. No currency, and allow the following for postage and packing:

1 book – 10p, 2 books – 15p, 3 books – 20p, 4–5 books – 25p, 6–9 books – 4p per copy, 10–15 books – 2½p per copy, 16–30 books – 2p per copy, over 30 books free within the U.K.
Overseas – please allow 10p for the first book and 5p per copy for each additional book.

Name ....

Address ....

....